Lule Musa, the minister's chief wife, was the kind of Ugandan beauty who attracted men. She certainly attracted me.

'My husband is in great danger,' she said, taking hold of my hand. 'You must fly him to safety.'

'The army are watching me,' I said. 'It's too much of a risk – Jesus!'

I cried out in surprise as she plunged my hand into her loose native costume. My palm met warm bare skin, fleshy and thick-nippled. They were the kind of tits that made me go weak at the knees – and weak in the head. What's more she was now unzipping my shorts.

'You will help us, won't you, Mr Wight?' she implored, manipulating me expertly.

'Please, Mrs Musa! What would your husband think?'

'He's too frightened to think,' she replied, going down on her knees – and not to beg for mercy . . .

Also available by Lesley Asquith

In the Mood
Sex and Mrs Saxon
Sin and Mrs Saxon
Lust and Lady Saxon
In the Groove
Reluctant Lust
Sleeping Partners
The Wife-Watcher Letters
The Delta Sex-Life Letters

In the Flesh

Lesley Asquith

Copyright © 1996 Lesley Asquith

The right of Lesley Asquith to be identified as the Author of the Work has been asserted by her in accordance with the Copyright, Designs and Patents Act 1988.

First published in 1996
by HEADLINE BOOK PUBLISHING

A HEADLINE DELTA paperback

10 9 8 7 6 5 4 3 2 1

All rights reserved. No part of this publication may be reproduced, stored in a retrieval system, or transmitted in any form or by any means without the prior written permission of the publisher, nor be otherwise circulated in any form of binding or cover other than that in which it is published and without a similar condition being imposed on the subsequent purchaser.

All characters in this publication are fictitious and any resemblance to real persons, living or dead, is purely coincidental.

ISBN 0 7472 5243 2

Typeset by Palimpsest Book Production Limited,
Polmont, Stirlingshire
Printed and bound in Great Britain by
Cox & Wyman Ltd, Reading, Berkshire

HEADLINE BOOK PUBLISHING
A division of Hodder Headline PLC
338 Euston Road
London NW1 3BH

In the Flesh

Chapter One

Shooting the breeze with fellow spirits and comparing notes on the usual subject, I can't recall anyone talking about a good fuck with their wife. Other men's wives, yes. Everyone agrees that the most memorable encounters happen by chance and the unexpected jump wins hands down.

So it was with Roberta, a Member of Parliament and Under-Secretary of State for Overseas Aid no less. I'd been her pilot on a fact-finding jaunt to northern Uganda to study an unexpected influx of refugees. Now, as I lay prone on her bed in her suite in Chobe Safari Lodge, I contemplated a fine specimen of the female bottom. Broad, curvy and full, it was a bum to be admired.

As she leant forward over the well-stocked drinks trolley, she revealed to me her full glorious cheeks, the cleavage between parted enticingly. The crinkled pucker of her tight rear entrance was exposed, plus an underslung cunt bulge with its curling bush and pouting lips. I'd seen worse sights, I had to admit.

There was no shortage here, I decided. I referred both to the array of bottles, paid for by you the taxpayer no doubt, and her heavy hanging-loose breasts proudly displayed as she turned to face me. The gleam in her eye and her cryptic smile, told me she'd had a lovely time imagining she'd been foully abused by a brutish man. She crossed to me, her extravagant tits wobbling as she handed me my reward, a tall vodka-and-lime tinkling with ice.

This was a brief interlude for refreshment, I imagined, but the Hon. Roberta couldn't forget her position. Or mine. She had to pretend that this behaviour wasn't like her. Not the done thing, at all. Why can't randy women come right out and admit they crave a good shafting? Life would be a lot easier.

'Don't make yourself too comfortable, this has gone far enough,' she stressed in her cut-glass voice. 'Drink up and return to your room, Mr Wight. I can't imagine why I'm letting you see me like this.'

That was rich. She'd come on as horny as a bucket of bullfrogs as soon as I'd been summoned to her presence to tell her when I would be flying her back to Entebbe the following day. That dispensed with, and offered a drink by a voluptuously built woman in a silk robe that left little to the imagination, I wasn't exactly blind to her intent. I've never been averse to being seduced.

When preliminaries were over and after some flirtatious talk about expatriate African life, I'd stood to leave. It paid off. 'Stay for a while, I want company,' was how she'd phrased it. Her invitation was an order with no hesitation in the voice, as befitted one who walked the corridors of power. It was obvious – under her cool exterior the lady was panting for a fuck. I was available. She became seriously determined, letting her robe slither dramatically to the floor. 'Take off your clothes,' she'd directed, ensuring I complied by starting to unbutton my shirt.

Once stripped, I managed a fondle and suck of her big tits and a quick feel-up of a well-juiced quim while she gave some expert rubs to my prick. As my erection sat bolt upright, I was pushed unceremoniously across the bed and straddled to the hilt.

In the Flesh

'Y-e-e-s-s,' I'd heard her grunt as she impaled herself on hard cock, working her thighs. She'd instructed me to lie still and I'd let her have her way, figuring my time would come. For the moment I'd enjoyed looking up at the bounce and sway of her large breasts, savouring her increasing excitement at being so well plugged. Her initial whimpers had soon turned into full-blooded cries and groans. With hips jerking furiously, she'd pleasured herself greedily astride my rigid bar of flesh.

It had continued until she could no longer hold back her crisis. With boobs swinging and bobbing, her head thrown back and unintelligible sounds issuing from her throat, she came to orgasm. The slap-slap of cushiony buttock cheeks on my thighs and the rub of her public bone on mine had me going too and I thrust up to match her downward lunges. We came together with loud gasps and in long shuddering spasms. As she collapsed forward over me in her final throes, Roberta called me a beast.

'Every inch of one, madam,' I admitted as she lay across me steaming. 'You really needed that, didn't you? Glad I was here to oblige.'

It was then she'd risen rather unsteadily to go to the drinks trolley and now she said my services were no longer required. I was being banished after practically undergoing rape. Offering me a farewell vodka-and-lime seemed poor recompense and I wasn't for giving up so easily. I desired further use of the comely body so close to me.

'You'd better get dressed,' she said as if reading my mind. 'I'd like you to leave.'

Beyond the bedroom I could hear the sounds of wild Africa at night. The distant rumble of the Nile cascading at Murchison Falls; the trumpeting of a bull elephant; drums beating out from the nearby Acholi encampment – all these noises were a world away from the luxury of a tourist hotel in the bush. The heat of the tropical evening, combined with her exertion, made Roberta's well-fleshed skin glisten moistly in the lamplight.

Beads of perspiration trickled down her neck to run into the deep cleavage of her bosom, the ample mounds drawn apart by mass and weight. Between her rounded thighs, a thick triangular growth of hair lay flattened and sweat-damp on the curved mound. Enough was enough. I took hold of her wrist and told her to come to bed.

'Let go of me,' she said icily. 'Return to your room.'

'The night is young,' I reminded her, intending to be reasonable. 'Why not make the most of it?'

'You take too much for granted,' came the haughty response. 'What makes you think I'd let you stay?'

'Because you want it,' I challenged her. 'Like I want it. Sleep with me. Let me have your lovely tits and arse beside me all night. Let's fuck all we want and then wake in the morning and fuck again.'

I saw that my crude words had her considering the possibilities. Drawing her down beside me, she sat on the edge of the bed. Encouraged, I slipped an arm around her, my palm cupping a heavy tit. The nipple was stiffly erect as I tweaked it. My free hand went to her crotch.

'I have my reputation to consider,' she began, her resolve weakening as I pressed a kiss to the soft join of her neck and shoulder. 'There's my position in the government as well as my prominent husband—'

'Your secret is safe with me,' I told her. 'We're a long way from Westminster and your old man. It's too late anyway. We've already fucked. I say we fuck some more.'

'How coarse you are,' she admonished, yet not preventing my hands playing with her tits and cunt. 'I've never been spoken to in such a manner.'

Which was no doubt what the hoity-toity bitch liked to

In the Flesh

think. I played up to her, certain she found the idea of a bit of rough intriguing.

'You've had *your* fun,' I said, 'now it's my turn. Pay-back time.'

'Is that so? You're not in any fit state,' she said, indicating my limp dick. 'What good could *that* do me?'

'With a little help from you it will rise to the occasion.'

'And how would I accomplish that?'

'Suck it,' I suggested, lolling back.

'This gets worse,' she observed. 'You're totally disgusting. I've never even done that to my husband.'

'So they all tell me,' I laughed, lowering her face over my spread thighs. I heard the word 'beast' again before the wet warmth of her full lips encircled my relaxed prick. She drew it in with increasing sucks as the throb and tumescence returned, my stalk stretching and thickening between her tongue and palate.

Roberta's head bobbed as she sucked harder, drawing my rigid flesh deep into her mouth as her letch increased. The lady liked sucking cock, I was convinced. If she really didn't do it to her husband, such was her expertise that some other lucky bastard was on a good thing. '*Umm*,' she mumbled as she got into her stride, greedy for it, cheeks hollowing and expanding, sucking as hungrily as a child at the breast.

'Quite a little cocksucker on the quiet, aren't you?' I felt bound to say about her enthusiastic gobbling. 'Hazarding a rough guess, I'd say you've done this before.'

She paused with my saliva-wet knob at her lips, looking up at me defiantly. 'I've been told I'm good at it. But you're still a filthy pig for expecting me to do this. I dread what you are going to do to me next.'

'Return the favour,' I said. 'Lick you out thoroughly before I fuck you. Has your prominent husband ever gone down on you? Tongue-fucked that greedy snatch between your legs?'

'You really know how to sweet-talk a lady,' she returned acidly, nevertheless she was turned on by my language I was sure. 'You're a complete brute, but as we've gone this far I insist that you lick me.'

'Among other things,' I promised, and the night hours that followed can only be described as delightful as we did everything sexually possible between willing partners. Daylight lightened the curtains while I was having her from the rear on all fours. Later I arose from beside the slumbering woman to go to my own room to shower and shave, pangs of hunger driving me down to eat a hearty breakfast.

Enjoying my bacon and eggs, I was joined at the table by Harry Saxon, the United Nations Food and Agricultural official who had flown north with us to the refugee camp. I'd been more than impressed by his dedication and his ability to create order out of chaos and start relief work.

'I see there's no sign of the Hon. Roberta Leigh-Pagett, M.P.,' he said cheerily, glancing around the dining hall. 'Doubtless the lady is having a lie-in after recent exertions. She does go at it, you know.' He studied the menu, grinning. 'That's one pushy woman. I'm sure Roberta hasn't got where she is through lying back on the job.'

'If you say so,' I answered, wondering what he was getting at and giving nothing away. 'How would I know? I'm only the pilot on this trip.'

'I looked into your room after dinner last evening, Ty,' he said, sounding mischievous. 'Thought we'd have a drink together. You weren't there, or anywhere else I could discover.'

'I was around,' I said, not committing myself. If women are good enough to let me fuck them, I don't tell tales.

'Couldn't locate Roberta either,' Harry went on, his grin

In the Flesh

wide. 'I didn't try her suite. Thought perhaps you two were together.'

'How could you think that?' I asked defensively.

'Because the lady's been desperate to get screwed this whole trip,' the UN man laughed. 'She tried to seduce *me* in my tent at camp. She'd evidently gone to seek you out first but I'd sent you off for supplies. So I was second best. Roberta tried to have her wicked way with me. You should feel flattered.'

'You should have given her one, Harry,' I advised, still not willing to involve her. 'She's a fine bit if you like 'em big-titted and round-arsed. Great knockers and bum on her.'

'She has that,' he agreed. 'Plenty of prime flesh. I wouldn't have minded but I'm a happily married man.'

'When did that stop anyone having a jump?' I asked. 'Roberta would hardly broadcast that you'd banged her.'

'I wouldn't be too sure of that,' Harry said wisely. 'Roberta has the kind of inflated ego that goes with positions of power. She'll be dining with my wife and I tonight back in Entebbe.' He shrugged as if entertaining the government official was a final duty he had to perform. 'I should be back with the refugees, they're flooding in from Sudan. But I've got to keep in with Roberta. Butter her up and send her home happy to press for more aid to be sent when she reports on the situation.'

'Then you should definitely have fucked her,' I said.

'With my wife acting as hostess tonight?' Harry pointed out. 'With the two women together, it could prove awkward if I'd screwed Roberta on an official trip. I wouldn't put it past the arrogant bitch to think she was one up on my wife and drop hints. Besides my guilt might show.'

'A wasted emotion,' I advised. 'I rather enjoy being

in the company of women I've fucked when they're all unaware of it.'

'It's good for the male ego,' Harry agreed. 'You're invited to dine with us, by the way. It's a pity Roberta didn't get laid this trip, all the same. I want to send her home in a good humour so she can demand we get help out here.'

'Are you serious about Roberta going back well-screwed?' I queried. 'Do you really think that good memories of her jaunt makes her more liable to press for aid?'

'I'm sure of it,' Harry confirmed. 'She came across as having the hots from day one. I suggested this stopover at the safari lodge to give her another chance of getting laid. I hoped you two would get together. You're footloose and fancy-free, a well-known horny bastard. Would it have been too much to ask?'

'Set your mind at rest,' I told him. 'The necessary was done. All through last night, in fact. Strictly between you and I, of course. The lady says she has a reputation to consider, plus a prominent husband.'

He held out his hand across the table. 'My lips are sealed,' he grinned relieved. 'Hard luck on hubby, a high court judge, but bully for you, Tyler. I owe you one. How noble can you get?'

'It was no chore,' I said. 'The Hon. Member fucks and sucks like it was going out of fashion. We did all the usual things plus some unmentionable ones. Once she's set on letting her hair down it's all systems go. You suspected, didn't you?'

'I had every confidence in you. You have your own reputation to consider,' he said, grinning. 'It's well known throughout East Africa.'

'All lies,' I protested.

'You will dine with us tonight?'

In the Flesh

'No can do, Harry,' I said, having something else in mind for my return to base. 'I'm fully booked.'

'No wife to go home to?' he asked.

'Never been so fortunate,' I said in sorrow. 'Nobody to nag me, spend my money, demand to know where I've been. It can be rough, chum. I'm forced to play the field.'

'You're missing out. Wait until you meet my wife, Diana,' Harry declared with pride. 'She'd make you change your mind about marriage.'

'I doubt it.' I dismissed his suggestion. 'The last thing I should have in my life is a wife. I can get into enough trouble on my own. I don't go looking for it, it seeks me out, always has. No doubt it will again.'

I could not know how true that prophesy would prove to be. Already, without my being aware, forces beyond my control were conspiring against me. I should be so popular . . .

Chapter Two

I was employed by Lake Airways, a small flying outfit occupying a far corner of Entebbe Airport. The trip with Roberta and Harry Saxon to the northern territory was just another job. My passengers alighted, and were seen on their way in the company Land-Rover, as the Cessna aircraft was towed into its hangar to be prepared for the next flight. I went into the company office, a wooden hut, to hand in my log book, draw my pay and, hopefully, quit for the day.

Malik Singh, the Sikh spare pilot who doubled as staff clerk, handed me my monthly salary slip. At last I was solvent again and had money to squander on the high life, something I was good at. To my relief, no urgent flying job had been booked for me. As I was about to drive off to my bungalow, I was collared by Bill Dove, the ex-RAF Wing-Commander who managed Lake Airways.

'I take it you're all set for this evening, Wight?' he demanded, referring to the opening performance of *An Inspector Calls*, put on at the Entebbe Club by his amateur theatrical players. 'I've arranged that you won't be flying again today, so whatever else you may have in mind, be there!'

'That's a threat?' I laughed.

'I know damned well the kind of life you lead,' he said. 'If you didn't fly my aircraft passably, you'd be out on your left ear. See you report early backstage.'

'Everybody's got me wrong,' I complained. 'I wouldn't miss this opening night for the world, Wingco.'

I threw him up a mock salute, liking the old aviator even as he shook his head at me disdainfully. It was Bill who had coerced me into becoming a member of the dramatic society. He had also given me my job, rescuing me from being a down-and-out in what I found was a tropical paradise for my style of life.* Owing him that, I'd agreed to become one of his players, though nothing could induce me to appear on stage. I operated behind the scenes. Helping work the lighting wasn't so bad – not as assistant to Chloe Warren.

It's an ill wind. Reporting for my first rehearsal, considering I had better things to do, I'd liked the look of Chloe right away. She was not only completely genned up on the switchboard, making my help extraneous, she quickly proved a more than friendly girl. A cuddly twenty-year-old English nurse employed at the local Grade A hospital, I had an immediate desire to see if her tits were for real. They positively bulged, an inviting pair in keeping with the rest of a voluptuous little body.

'It's an easy one tonight,' she said on my late arrival. 'Just one set, the dining-room. The first act has just started.' Her wicked smile was an open invitation. 'There'll be nothing much for us to do back here all alone, will there?'

'I'll have to think of something,' I said, advancing and pinning her against the switchboard console. Her cushiony breasts flattened against my chest and my prick stirred as it nudged into her pliant belly. Close by we could hear the play proceeding. 'How about some more of what we did at the dress rehearsal?' I suggested.

'It would help pass the time,' she giggled, working her crotch up into mine. 'Gracious, did I do that to you?' she

---

* See *In the Groove*, also published by Headline Delta.

In the Flesh

said, referring to the hardness against her mound. 'It's really huge tonight.'

'And it's all yours,' I said, one palm cupping a luscious tit while the other was filled with her left buttock cheek. I kissed her and she reciprocated fiercely with open mouth and probing tongue. No time waster, her hand went between us, drawing down my zip. 'You're everything I like in a girl, Chlo,' I said. 'Lewd, lecherous, wanton, randy as hell—'

'And someone to fuck,' she completed for me, my stiff dick now gripped in her hand. 'Fuck me with this then. Make the most of it because it's your last.' She kissed me lingeringly. 'After the show tonight Heinz and I are announcing our engagement.' Again she gave her wicked giggle. 'He's going to make an honest woman out of me. About time, isn't it? We really shouldn't be standing here with your cock in my hand and you feeling my tits.'

'Blast! I intended to marry you myself,' I said. 'So young Herr Doktor at the hospital has popped the question? He's getting a fucking machine, lucky boy.' My hand behind her rucked up the light cotton dress and met smoothly rounded bare skin. 'Oooh, I feel a perfect arse,' I joked.

'Knowing you, I dispensed with my knickers,' Chloe said, her voice husky with arousal. 'It's that lovely big prick of yours, Tyler Wight, that's made me such a slut. Fuck me! Fuck me good and hard so I'll remember it. Put it in me now!'

'You've got hold of it. You put it in,' I said. 'You know how, its been there often enough.'

'Poor Heiny doesn't deserve this,' she said plaintively.

'He's not getting it,' I retorted, the time for pleasantries over. I fingered a plump little quim saturated and pulsing like a heartbeat. *Like a knife through butter*, I thought as she guided me in, thrusting her pelvis hard to me and gaining deep penetration first go. I prefer beds when screwing and knee-tremblers are not my first choice, but beggars can't be choosers. Our bellies slapped, matching heave for heave as I pistoned my cock up a receptive cunt. Soon we were jerking in complete abandon. Muffled gasps and cries plus long shuddering spasms told me she was coming. Waiting for that sign, I let go, pumping my tribute up her in long spurts.

'God, I'll miss it if Heiny doesn't make me come like you do,' she mumbled breathlessly, leaning into me. 'He'd better.'

'You've become engaged without finding out?' I said, surprised. 'What does he expect, a virgin?'

'He is,' Chloe chuckled, 'and I'll be one on our wedding night. Now, since you've corrupted me entirely, will you corrupt me some more?'

'That's my girl,' I said. Kisses, cuddles and fondles led to one more fuck for luck during the third and last act. This time Chloe leaned forward over the switchboard with her dress rucked up to display her lovely young arse. I took my time in a long and leisurely screw, giving her several strong climaxes before shooting my load into her, buffeting her comfy rear as she stifled her cries while coming off. I've long considered the main pleasure of sexual activity is to have the female on the end of one's prick going out of her mind. Chloe was a natural, one might say a girl who shared the male complaint of premature ejaculation – her climax was triggered almost on insertion.

When the play was over, I joined the company in the adjoining club bar to find it decorated with balloons and streamers for the young couple's engagement. Heinz Muller, her German doctor fiancé, stood with his arm about her proudly. I went out of my way to offer him congratulations, getting an appreciative nod and smile from Chloe. Beside them stood a couple I guessed were her parents, an attractive mother in her early forties, almost a double of her daughter.

In the Flesh

I had judged correctly. 'Mummy, this is Ty. Tyler Wight, a daring bush pilot and a fellow member of the dramatic society. He's a good friend. And Tyler, this is my dad,' said Chloe.

I shook hands with the mother. 'I hope you enjoy your stay in Uganda, Mrs Warren,' I said, observing she had the same shapely tits as her daughter, only even larger. 'Heinz is a very lucky man.'

'Very lucky,' Heinz agreed, hugging Chloe fondly. 'We do not intend a long engagement, do we, *liebchen*? First we go to Germany so that my parents meet my future wife—'

With Chloe distracting me with a sly wink, I realised I still held Mrs Warren's hand. 'A bush pilot, how exciting,' she enthused as I relinquished my hold. 'All this is such a change from our home in Harrowgate, isn't it, Arthur?' she prompted her husband. 'I often think we've never really lived.'

'I don't know,' her Arthur commented. 'We have our interests. The golf club, our caravan holidays in Devon. I'm not keen on a hot climate or flying either. The flight out was extremely bumpy. Turbulence, you know.'

'I enjoyed it. It was exciting,' his pretty wife declared.

Her husband was obviously a solid Yorkshire business type, out of place in a floral shirt worn loose over shorts, more used to wearing a dark suit for the office. He was short tubby and florid-faced. I left their company to go to the bar, and was having a beer with Bill Dove when Chloe disengaged herself from her fiancé to join us. The Congolese band hired from the Lake Victoria Hotel had been engaged for the night and dancing had started.

'One of you two men ask my poor mum for a dance,' she said. 'Daddy doesn't know a step and Heiny has given her several, but I know she'd like a change. She's sitting at our table tapping her feet.'

'That rules me out,' Bill Dove excused himself. 'I'm like your father, never able to master any dance. Two left feet. How about you, Wight? Would you see a lady in want of a partner?'

'He can dance very well,' Chloe said positively. 'We've danced before. Do as I say, Tyler. I order you.'

I crossed over to the table where Chloe's parents sat with Heinz, noting that Arthur Warren's florid features had grown even ruddier in the close atmosphere of the tropic night. He mopped his brow, looking rather unwell. 'Would you care to dance, Mrs Warren, if your husband doesn't object?' I asked politely. She stood at once and I felt big firm breasts pressing against my chest as we circled in a slow foxtrot. Her belly and crotch were too close for comfort as well. The warmth of her body in the light dress she wore transferred its glow to mine disturbingly.

'This is such a pleasure. I'm glad I nagged Arthur into flying out for Chloe's engagement,' she enthused. 'He's such a stay-at-home these days – golf, bowls and television – I could scream. My daughter tells me you live quite near her bungalow.'

'Hardly ten minutes walk, Mrs Warren,' I said, thinking of all the times I'd slipped out at dawn after a night spent with the nubile young nurse. Leaving before anyone was about to start a scandal. It was best that way for her sake, people locally had given up on me.

'Please call me Margaret,' she smiled. 'Mrs Warren is so formal. I find it exhilarating being here – the sights and sounds of Africa. I'd love to go upcountry on safari to see the wild life, but they say it's not advisable at present.'

'It's a little unstable outside Entebbe and Kampala,' I agreed. 'There's rumours of a coup, with the army

In the Flesh

overthrowing President Obote and his government. The usual power struggle and nothing new in Africa. It would be safer to stay around here.'

Her closeness was beginning to tell despite my resolve. Apart from her cushiony tits flattened to my chest, her mound rubbed against mine with each twirl as we danced. My prick, always an unruly appendage, was eager to be given its head. I was relieved the following dance was the twist and parted us, after which I escorted her back to the table. I considered her to be a respectable middle-class housewife and mum, wholesomely attractive and living a very mundane existence. I wished the party goodnight, intending to venture out into the night and seek better sport at a local bar.

'Thank you for the dance. Don't be a stranger while we are here,' she called as I turned to leave.

Passing through the verandah to the steps leading from the club premises, I met Harry Saxon. With him were the Hon. Roberta and a woman I knew must be his wife. At once I was smitten, never before having seen such beauty in a woman. Burnished auburn hair surrounded a lovely oval face. She had dark hazel eyes bright with the love of life and full red lips parted in a smile to reveal even, white teeth. I noted a superb figure encased to best advantage in a simple floral dress.

'You're staring, Tyler,' Roberta said sharply.

'Diana has that effect on men,' her husband said proudly. 'Didn't I warn you, Ty, she'd make you change your mind about marriage?'

'Do shut up, Harry,' his wife laughed. 'You embarrass me.'

'No woman would have him,' Roberta stated, linking her arm in mine firmly. I guessed from her demeanour she had been drinking and was merry, part of Harry's plan to send her home happy, no doubt. 'I hear music in there, I want to dance.'

She led me off, imperious as ever. Again I had a warm and pliant body in my arms as we joined the dancers thronging the floor. This time I did not mind my dong erecting to nudge into the soft underbelly pressed against me. 'You're still totally disgusting,' I was reprimanded. 'Have you a car outside?'

'Of course. It's too dangerous to walk at night.'

'The Saxons were driving me back to the hotel when they stopped off to show me this club. You can drive me now.'

'My pleasure,' I assured her, envisaging another night sleeping together. 'We'll tell them. Just ease away to let my hard go down.'

The music ended and I walked her to the bar where Diana Saxon and her husband were waiting. Harry immediately turned the conversation to the plight of the refugees, taking every advantage to impress upon Roberta how vital her help would be. 'He's on his favourite subject,' I said to his wife. 'Would you care to dance, Mrs Saxon?'

'I'd love to,' she said, fitting into my eager arms as we glided away, earning an angry glare from the impatient Roberta. 'I think our important visitor is anxious to be off for some reason. I wonder what it can be?' Diana added playfully. 'Do you think she's looking forward to being in bed?'

'Maybe she is,' I answered, playing the innocent, 'but she can wait until we've had this dance. Before I drive her to the hotel, I mean.'

'Of course,' Diana smiled. 'It was kind of you to offer.'

'Are you aware you're by far the best-looking woman here?' I said to change the subject.

'Be careful, Mr Wight,' she warned mischievously. 'You evidently have an ardent admirer in Roberta and she's not

In the Flesh

to be trifled with. But I'm led to understand that you trifled with her somewhat during your stay at the safari lodge last evening. All in the line of duty, of course.'

'Your husband told you that?' I said, shocked.

'After I'd learned it from the most reliable source,' she laughed, amused by my reaction. 'Harry is indebted to you. He said that to make that woman's trip memorable, he'd have obliged her himself. At least, he thought about it. Poor Harry, he does take his responsibilities seriously.'

'And you wouldn't have objected?' I asked.

'In the event I didn't need to, did I?' she said as if finding the whole idea hilarious. I could only think what a special kind of woman she was proving: beautiful, with a sense of humour, and above possessiveness in relationships.

'I think I'm falling in love with you,' I said, only half in jest. 'You wouldn't care to run away with me, would you?'

'And risk the wrath of Roberta?' she laughed lightly. 'Thanks to your efforts she was full of praise at dinner for what was laid on for her during the trip. She solemnly vowed she'd use every effort to rush aid to Harry's refugees on her return. Both in parliament and by using the media to get donations from the public.'

'I'm happy to have helped out in a small way,' I said wryly.

'Not so small, I heard,' Diana teased. 'Not from what Roberta told me in private this evening. She's a kiss-and-boast female. If my Harry had been with her sexually, wouldn't she just have loved rubbing my nose in it? As if it would have mattered? I mean if Harry had bonked her. It wouldn't have been the end of the world, would it?'

'Not in the cause of humanity,' I laughed with her, swinging her around as we danced, intoxicated by her nearness and smell, a fragrant mix of an unobtrusive perfume and clean female scent. 'You're some kind of lady, Mrs Saxon. You've got Roberta's number all right.'

'I don't resent her wanting a fling away from Westminster,' she rebuked me kindly, 'among you macho men. She's really very attractive. I'm sure you didn't find it too hard.'

'You're truly beautiful,' I told her. 'Inside and out.'

'But I'm not,' she protested. 'My mouth is too big, like my bust and bottom. And I have freckles all over.'

'Prove it,' I grinned.

'Are you trying it on with me?' she laughed.

'Your husband is a good friend of mine,' I objected. 'Of course I'm trying it on. Give me half a chance.'

'When the music stops,' she said firmly, 'Roberta awaits you. I want my husband to myself for the first time in weeks.'

'Lucky Harry,' I said, at that moment feeling a hand on my arm and Roberta moving in between us. She held on to me tipsily as Diana stepped away, cutting in to continue the dance by pulling me around the floor. 'You're pissed,' I accused her, breasts and crotch thrust into me. 'Pissed and randy.'

'More randy than pissed,' she stated. 'Never felt better. Is there somewhere private in this place? I need a fuck.'

'Can't you wait until you get to the hotel?' I asked, being reasonable, I thought. All the same, her nearness had my prick standing in the fork of her thighs. 'I suppose we could find somewhere if you're desperate.'

I waltzed her to the back of the hall and found the door of the billiards room. Luckily none of the regular snooker fanatics were present. It was a place I never used myself and I looked for the first time at the two full-sized tables and racks of cues, the wall hung with fading photographs of colonials of years gone by standing beside dead lions and elephants with poised rifles.

In the Flesh

While observing this, Roberta locked the door and advanced on me. I felt my trousers and pants pulled down as she knelt before my legs, gripping my prick and covering it with her mouth, sucking avidly to bring it to full size for her use. Moments later, she stood to remove her knickers, rucking up her dress and climbing on the table to lie prone on the green baize cover. Legs apart, feet braced, cunt tilted for penetration, she was on offer. I joined her, her legs curling around my back and her hand guiding my rampant stalk to her outer lips.

I had fucked in more comfortable places, but Roberta's body was made to cushion the buffeting I gave it as our ardour grew. She deserved full marks for enthusiasm, heaving back to me in her throes, groaning in her heightening pleasure, croaking out that I was making her come and, as ever, reminding me I was a beast. In time she lay back recovering, with my load up her, both of us satisfied and sobered up somewhat. Suddenly she asked me what I thought of Diana Saxon.

'I hardly know her,' I said. 'She seems a nice woman.'

'Is that all?' Roberta said snidely. 'I watched the pair of you dancing and getting chummy. You'd like to fuck her.'

'Chance would be a fine thing,' I admitted. 'Get your knickers back on and I'll drive you to the hotel. Will my services be required again tonight, madam?'

'Come along and find out,' she offered provocatively. 'Tomorrow I must return to reality. Make tonight one to remember.'

It was going to be. More than we knew.

Chapter Three

Escorting Roberta to my car, a humble Morris 1000 Traveller that had seen service, I drove her a mile or so in the night to the Lake Victoria Hotel. Walking her through the foyer with its mounted heads and tusks of the local wildlife, I was accosted by Miklos Dimitri. A handsome Greek, the owner of Chez Miklos, Kampala City's best restaurant, he was known to me as a wheeler and dealer, into anything straight or crooked that increased his wealth and standing.

Miklos was out of my league and he usually ignored me. I had never sought his company. With his powerful political and military connections he was a potentially dangerous man to know in such a volatile country. I prefer the quiet life.

He came up with a darkly beautiful Turkish woman in tow, one I liked the looks and body of immediately. Full of good fellowship, his interest was patently centred on the well-stacked white flesh of Roberta.

'Tyler, you old flying fool,' he greeted me heartily in his accented English, slapping my back. 'We haven't seen you at my place for too long. My girls are always asking for you. I insist you introduce me to this charming lady.'

I saw Roberta frown, unsure of the larger-than-life character who had intruded on us. 'This is Bertha,' I said, guessing that she would prefer to remain anonymous. 'Miss Bertha Westminster. An old friend who is staying at the hotel overnight and leaving for England in the morning.

An early flight,' I added, 'so Miss Westminster is retiring for the night.'

'Surely not,' he protested, clasping Roberta's hand and retaining it. 'Miklos is the name, beautiful women is my game. I am the proprietor of Kampala's most exclusive restaurant. Why have I never seen you there, Bertha? A lovely name for a lovely woman.'

'I've never liked it myself,' Roberta said, her eyes twinkling, enjoying the attention of the forward Greek. 'And I've never been to your restaurant because I'm just passing through Uganda.'

'From Australia,' I put in, to add to the deception. 'Bertha is going to England to look up relatives. And you're full of shit, you whore-master. If you don't mind, we'll be on our way.'

'Always the joke, Tyler,' Miklos said unperturbed but his dark eyes flashing a warning to me as he bent to kiss Roberta's fingers. 'Surely a farewell drink is not too much to ask? The lady with me is my cousin, Fatima. We could make up a very pleasant foursome.'

'Why not?' Roberta answered pleasantly. 'That would be fun.'

'You don't know what you're getting into,' I warned her as Miklos led the way into the lounge bar. 'Fatima's no more his cousin than I am, in fact they say she's his wife. Anyway, she's one of his upstairs performers, a whore.'

'You should know,' Roberta countered. 'I don't meet these kind of people normally. I'm intrigued.'

'So is he,' I said. 'I know the kind of foursome he has in mind as well. But have it your own way. What happened to the parliamentary patrician I used to know? I'll fuck you all you want. You fancy slumming with *them*?'

'I'm Bertha Westminster tonight,' she reminded me. 'My own woman and a big girl. When else do I get the chance

In the Flesh

to mingle with such colourful characters? I'm enjoying myself.' She had wined and dined and was feeling randy, teasing the Greek. Seated on a bar stool with a generous gin and tonic, I saw her allow Miklos fondle her thigh. I stood beside Fatima, who was watching with amused interest.

'What is that woman to you?' she asked casually. 'You know that Miklos intends to fuck her?'

'The thought had occurred,' I agreed. 'As his wife, do you object? For myself, if she wants to sample his dick, I don't give a flying fuck. She's nothing special to me.'

'I think she is someone,' Fatima gauged shrewdly. 'Of a good position and family, probably with a rich husband. You see her rings and jewellery? This is her way of being different, I think. You are worried about her being with him.'

'Only for what she might regret in the morning,' I shrugged. 'She's a grown woman.'

'Very much so,' Fatima nodded. 'The kind Miklos likes. For myself I would like to see him fuck her and make her do the things he likes. I wouldn't mind having her for myself too. She's so soft and white.'

'And asking for it,' I said, watching the Greek kiss her neck while she giggled. 'Knocking back the gin too.' I thought of Harry Saxon and his concern that Roberta returned safely home with memories of a pleasant sojourn. Going up to her, I took her wrist.

'Miklos has invited us up to his room,' she said defiantly, pulling away from my grasp. 'I'm going . . .'

'It will be more private,' the Greek said with a look that warned me to keep my nose out of it. 'A little farewell party for Bertha. There will be champagne. You are welcome, of course. He winked at me slyly. 'I'm sure you'll find Fatima excellent company.'

I was sure I would, I thought as I followed the others to

the stairway leading to the first floor. 'She will learn,' the buxom Turkish harlot said to me. 'Perhaps your friend will like the experience. She will have to do as he pleases. It has always been his way. Would you object to joining in?'

'It's out of my hands,' I said, giving her waist a squeeze and feeling her raise my hand to cover a plump tit. The room lying in wait for us was clearly in the whore's boudoir class. It reeked of perfume, with deep carpets and a huge bed strewn with soft cushions and silken ivory sheets. Large mirrors lined the walls, with one strategically placed directly above the bed. Subdued lighting threw a warm rose-tinted glow to every corner. The array of drinks on a long sideboard included the best champagne on ice. The Greek had obviously envisaged an orgy and ordered accordingly.

'This is going over the top, you horny Greek hound,' I was forced to say in grudging admiration. The two women had gone into the adjoining bathroom, leaving me with our host as he opened the champagne. 'I know this hotel well but never knew of this lovenest. Isn't your pleasure palace in Kampala enough for you? This must cost a bomb to maintain, just to lure unsuspecting women here to fuck.'

Miklos shrugged. 'The money is nothing, I have plenty. This room has a value apart from what we'll use it for tonight.' He grinned at me shrewdly. 'You know the situation in Uganda. I'm informed you know General Amin well and have flown secret missions for him – unofficial flights for his own devious purposes.'

'Only with a gun at my head,' I protested.

'I could lose everything, including my life, on the whim of a senior army officer like him. One day he'll be making himself president of this country. I own much they'd like for themselves, so I keep well in with him and his colonels. They have free access to this room and my girls: European,

In the Flesh

Asian, African, any time. There is a key left at reception for their use.'

'Insurance,' I said, impressed, never keen to fall foul of anyone who could get me deported or worse. 'I prefer to keep Idi Amin at a safe distance.'

'Well, tonight is for us,' Miklos declared, handing me a full glass. 'I intend to screw the arse off your classy friend, among other things. And then wipe my prick in her hair. Fatima will want her too and then there's yourself. By morning she'll know she's been fucked front, back and sideways.'

'What did he say? Did I hear right?' Roberta demanded uneasily, returning from the bathroom with Fatima. 'Tyler, what is going on here?'

'What I warned you about,' I reminded her. 'And what you chose to ignore. It was you who was so bloody keen to come here. His kind are above the law here – what there is of it. Whatever happens, lie back and think of England. Put it down to experience.'

'I don't think so,' Roberta said icily, sobering up with shock and reverting to her authoritive voice. She refused the glass of champagne Miklos offered. 'It's been interesting meeting you and your wife, Mr Dimitri,' she said, offering her hand as if dealing with civilised people. 'I do have to leave. Early flight, you know.' Her hand was withdrawn as Miklos ignored it. She turned to me, now noticeably apprehensive. 'See me to my room, Mr Wight.'

'Stay,' Fatima urged seductively, going behind Roberta and grasping her wrists. 'I am here with you; another woman. There's no need to be afraid, Englishwoman. I promise you will enjoy—'

'Let go of me,' Roberta ordered. 'At once.'

'I don't think so, madam,' Miklos said, a hard edge in his voice. He spoke as Fatima tightened her grip on Roberta's

27

wrists, pinning her arms behind her, pulling her back until her appreciable breasts thrust out. 'She has good big tits,' he observed. 'I want to see them. Maybe I shall fuck them.'

He raised his hands and grasped Roberta's breasts, squeezing them callously. Her look at me as she shrieked out in anger and surprise was a mix of disbelief and fright. Miklos and Fatima threw her rudely across the bed. It took the two of them to hold her down and pull off her clothes, her screeches silenced by Fatima raining a flurry of sharp smacks to her bared buttocks as she twisted about.

'This is an outrage,' Roberta protested breathlessly, trying to maintain some dignity but remaining still with her thrashed bottom smarting and Fatima's hand poised above it. 'You beasts, you *dare* to smack me! This will be reported to the proper authorities.'

'What authorities?' Miklos mocked. 'Madam, you are in Uganda. Be a sensible woman and behave.' He freed her panties from an ankle, tossing the lacy briefs aside. 'We are only going to fuck you, not kill you.'

I saw her look at me pleadingly. 'You're an Englishman, are you going to allow this?'

'Nationality has nothing to do with it,' I had to say. 'You came up here despite me trying to put you off.'

'I didn't know you were being serious about these awful people,' she bleated. 'I can't have sex with all of you. I was only being friendly. Tell them I'm sorry if I gave the wrong impression.'

'You did,' I said. 'I'm sorry, but you'd better let them have their way. These low-lifes could make us disappear, with the kind of friends they have . . .'

'Do they have any idea who I really am?' she began pompously but a warning look from me made her shut up. Sprawled enticingly naked across the bed, I was sure they didn't care.

In the Flesh

'Better they don't know,' I advised. 'Think of your reputation, your husband. You can't afford to kick up a fuss.'

'Enough talk,' Miklos cut in impatiently. 'I don't give a damn who this woman is, only that she's going to get fucked good. Fatima, play with the bitch, arouse her,' he ordered sharply to his wife. 'Let's see if there's any life in the gabby cow. I've never heard anyone go on so much about a natural thing like being screwed.' He grinned in my direction arrogantly. 'It's obvious you never had any joy with the frigid bint. We'll show you how it's done.'

"Bitch", "gabby cow", "frigid bint" – these were hardly descriptions of herself Roberta was accustomed to hearing. I had to stifle a grin, despite her situation, seeing her glare of displeasure. My attention was then wholly diverted by Fatima who had stripped to her bare brown skin. I was mesmerised by such voluptuousness. Extremely comely if a trifle over-developed in the fashion beloved by Turkish connoisseurs, she was eminently beddable to my greedy eye.

Her dusky teats were huge, peaks firm and uptilted, defying gravity despite mass and weight, the nipples dark and outstanding in thickness and length. Her thighs and buttocks were amply proportioned, the mat of thick black hair on a thrusting cunt mound matching the unruly thatch in her armpits. She was some woman. My prick, ever appreciative of such charms, twitched and stirred instinctively.

Fatima had a job to do and she went at it with a wicked smile. Kneeling on the bed beside Roberta, who watched as if hypnotised, Fatima's hands gently smoothed, stroked and fondled the apprehensive subject's breasts. She gave a lingering kiss to a startled mouth before lowering her lips to nuzzle and suck upon each nipple. I heard Roberta expel a low moan, as if in an agony of despair, as the other woman increased the suction, drawing breast flesh into her wide mouth. Miklos gave me a knowing look as he drew his shirt over his head, tossing it aside. His trousers followed.

'Relax, enjoy,' he ordered Roberta harshly. 'Go with it, woman. This is just the *aperitif*, so there's plenty more to come. You'll soon warm up.'

'No! *Please*,' Roberta now whimpered, her arrogance gone. Miklos calmly stated that progress was being made and I had to agree as I watched her struggle to resist giving way. One of Fatima's hand-cupped fat tits was being pressed to her face, the hard nipple forced to her lips. For a long moment Roberta suckled almost as if grateful for the comfort, before tearing her mouth away.

'You will obey!' Fatima said fiercely, giving a warning slap across Roberta's breasts before inflicting a further indignity. She roughly pulled apart the knees of the woman below, revealing all, the hair-covered cunt and anal ring. 'I do not know what she complains about,' Fatima observed, curling a finger between Roberta's outer lips and venturing beyond, bringing a groan of dismay. 'This is a much-fucked pussy, this one, wet for want of more prick. Miklos, be ready. I will bring her on more. I know she likes it.'

'I – I *don't*, I *don't*!' Roberta pleaded, her cunt being probed and no doubt, considering Fatima's skill, her clitty excrutiatingly tickled. 'I've said I'm sorry if I led you on. Don't shame me any more, *please*.'

A glance at the flushed faces of Miklos and Fatima told me she was wasting her breath, what there was of it, as her breasts heaved in panic or excitement. Her tormentors stood on either side of the bed, looking down on their naked victim with lustful intent, Miklos sporting a huge veiny erection. Roberta, I suspected, despite the token opposition, had now resigned herself to her fate. In such a situation there are women who find it erotically arousing to be used as if against their will, the bitter-sweet humiliation acting as a

In the Flesh

powerful aphrodisiac. I could see that Roberta fell into that category. It did not make me feel so bad at not trying to halt the romp.

'Yes, the bitch likes it,' Miklos said, echoing my assessment as Fatima worked long fingers into the parted slit and Roberta's belly and thighs quivered, vainly trying to stem her mounting arousal. Her breasts were swollen from being sucked, the nipples engorged and stiffly erect, saliva wet against the pink areolae. Miklos seemed content to idly stroke his upright prick and watch his wife compel another woman to respond against her choice. It was no act on the part of the Turkish whore, her own wantonness evident as she used mouth and fingers to reduce Roberta to lewdness. My dick was painfully erect. It was to be one of those nights, I knew, as I took off my clothes.

'Have you ever been loved by another woman, fine English lady?' I heard the salacious Fatima coo into Roberta's flushed face. She flicked a long wet tongue over the taut nipples, working her wrist as the fingering continued below. It was not my imagination that the Hon. Member of the Mother of Parliaments sighed languidly, her legs widening and toes curling. 'See, the men are watching us,' Roberta whispered. 'They like to watch women make love. We've made them big and hard to fuck us. Is it not exciting?'

Her voice tailed off as she slid down, positioning herself between Roberta's spread thighs. Her palms widening the rounded flesh surrounding her head, Fatima placed her full lips over Roberta's pouting cunt and sucked greedily. I had no doubt it was followed by a deeply delving tongue as Roberta groaned mightily and bucked her hips, grasping at Fatima's thick hair. Her arse bouncing on the bed, Roberta muttered, 'Yes! There! Oh, heaven, you're making me – making me come – COME! You've made me . . .'

'She has a pretty mouth,' Miklos observed. 'For a start I'll let her suck me off.' He got on the bed, kneeling beside Roberta's head, holding his stiff cock before her face. 'How about it?' he asked wickedly. 'I'll bet you've eaten cock before now. Open up!'

Engrossed as she was by being licked out by another female, Roberta turned her head and took his prick into her mouth, sucking immediately as if welcoming the intruder. I hardly noticed, my full interest being centred on Fatima's magnificent out-thrust arse. Kneeling forward from the edge of the bed, her back dipped as she concentrated on lapping and tonguing Roberta to repeated climaxes, an utterly irresistible bottom was tilted to tempt me. *Fuck it*, an inner voice urged. *Go in like flint*.

I touched up a plump fig-like quim nestled between the solid moons of her cheeks, finding the silky soft inner walls slippery with juice. My probing encountered a hard projection big as a thumb, a clitty of abnormal size that I strummed with my finger. In return I got an encouraging wiggle of her buttocks, plus a strong backward surge against my hand.

'Yes, fuck me! Fuck me now!' I heard Fatima gurgle into Roberta's thrusting crotch. To hear is to obey. I parted the plump cheeks with my palms and gave my all. Lubricated as she was, I penetrated full length first thrust, going in to my balls to bury every last inch. I interpreted her grunt as one of appreciation, her cushiony arse grinding back to my belly as I shafted her lustily. Experienced in the art, she contracted and relaxed her cunt muscles to match my thrusts, milking my stalk and adding greatly to the pleasure. I ordered myself to contain my surge, determined I'd have the big Turkish houri exploding before I let go.

On the bed I saw Roberta quivering in her throes, tits heaving and face turned to the kneeling Miklos. A hand

In the Flesh

squeezed his balls while her mouth sucked like a glutton on his prick. Then Fatima was squealing, bucking wildly back to me in convulsions as she came. Timed to the second, I let go, emptying my balls into her, buffeting her arse in the long series of spurts.

It was time to return to the champagne. Four naked bodies sat on the bed, recovering from the opening bout and preparing for the next. Now at the point of no return, Roberta rolled over obediently when ordered to do so by Miklos. His erection regained by his wife's employment of her mouth, he began fucking Roberta in the cunt before buggering her.

I led her away after that, using her early flight as my argument. For want of finding a bed in the wee small hours, once in her room I got in beside her. Awakening next morning I found her sitting up, breasts stretching as she yawned pleasantly, a smug smile on her face. This cat had enjoyed the cream, all right.

'That was really beyond belief last night, wasn't it?' she said, unable to hide her satisfaction. 'I didn't know such vile creatures existed. Would you believe what that dreadful Greek pervert did to me?'

'The bastard brought you off at least twice,' I said. 'Front and back. Plus his wife did the same. Are you complaining? It beats the hell out of a late-night sitting in the House of Commons, doesn't it?' I felt her hand sidle over my thighs, giving a little jiggle to my penis. 'If you insist on continuing that,' I warned, 'you'll have to climb on top of me. The rest of my body is still asleep.'

'I really didn't mean things to go that far, whatever you think,' Roberta insisted, not able to wait until I was fully erect before throwing a leg across me. 'It must never be known. God, it's got big and hard in there now,' she added. 'Let me fuck you nice and slowly. There's time enough before I get ready for my flight. I want to ride up and down on that lovely stiff thing. You'll never reveal to a soul about last night's orgy, will you?'

'What's to tell?' I grinned, enjoying her grinding down on me. 'We carry on like that all the time out here.'

'Do you people really behave like that often?' she enquired later, having satisfied her urge. 'I must visit again soon,' she laughed. 'Meantime I'm sending a friend of mine out here, someone who claims she's never experienced an orgasm with a man. She's a doctor who's expressed a wish to work with Harry Saxon's poor refugees. I'm sure she'd love to have one. An orgasm, I mean. Would you be kind enough to oblige?'

'I can but try,' I promised. 'It offers a challenge.'

It was something to look forward to, I decided, not knowing the half of what I would be letting myself in for.

Chapter Four

I entered the airport departure hall with Roberta clinging to my arm possessively, meeting Harry Saxon and his wife waiting to bid her farewell. The amused smile Diana reserved for me said, I know how you two spent the night. Why did that make me feel awkward in her presence? She was not judging me, rather enjoying a little harmless kidding. Usually I didn't give a monkey's what women thought of my philandering, but I remembered the dance we'd had together, her scent and the arousing feel of her lovely body in my arms. That had been an experience to savour, wondering what I felt for this woman, another man's wife. Not going soft, Wight, are you? I asked myself. That was not my style.

I got a full kiss on the mouth from Roberta as she prepared to board the jetliner. 'Be nice to my friend when she arrives,' I was reminded. 'The two of you should get on splendidly. I insist that you do.' She added to Harry, 'Cynthia Pellow is an old schoolgirl chum of mine, now a doctor of tropical medicine. She expressed a wish to me to work among refugees. Now that I know she'll be in safe hands, I'm glad to advise her to come.'

'We can use all the help we can get,' Harry said, carrying her hand luggage, no doubt impressing on her right up to the aircraft how much depended on her influence. I was left with Diana Saxon, stuck for once for something clever to say to a beautiful woman.

'You obviously made a deep impression on Roberta,' Diana said with that same amused smile. 'She wants you to look after her doctor friend because she knows the lady will be in safe hands.'

'You are taking the proverbial piss and you know it,' I replied, accepting her sense of fun, finding it extraordinarily pleasant being with her. 'So I've slept with Roberta. I'm glad it amuses you. I'd much rather have slept with you.'

She laughed delightfully as she shook her head. 'You really are all they say about you. Roberta certainly went away happy. But I don't believe you're as bad as you like to make out.'

'What don't you believe, Diana?' her husband asked, returning to join us.

'That I'm not a complete degenerate with an eye always on the main chance,' I answered for her. 'I've informed your wife I am.'

'He's right, dear,' Harry agreed. 'In fact his estimate of himself is rather generous. Have nothing to do with him. Apart from that, I like him. He's even willing to risk his neck flying me into hostile territory.'

'I've heard enough,' I said. 'I'm leaving before you ruin my bad name. I'm off to bed for the rest of the day.'

'Making up for lost sleep, I'm sure.' Diana teased again. 'Alone at last. Or is that too much to expect?'

'With my teddy bear,' I said. 'Harry, your wife regards me as a figure of fun. Warn her how dangerous I am.'

'I already have,' he said. 'Get your sleep, Ty. You'll be flying me back up north tomorrow. I'd be going today but I can't get the medical supplies delivered in time. Diana and I are driving two cars to Nairobi to pick up the goods. Be

In the Flesh

ready to fly early morning. Don't do anything I wouldn't do until then. As if you would!'

Looking at his wife, I thought how much I'd like to do to her what he would no doubt do before leaving her again. 'Safe journey,' I wished them, for the long road leading to Kenya had its hazards, getting a kiss on the cheek from Diana for my concern. I drove to my place by the lake shore, a rambling colonial-type bungalow surrounded by encroaching bush and scrub populated by chattering monkeys. Shamba, my ragged Kikuyu garden boy was as ever busy hacking back the undergrowth which threatened to take over the dirt track leading to my verandah. He gave a cheery wave of his razor-edged machete to remind me it was pay day.

Jovial Nkutu, my house servant, was dressed in her best native busuti costume, a basket balanced on her handsome head and about to leave on a shopping expedition. It was something I left entirely in her hands with all other household chores. Tall and statuesque, she greeted my arrival with a wide white smile. 'Welcome home, bwana,' she said. 'Will I make you breakfast before I go?'

'I've eaten, thank you, Jove,' I said. 'I'm going to bed.'

'Shall I come with you, sir?' she asked. 'I can shop tomorrow.'

'Later, I've no doubt, when I've caught up on some sleep,' I said to her offer. 'I know you like to meet your sister at the market. I won't surface until evening.'

So I intended, drawing the curtains in my bedroom before falling into a deep sleep. When I came to, my watch showed three in the afternoon and I felt remarkably rested. I was revived enough to awaken with a great straining erection which made me wish that Jovial was beside me to relieve it. I arose to shower, deciding I'd drive to the hotel to dine in style and see what talent there might be there. Visiting air hostesses from the major airlines were always a rich field of opportunity.

With that pleasant prospect in mind, I drew back the curtains to let in the afternoon sun. The view from my bedroom was of the garden with its lawn, flame trees, and the wide sparkling expanse of Lake Victoria beyond. I still had the most tremendous hard-on thrusting before me, thick and erect as a flagpole. Before me, too, through the window, I saw Chloe Warren's mother, Margaret. Her hand shot to her mouth as if to cover the shock, seeing me suddenly appear with a rearing cockstand. Face flushed, she lowered her eyes and stared hard at my erection for a long moment as if held captive by the sight.

Drawing the sheet from my bed to drape around my waist, I made a signal for her to go to the door on the verandah. Quite liking the situation, keeping the sheet as my sole covering, I let her in. Still uneasy, she entered to look around my sparse lounge with its wicker furniture, all at least kept neat and shining by my faithful Jovial Nkutu.

'I – hope I've not disturbed you, Mr Wight,' she began. 'Arthur, my husband, you remember, and I are staying at my daughter's bungalow nearby. I was out for a walk after lunch and came across yours.' She swallowed, attempting to quell her obvious embarrassment. 'I did knock but got no answer. Then I went into your garden thinking perhaps you were sitting out there.'

'You caught me unawares but you haven't disturbed me, Mrs Warren,' I assured her, meaning no way was I mortified by her seeing me so rampantly erect. My prick still firmly tented the sheet wrapped around me. 'I'm delighted you thought to visit. Forgive my state of dress, I was about to shower. Can I get you some refreshment? An orange squash or something stronger if you wish.'

In the Flesh

'I think I'd better, I feel I need something,' she said, allowing a first little shy smile. 'Would it be naughty of me to ask for gin to be added to the orange?'

'You can be as naughty as you wish with me,' I said suggestively. 'Of course, have a gin. I'll join you.'

As I had the previous evening, I admired the wholesome *niceness* of this attractive woman, so neat and to me vulnerable in a pink cotton frock that accentuated her figure. She sat in the best wicker chair looking around to avoid my eyes. The walls held African artefacts: crossed spears over a Masai shield, carved native masks, all left to me by a previous occupant. Impressed, she said, 'How full your life must be. Mine is exceedingly safe and dull.'

'We must make it more exciting for you while you're here,' I said, watching her swallow the stiff gin I'd prepared. So Mrs Saxon did not believe I was as bad as reputed, did she? Seduction of Margaret Warren was foremost in my mind. I refilled her glass.

'I shouldn't,' she said, accepting the drink. 'We had wine with lunch at Chloe's. You'll have me tipsy.'

Tipsy and naked, I envisaged. 'Where's your husband?' I asked.

'Arthur's not at all well, I'm afraid,' she said. 'The heat is too much for him. After lunch he had to lie down.' She drank at her gin, looking at me. 'He won't leave the house today.'

'Too bad,' I murmured. 'So you sought me out.' Perhaps my leer was too obvious, scaring her. 'Any special reason?'

'I don't know what you mean,' she protested nervously, her face blushing deeply again. 'I think I had better leave.'

'You know where the door is,' I told her, guessing she needed firm treatment and would probably welcome proceedings being taken out of her hands to assuage her guilt. I enjoyed the bounce of her substantial tits as she stood in confusion. 'Don't complain to me about life being safe and dull if you won't do anything about it,' I said sternly. 'Now's your chance.'

'Am I right in thinking—' she said hesitantly. 'You mean you want – want me – want to make love to me?' Remaining standing, confused but tempted, she admitted almost inaudibly, 'I won't say I wouldn't like to, but it's not right. I have a loving husband. I hardly know you.'

'What better way to get to know each other,' I insisted, letting my sheet fall to the floor and clasping her hand around my stiff tool. 'You want it and I want to give it to you. Have you coming till your teeth rattle. Does Arthur get you that way? He doesn't look the kind.'

'That side of our marriage was never like that,' she admitted, unable to withdraw her hand from my prick. 'Arthur is a good provider but not that kind of husband.'

'Did he never give you a good strong come, the kind that curls your toes?' I challenged. 'Have you ever had a come?' There were women who had never, I'd heard, and was interested. Added to that, salacious talk often increased the hearer's arousal.

'You want to know such personal things,' Margaret said, adding with a shy giggle. 'Of course I've had a come, a climax . . .'

My fingers were busy, down to the third button from the neck at the front of her dress. 'How?' I asked firmly. 'How? Other men?'

'How what?' she said shyly.

'How did you climax? I'm certain it wasn't Arthur. So?'

With the buttons undone to her waist, the high slopes of her breasts were revealed, rising and falling in her

In the Flesh

breathlessly excited state. Her eyes lowered as I insisted that she answer me. Pulling aside the dress showed a well-filled bra.

'There were no other men. I masturbate,' she confessed in a voice so low I made her repeat the shameful word. 'There, if you must know, I bring myself to it.' Looking up at me, she murmured, 'it was the only way. My husband never could – give me full satisfaction.'

'This is your lucky day, I guarantee it,' I said, convinced she was discovering erotically arousing emotions churning her innards by revealing sexual secrets. Saying them aloud to a man, and despite or perhaps because of the humiliation suffered, would make it all the more pleasurable. I kissed her long and passionately with my tongue deep in her mouth and my prick held hard against her lower belly. I felt her tremble and, after a moment, return the torrid kiss. 'It's time a real man taught you the facts of life,' I said to her face, determined to give her the star treatment. 'Me, for instance.'

'But we shouldn't,' she still protested between further long kisses. 'I've been a faithful wife . . .' Her expected objection was no doubt a salve to her conscience and merely added to my enjoyment. I like a show of reluctance, even if not entirely genuine. 'Believe me, I've never done anything like this before,' she moaned as my tongue left her mouth and I gave both tits a squeeze. 'Poor Arthur,' she added, as if an afterthought. I had no doubt that increased the wanton feelings she pretended to resist.

A determined tug brought the dress down. She wore neither slip nor stockings and was left only in the bulging lacy bra and matching briefs. She blushed as I ogled her shapely figure, the uplifted spheres of her large breasts and, below, between surprisingly strong thighs the dark outline of her pubic bush showing through the thin material.

'Unhook your bra and let me see those lovely tits,' I ordered, feeling crude talk was right for the situation and she wanted it. 'Drop your knickers too. You're too pretty to stay covered, don't you know?' To encourage her, I stood feet apart, rampantly erect. 'I don't mind so why should you? Get 'em off.'

'I don't know what my husband or daughter would say if they could see what you are making me do,' she whimpered, harking back to the theme that no doubt excited her. She unhooked her bra with trembling fingers, letting it fall to the floor and standing as if in an agony of embarrassment. Her tits were beauties, opulent globes of flesh that she tried to conceal. I drew her hands away and nodded to her lower region.

'*Please*,' she begged. 'Must I take more off? Don't make me.'

I'll make you, if that's how you intend to draw out this charade, I thought, my cock growing impatient to be at it. *Your daughter doesn't make all this fuss about me fucking her*, I could have said. I took her wrist, directing her through to my bedroom. Sitting down on the edge, I pulled her across my knee, my left hand with a firm hold on her neck. Thus placed, breasts dangling, stomach lying in my lap, she turned her face questioningly to me. *You wouldn't, would you?* her expression said. *Smack my bottom? I believe you would.*

With a deliberate movement I used my free right hand to draw her briefs down over her ankles and cast the garment aside, baring a delightfully rotund and full-fleshed bottom. I tested the silky smoothness of the cheeks with my palm and gave them a tentative warning slap. 'You came calling wanting me to fuck you, Mrs Warren,' I said accusingly.

In the Flesh

'All this protesting your loyalty to your husband has gone far enough. You fuck or I throw you out. Why so bloody coy? Do you need your arse smacked to make you admit why you came here?' Looking down at her quivering buttocks I knew I couldn't resist. I raised my hand and brought it down with a pistol-like crack on her naked flesh.

'Ohh! *Oww!*' Margaret howled as the sting burned her spanked rear. '*Please*, that hurts.'

'It's meant to,' I said, delivering smart smacks to her reddened cheeks, the imprint of my hand clearly impressed. *Owww*, she wailed, while I whack-whack-whacked and her lovely arse clenched. 'Fess up,' I ordered. 'Say you came dying to try out another cock. To sample a real come, not one brought on by yourself. Say it!'

'I did, I did,' she sobbed. 'I've got what I deserved. I – I – hoped you would – *fuck* me. There, I've said it. Please don't punish me any more. Fuck me if you still want to. I want you to.'

I placed her across the bed, lying stretched out quietly and self-consciously naked while I inspected her charms. I lifted each weighty breast, pinched each taut nipple, trailed my fingers lightly over her cunt lips to find them moist. She drew in her breath at my touch. 'Please, this is new to me,' she whispered. 'I want you to do things to me, even the smacking of my bare bottom made me very aroused. What else will you do?'

'Everything,' I promised, joining her on the bed, 'if you must know. I'll play with these gorgeous tits, even fuck them.' My hand went to her cunt, inserting a finger which made her arch her back. 'I'll enjoy licking out this tight little quim, making you come a storm. And you've a lovely cheeky bottom, I noticed while I was thrashing it. We mustn't ignore that.'

'You wouldn't,' she gasped, blushing furiously. 'It's not decent, not possible.'

'Anything's possible,' I said, parting her thighs with the palms of my hands, looking directly at her cunt with its surrounding thatch of softly curling hair. I heard a low moan as my tongue rasped over her outer lips before probing inside. The tip enclosed in warm moist folds of flesh, I flicked and swirled it around the taut bud of her clit. In response she squirmed her crotch, crying out that I continue, discovering a new delight and loving the experience.

'*Ohh*, you dirty, dirty thing,' she wailed out in her excitement, certain I was sure, that she basically considered the act disgusting. And that despite her reaction: arse wildly gyrating, cunt tilted and thrusting to my face, hands pulling my head into her parted thighs. 'Oh, Lord, I never, *never*,' came her cries. 'It's heaven, *heaven*—'

'Your husband never does this to you?' I taunted, judging she'd never been tongued to the brink, hearing her anguished cry as I drew my mouth away. 'Make him in future. You love it, love having your cunt licked.'

'I do, I do!' she moaned, clawing at my head to haul me back. Even though I kept my mouth from her, the surge continued and she jerked and pounded the bed in the throes of a formidable climax. It was satisfying for me too, bringing her off so strongly I could watch her cunt convulse.

I arose between her sprawled thighs, eyeing her meaningfully, my prick rearing and held directly at her parted quim. 'It looks so huge and hard now,' she said almost reverently, her eyes fixed on the rampant stalk. 'My God, can I take all that?'

'It's always gone in before,' I assured her, going forward, my aim good and true. The first thrust penetrated to the hilt, finding a receptive channel, tight but saturated. My balls thudded against comfortable arse cheeks as I shunted deep and hard; in to the meeting of our pubic bones, out to the knob before plunging in again repeatedly. Her arms and legs clasped about me as she returned thrust for thrust, wild to repeat the wonderfully abandoned deliverance of her previous come. Yet even in such heightened coupling she did not forget this was forbidden fruit, made more lewd by the thought.

'What am I doing?' she croaked out, buffeting my crotch as we increased pace, bellies smacking noisily, tacky with our sweat. 'Oh, Arthur, this man is having me, *fucking* me. Fucking your wife!'

'Damn right, Arthur,' I gritted, determined to hold back my own supreme moment until she'd had the ride of a lifetime. Mrs Warren climaxed strongly, urging me to go on, shove it up, and not come. At times only her head and shoulders remained on the bed, heaving up to me with a strength expended that would later leave her drained. To pull her even closer, my right hand went under to cup her writhing buttocks. In its working the cheeks were parted, hot and damp. I went in, wrist deep, a finger finding her anal pucker, inserting itself to the second knuckle while she squealed and bucked in even greater agitation. It was an old trick of mine and, when used at the appropriate moment, it added to the wantonness of a woman already out of control.

With Margaret it certainly added impetus to her already wild responses. She cried out she was coming, inhibition a thing of the past, urging me on in the lewdest words, ordering me to keep fucking her. *Harder, deeper, faster*! She howled out her demands like a demented soul, rolling her bottom around, exploding when the angles of my penetration poked at the places she liked best. She came at least four or five times before I let myself shoot a long-delayed volley into her begging crack. Finally our spasms subsided and, with murmurs of pleasure, she nestled in my arms and we both slept, sated and spent.

I woke up to the sound of loud knocking at the verandah door. Margaret sat up, immediately apprehensive, her face fearful. I drew on my dressing gown and prepared to find out who had disturbed us, hoping it was not an irate husband.

'Don't worry,' I said, covering my own concern. 'It's probably my housegirl enquiring what I'll have for dinner. Or I'm being called in for an emergency flight. Whoever it is, I'll send them away. Stay there and don't move.'

I left the frightened woman, closing the bedroom door behind me with a finger at my lips to assure Margaret our secret was safe. In turn she forced a wan smile, the ripeness of her breasts rising and falling with the pounding of her heart. Between her thighs, apart and uncaring now of what she revealed, the pouted outer lips showed glistening pink inner folds of flesh. That was my doing, I reminded myself, renewed by rest and suddenly eager for a resumption of fucking. Whoever was at the door, I determined to see them off with a reasonable excuse or even a downright lie.

Padding barefoot through to the lounge, I saw Margaret's daughter Chloe outside on the verandah, pacing about impatiently. Seeing me appear she shouted, 'What kept you? I've been banging for ages.'

'You certainly have and none better at it,' I replied, opening the French doors to let her in, thinking how young and pretty she was in a long red evening dress. My remark did not amuse her, noting her annoyance. 'I was fast asleep,' I said. 'You woke me up.'

In the Flesh

'We've lost my mother,' she said accusingly. 'Why is it I've got a horrible feeling she's here with you? I know where your bedroom is, you've had *me* there often enough. Out of my way and let me through.'

Chapter Five

'Whoa, Chlo,' I objected, adopting a hurt expression, standing to bar her progress to the bedroom. 'Cool it. Are you suggesting I've got your mother here?' I played for time, my mind racing to come up with a plausible alibi. To my relief, she shrugged and relaxed somewhat.

'Even you wouldn't sink that low, I suppose,' she said, 'but she did ask me to point out your house through the trees, so I assumed she came here. Bother mother. Heinz and I are due in Kampala. German friends are giving a dinner to celebrate our engagement before we fly to Munich tomorrow to meet his parents. My father is in a darkened room with heat exhaustion and now mum goes missing. This is Uganda. We're very worried about her.'

'Well, don't,' I told the girl, suddenly inspired. 'Mrs Warren did call here. She'd heard of the tennis tournament at the club today and expressed a wish to see it. So I drove her there and came back to catch up on sleep. Later I shall go and fetch her as promised and deliver her home safely. And you come along here with such a rotten accusation. She's your *mum*. As if I would!'

Chloe nodded in relief, swallowing my story wholesale. Her worried attitude changed and she giggled irreverently. 'I don't think mother would have minded,' she said wickedly. 'My father is not exactly a sexual athlete, like some people I could name. I've heard my mum complain about sex, or

Lesley Asquith

the lack of it in her life. Knowing too well how good you are at pleasing women with that big thing of yours, maybe I shouldn't mind if you had her through there in your bed. How is your dick today, by the way? Primed as usual?'

Her hand slid between the folds of my dressing gown and soft fingers circled my drooping dong. It immediately responded with a twitch and throb, thickening to stretch and rear its bulbous head as she massaged it. It felt too good to stop her. I only hoped her mother was obeying my instruction to stay where she was. Her daughter, growing horny with the hot stalk stiffening beautifully as she rubbed the outer skin, pushed aside the dressing gown to see what she'd achieved. Bending, she gave it a lick and a smacking kiss.

'I'll give you an hour to stop that, you randy girl,' I grinned. 'Young Heiny hasn't been doing his duty, has he?' I held apart the dressing gown for her better access, legs braced apart. 'Didn't he fuck you last night to seal your engaged state?'

'My fiancé isn't like that,' Chloe laughed cheekily, withdrawing her lips from my prick. 'He wants a virgin on his wedding night, so I've got to be a good girl until then, haven't I?' She rubbed me harder. 'I can wait, if this is available. Like always.'

'I'll be glad to oblige,' I promised, a churning in my balls at her insistent rub-rubbing. 'Keep going.' My voice lowered to contain my mounting excitement. 'Finish it in your mouth, or shall I fuck you across the couch?'

'Nope,' she teased, withdrawing her hand. 'It will keep you eager. Besides, Heiny is waiting outside in the car. You don't think I walked here in this evening dress, do you?' She pressed a tongue-probing kiss to my mouth and gave my prick a final squeeze. 'Keep it up like that for me, won't you, Ty?' the pretty young thing giggled. 'I'll probably be

In the Flesh

in need of a good ride when I get back from Germany. You won't forget to fetch my mother, will you?'

How could I forget her, seeing she was lying naked on my bed? Now with a good excuse to keep her there. Closing my dressing gown over a straining cock that felt rock-hard and permanent, I went back into the bedroom confidently. Now that the coast was clear, I decided a little erotic exercise with her would be in order. Margaret lay on her side, a knee drawn up to reveal the lovely curve of her divine bottom. Her anxious glance asked, why were you so long?

'It's nothing at all to worry about,' I said, explaining her daughter's visit and the time we now had that her absence had been quite satisfactorily covered. I admired the way she rolled over on her back, stretching languidly, her splendid breasts lifting and drawing apart. She cupped them in her palms, smiling at me, parting her legs to show off her enticingly curved mound with its furred triangle around the slit. 'Glad to see you've got over any shyness,' I said, shedding my gown to show off my rampant prick.

'Why has it got big again?' she giggled.

'Seeing you lying there so seductively,' I said. It would hardly have done to say her daughter had made it like that. 'Now where were we?' I sat on the bed and took her in my arms, kissing her mouth, both taut nipples, my fingers trailing over the silky soft outer lips of her quim. 'Shyness and guilt are hang-ups when it's not in your nature. But there's hope for you. You came seeking me out.'

'Because I needed a man, was desperate for one,' she confessed, tilting her cunt to encourage my touching her up. 'I've never wanted to be shy or feel guilt. I'm trying. You don't know the real me. Nobody does. I'm a sexually frustrated woman who secretly longs to have a man do the things you do to me. I've been like this ever since I was a young wife.'

'And remained frustrated and unsatisfied,' I sympathised to gain her confidence, all with a motive in mind. 'You can say what you like to me. It's good for you to get it off your chest.'

'Would you believe that I've fantasised the most awful things while – masturbating – to relieve my feelings?' she asked as if forcing the words out. 'Truly disgusting thoughts and acts I'm ashamed to admit, even to myself.' She suddenly embraced me passionately, her lips clinging to mine. 'You have made me see I'm not perverted, at least not entirely. That the urges I have are not unnatural. But kind as you are to be so understanding, I could never reveal such secret thoughts.'

'Admit them and even enjoy them,' I advised playing the wise counsellor, eager to hear what lewd hankerings such an obviously respectable wife and mother came up with in her randier moods. 'It's normal to have such thoughts,' I encouraged. 'It's known as therapy to acknowledge them, more so to discuss them—'

'Isn't what you're doing to me enough?' she asked, smiling shyly, her hips squirming as I tickled the hard nub of her clit. 'I've let you see all of me, feel me, lick me, fuck me; someone else's wife. I *couldn't* tell you what thoughts I have, not even to you. Not even if you smacked and spanked my bottom again.'

'You liked that, didn't you?' I said. 'But there's still a bit of the puritan in you. It's no wonder you bring yourself off with lewd fantasies, the husband you've got. What's the big deal?'

'You just want to hear what they are,' she moaned in her arousal. 'I could never look you in the face again. Oh, you're starting to make me come again with your fingers and your talk.' Her hand reached for my prick. 'It's ready. Fuck me. I'd rather you fucked me.'

In the Flesh

'In time,' I promised, taking her hand away. 'Tell me what goes on in those lurid thoughts that shame you so. Maybe we can act them out.'

'I believe you're enjoying this,' Margaret complained. She did not resist as I sat up with my legs over the edge of the bed, drawing her across my knees again. 'Why won't you fuck me? I've asked you; that's not easy for a woman. You're arousing me deliberately.'

And making a good job of arousing myself too, I could have said, looking down upon a narrowing waist that curved out to shapely buttocks. I parted the cheeks, trailing in a curved finger to touch up both orifices while she moaned and stiffened.

'Don't *stare* so at what's in there,' she pleaded, her head turned to me. 'It's not *nice*, it's disgusting.'

'But it excites you,' I said. 'I'll bet it's one of those naughty ideas you dream up when on heat. Held over a wicked man's knee with all your secret charms revealed to his eyes, opened up to be fingered as he likes. Helpless even if he smacks your bare arse to make you do things against your will. Only it isn't really against your will, is it?' I gave her bottom one good warning whack. 'Admit it!'

'No,' she whined almost inaudibly. 'You make me.'

'It's time someone did,' I told her. 'Come up here, I'll teach you a new trick.' Lifting her bodily, I arranged her standing, facing away with her back to my chest. My rearing stalk's knob nudged into the hot damp groove of her arse, touching the outer lips of her cunt. 'Remain standing,' I ordered, 'much as you want to sit on it.' I felt a tremor in her bottom, halting further movement with a slap to her thigh. 'It goes right up straight that way, bolt upright. Women love it. Have you ever had a prick up you that way?'

'No, *never*. Can I put it in, *please*?' She eased down

slightly on the balls of her feet, the bulbous helmet of my tool parting her nether lips the merest bit. 'Don't make me beg. You've humiliated me enough.'

'Have I?' I questioned. 'Isn't humiliation part of the fantasies you have? It's a common theme. Admit all and you can squat on it to your heart's content, impale yourself on every thick inch.'

'How cruel men can be,' she said. 'If you must know, I have had thoughts of being humiliated. By both men and women. There, does that please you?' She eased herself down over me with an anguished sigh, my prick engulfed in a clinging channel. 'People arousing me like you are, making me ashamed.' She began to jiggle her bottom tentatively with the upright root deeply enclosed, stopping when I ordered her to. 'Taunting me, tormenting me, the way you are doing.'

'And you're loving it,' I breathed into her neck, my cupped hands going around to grasp her weighty breasts, thumbs flicking the elongated nipples, my balls cushioned in the parted cheeks of her behind. Much as I desired to let her arse squirm I determined to make her confess more. 'Believe me,' I said, 'this is like an experiment. Living out your fantasies. It's harder on me than you. Tell me everything.'

'Thank goodness my husband can't see me now,' she began.

'Sure. That's part of your routine too, isn't it? Getting a big buzz out of dreaming up how you're being unfaithful to your loving hubby. You've harped on about it. Confess the rest, Mrs Warren.'

'It's worse when you call me that,' she moaned, the prick up her filling her, desperate to jog on it. 'I've been a good wife.'

'A good wife wasted,' I said.

In the Flesh

'When I – I – get the feeling,' she began hesitantly, as if deciding she had to, 'I go upstairs. It can come over me any time of day when I'm alone, when I'm dusting or baking. I can't help myself. It's always as if I'm in a trance going up to the bedroom. *There*, there I do you know what.'

'I don't,' I argued. 'Explain fully, please.' I permitted her to rotate her bottom to get more firmly on my dick. 'I'm no mind-reader.'

'I undress and touch myself. Sometimes in front of the long mirror, or I get on the bed. I play with myself.'

'Where?' I insisted.

'My – my breasts and nipples at first. Then lower down, between my legs. I suppose you want me to say my cunt?'

'That's what it is,' I said cheerfully. 'Good to say it, isn't it? You're doing fine so far. What do you use, fingers or other ways and means?' I eased myself up to give her a taste of my prick probing her innards. It had its effect, making her writhe on my lap and utter little whimpering sounds.

'Fingers, what else is there?' she asked tremulously.

'Vibrators, dildoes, bananas. Cucumbers for those who think big,' I suggested. 'Didn't you diversify?'

'Only fingers,' she insisted. 'They were enough – enough to give satisfaction. With the thoughts that always came.'

'Who or what was in those thoughts?' I enquired. 'Tell.'

'Men and women,' she admitted, choking on the words, but brought to a peak of arousal by deep penetration and our question-and-answer session. 'I couldn't help it. The thoughts just came.'

'Naturally. We all have them,' I sympathised. 'Continue.'

'Several men and somehow women appeared too,' I heard

55

in her mumbling. 'Having me two or three at a time, with my husband forced to watch. Oh God, making me do everything.'

'*Everything?*' I said, striving to keep the glee out of my voice. I took one of my hands from her breast, sliding it between my lap and her buttock cleave, inserting the tip of a finger in her rear hole. She stiffened in alarm, squeaking a protest. 'Even there?' I demanded of her. 'I'll bet so.'

'Don't make me admit *that*,' she objected, but beyond control she began to bounce up and down on me, gyrating her arse, thrusting and dipping, fucking wildly. 'I told you the thoughts come without me trying, damn you! *Honestly* they do!'

'It's your subconscious saying what you'd really like done to you,' I gritted out, heaving back to her and both of us unable to stop the shuddering climaxes that followed. She lolled back against my chest, still gripping my shrinking cock in her, both of us fucked to a frazzle and gasping as we fought for breath and recovery. A burst of loud hand-clapping from the suddenly wide-open bedroom door made us turn in alarm, Margaret falling from my knees to the floor as if in a faint. Miklos Dimitri stood there with the widest of grins, applauding our performance.

'How excrutiatingly pleasurable for your lady friend, being made to reveal such intimate details,' he said, coming forward to join us with the front of his drill trousers bulging. 'And how she fucked so wantonly on the strength of your interrogation, Tyler. I have revised my estimation of you. Beautifully done.'

He leaned forward, arm and manicured hand extended gallantly to a startled and petrified Margaret on the floor. She cowered before him, one hand covering her ample tits and the other over her cunt. 'Allow me to help you to rise,

In the Flesh

madam,' he offered chivalrously. 'I insist that you introduce us, Mr Wight.'

'You can fuck off, you Greek slimeball,' I said furiously, getting between him and the prone Margaret. 'Who gave you the right to come into my house? How long have you been here?'

'Long enough to be behind the door and hear the confessions you've wrung out of this delightful lady. I saw and heard all,' he said. 'Highly arousing words *and* the bout that followed. They've had the usual effect on me, as you can see.' He spoke calmly, menace in his voice, his dark eyes fixed on Margaret's nude body. 'Don't be alarmed, I just want to join in. I greatly admire you both.' He drew off his bush shirt, obviously intending to undress. 'Eroticism is a dying art, I find. People just fuck like animals. How refreshing to find true sensualists alive and well. I'm honoured to join you. Two's company but I've always found three the more pleasurable. More so for the lady.'

He posed naked before us, barrel chest furred with a mat of black hair. A prick of admirable length and thickness thrust out over heavy balls. Margaret, as if mesmerised, giggled as if all were beyond her. Cooling down myself, amused by his arrogance, always willing to see the funny side, I strove to maintain a stern face without the grin breaking through. I had been in similar situations as the gate-crasher myself.

'This is a private party, Dimitri,' I said. 'Get back into your clothes and piss off. Your services are not required. What the hell are you doing here, anyway?'

'Business initially,' he said, 'although I seem to be making a habit of having your women. I've a flying job for you. One you'll be extremely well paid for.'

'Something highly illegal, no doubt,' I said. 'I don't wish

to know.' I put a hand on his chest to prevent him stepping around me to see Margaret crouching behind my legs. 'As for having my women, as you put it, no way with this lady, you bastard.'

'You've no say in any of it, my friend,' Miklos said casually, and the more sinister for that. 'I have people in high places who ask that I obtain your services for them. You wish to continue living here, I presume?' He sidestepped me, smiling down at Margaret genially, again offering his hand to help her rise. She accepted it to my surprise, but who can tell what a woman will do? Raised to her feet, stark naked and with her breasts lifting with excitement, she allowed him to kiss her hand.

'What did you say about having Tyler's women?' she asked, more intrigued than offended, I suspected. 'Did I hear right? You have *shared* another woman?'

'It wasn't like that—' I began angrily.

'But it was,' Miklos said snidely. 'Tyler's a generous man. The lady was lovely, just as you are, and most appreciative of the attention and pleasure two can give. Do not be afraid. Think of my timely arrival as a further humiliation to be savoured, if that is your special pleasure. And why not? I have heard you admitting you fantasise about two men having you, making you do all kinds of things you have only imagined. Arousing as that may be to think about, the real thing is so much better. Let us show you.'

'I shall have to take your word for that,' I was glad to hear Margaret say, her nervousness decreasing. She was enjoying being naked before us and was growing flirtatious. 'This day's events have already exceeded what I should have allowed. If you're a gentleman, sir, you'll dress and leave us. Thank you for the offer, but I think things have gone far enough.'

In the Flesh

'You heard her,' I put in. 'We don't need you. On your way.'

'The lady might be made to change her mind,' Miklos said, as ever confident. 'I heard repeated references to a husband during your game of confessions. A daughter too. No doubt a happy family. How could your afternoon's orgy be excused by them, if informed? Further, as Tyler well knows, a word in the right ear, a telephone call even, could get you all deported by this evening. Come, surely allowing me to join you in your romp is a small price to pay for my silence?'

'What is he saying, what does he mean?' Margaret bleated in fear, her capricious attitude vanquished.

'That this apology for a human being would see that your Arthur knew all about you visiting me. He could also get us thrown out of the country if you don't give him his way,' I had to say. 'He'd do it without a qualm. I'm truly sorry this has happened.'

'She won't be,' Miklos said. 'Not when I've done with her. It will be my pleasure to fuck such a fine woman. Lie on the bed, madam, prepare to do everything I want. Forget him. He's had his turn, now it is mine. Please me and I will not be ungrateful.'

Chapter Six

It had been my good fortune up to this point to have had little to do with the lecherous Greek. Now, twice in as many days, he had intruded on my space and helped himself to my female partners. First Roberta and now Margaret. I seethed, watching as he stood over the bed, gloating at her comely nakedness while she cringed before him.

'Tyler,' she whimpered pitifully, 'I don't want to do this. Won't you stop him? Please make him go away.'

'I'd love to punch his lights out,' I said, my fists bunched. 'Say it and I'll do it, whatever the consequences.'

'No, no!' she pleaded, changing her mind. 'I – I – couldn't risk all this becoming known to my husband. And Chloe too. I'd die of shame. Let him do what he wants.' I was relieved to hear it.

'Now we're being true to form,' said Miklos. Unresisting, she let him test the ripeness of her breasts, shivering as he squeezed them and plucked hard at the nipples. 'Her reluctance doesn't fool me, I've seen the way she fucks,' he added meanly. 'I like that for a change, getting off on deluding herself she's being forced to undergo such demeaning sexual acts.' He parted the outer lips of her sex, probing the inner folds of soft flesh while Margaret moaned. Two fingers worked on her, delving in until I saw her bite her lip as if to resist the ripples of pleasure surging through her already inflamed cunt. She craned her neck to look at his hand shunting at the forested patch of hair on her mound below her smooth stomach.

'Please, *please*,' she appealed, disturbed at her response, as if submitting to him would prove his point. 'Ohhh, *please*—'

'I aim to please,' Miklos said crudely. 'Your little games have got her juiced up nicely for me, Tyler. She's wet to the core.' I heard Margaret give a howl of distress and real embarrassment at his words, making him laugh callously. 'You won't mind if I take over from you, I'm sure.'

'Be my guest, you Greek pig,' I said, boiling inside, determining in time I'd get my revenge. 'Fuck her and fuck off.'

'Don't be a sore loser,' he advised, his two fingers still agitating Margaret's quim while she struggled to contain the occasional writhe she could not prevent. 'We're doing the bitch a good turn. You by providing the *hors d'oeuvres*, me by adding the main course. Don't glare at me, friend. I can compel her to allow me to do anything with that beautiful body but I think that is hardly necessary. Is it, Mrs Warren? That's what I heard him call you. Or do you prefer Margaret?' he asked to her frightened face. 'You want it, don't you?'

'If I have to,' she whimpered.

'But you do,' he insisted. 'I heard you say you're a neglected wife. A masturbator and fantasiser.' This too had her starting to sob. 'A very neglected wife, I'd say,' he added, aware despite her apparent despair that his fingering had her arse squirming on the bed. 'Ripe for plucking.' He grinned evilly at me. 'And fucking.'

'A comedian you're not,' I said drily. 'Stop tormenting her. Do what you're going to and get out.'

'I like them obedient. Be sure to take note,' he boasted.

In the Flesh

'You'll learn how it's done. When I've screwed her front, I'll attend to her lilywhite English ass.'

'No!' Margaret cried in alarm. 'Not *that*. I wouldn't like it.'

'You never know until you try,' Miklos informed her. 'I'm very sure friend Wight had it in mind. Do not concern yourself, all this is not entirely for my pleasure. First I'll make you willing and eager for any variation I choose, want it or not.'

'I don't want it,' Margaret begged.

'I'll be the judge of that,' she was told. No slouch in the art of titillation, I had no doubt he was cunningly stimulating her clit. That he was winning was plain from the suppressed sighing and soft moans issuing from her clenched lips. With his free hand he stroked her unconstrained breasts as they lifted in her breathlessness. It was getting harder for her to subdue an uncontrollable frenzy pulsing through her loins. She arched her back, shuddering and bucking her arse. Miklos knew he had her, and withdrew his fingers. For a long moment, she continued to thrust her pelvis up into the empty air. Baulked on the verge of climax, realising the pleasuring hand had been withdrawn, she cried out in her frustration.

Miklos stood by, patently amused, almost smirking. Much as I disliked him, I grudgingly gave him full marks for a devious skill that had reduced Margaret to a quivering mass. Coming to somewhat, she looked up, totally ashamed, to see the way we two men regarded her. Her eyes appealed to me. 'I couldn't help it,' she moaned.

'I know,' I said to console her. 'He forced you.'

'Worse than that,' Margaret cried, mortified. 'He – made me want it – want him want him to continue,' she sobbed. 'I should loathe him. But he stopped and I – I – didn't want him to.'

63

'Now we're getting there,' Miklos observed, laughing at her turmoil. 'So no false modesty, madam. Tell me what I should do to that greedy cunt. Name it and I'll do it.'

Margaret's tear-brimmed eyes raised gratefully. 'Anything,' she said hoarse with arousal. 'Please, you've got me in such a state. Do it to me.'

'I intend to fuck you later, when you'll go on your knees to beg for it. Right now, do you want to be finger-fucked or sucked?'

I watched Margaret, her face set, struggling to force her choice from a dry throat. 'S-s-sucked,' she said in her shame, the admission made in a tortuous whisper. 'Please.'

'I didn't hear that,' Miklos said. 'Speak clearer.'

'*Sucked*!' Margaret almost shouted, desperate and unable to keep her own fingers away from her inflamed pussy. 'You've humiliated me enough, haven't you? Well, suck and lick out my cunt, damn you. Lick me clean. Tongue-fuck me, only for pity's sake let me *come*!'

'Words I love to hear,' Miklos said snidely, glancing at me to make sure I recognised talent. 'Loll back, raise your knees, tilt your cunt,' he instructed. 'Let the master get to work.'

'Big-head,' I scoffed. 'Fucking big-head.'

'No, good-head. I give excellent head, in fact,' he returned, unperturbed as he bent to his task. I saw Margaret look appealingly at me as his head went between her drawn-up thighs, her eyes pleading for understanding. The throb in her cunt would not be denied. Even as she reached for his head to draw his mouth closer, I saw tears of mortification had wet her cheeks. She groaned gratefully as his tongue lapped.

Nose brushing her bushy mound, his hands spreading wide her upper thighs, a long pointed tongue parted the

In the Flesh

outer lips and delved inside. Margaret drew in her breath, and angled her cunt to his probing. I could imagine him exploring every delicious nook and cranny, flicking at the vulnerable clit, tongue-fucking her avidly to get the desired effect. Margaret began to respond frantically and soon the Greek had reduced her to a convulsing, groaning mass of sensation.

I could only shrug, deciding Margaret was a gone goose, anybody's at that moment and certainly his. It was erotic viewing as well, my prick responding to the sight before me, urging me to get in on the act. 'Ohhh – aaagh – ooooh – *more*, make me come!' I heard Margaret wailing, surging upwards with her hips. One hand cupped a breast and crushed it as if to quell the agony of the ecstasy she felt; the other employed two fingers to widen the lips of her splayed quim for Miklos's access. 'Go on, on,' she urged. 'I'm nearly there, I can't stand it any more. I want you. Get on me—'

'Get on me?' Miklos said sarcastically, raising his mouth. 'Use the right words. Say what you want.'

Margaret was too far gone now to hesitate. 'Put your prick up my cunt and fuck me,' she ground out. 'Fuck me. Fuck all you want. Do it! I'm dying for it!'

I guessed that saying the words, not terms ever used by her before outside her fantasies, aroused her to an even higher pitch. All propriety and reason seemed beyond her as she cradled Miklos in her strong thighs and clung with legs crossed about his waist and hands hauling at his arse as he penetrated her. I did not credit Miklos or myself for getting her in this state. Margaret was a hot-blooded fuck, a natural, and making up for years of deprivation.

With that clear in my mind, I gave up worrying about Miklos's intervention or the effect it might have on her. She was thriving on every lunge up her cunt, going wild. 'Fuck her, fuck her good!' I heard my voice encouraging him. 'Fuck her rigid or I'll drag you off and get across her.'

'Not a chance,' Miklos shouted, but Margaret's abandoned response making him no longer able to control himself. 'Take that!' he yelled, savagely thrusting his bursting prick into her hairy slit and pounding away. It was obvious from her spasms that she had climaxed more than once. It seemed as if a rapid series of electric shocks surged through her body, convulsing her helplessly. 'Keep fucking, keep fucking me!' she screamed out, her orgasms continuing, heaving in great throes as the sensations rolled over her. It was a tremendous fuck by any standards.

I considered it should have been my pleasure to have got her in that heightened state. I cursed Miklos. Her eyes rolled up to the ceiling. Rocked by the explosions in her loins, her tits bounced and heaved to the pounding of her heart. Miklos croaked out he was coming, his arse cheeks clenching as he shot his load. The Greek slumped forward to rest on her cushiony body. Margaret stirred under his bulk, looking up at me almost as if for approval, even a little smugly and increasing my annoyance. There was little doubt she was well on the way to accepting that she was highly sexed and glad of it.

'Get off her,' I ordered Miklos sternly. 'You've had your fun. Dress and get on your way. That's your lot.' I grabbed his arm but he shook me off, again menacing me with his dark eyes.

'Miklos never fucks just once,' he said arrogantly. 'He does it as many times as he likes. *You*,' he threatened, rolling aside from Margaret and jabbing a finger at me, 'forget your place. With my connections I do not make a good enemy. I could be your friend, make you more money than you know.'

'With a friend like you, who needs enemies,' I said to

In the Flesh

annoy him. 'As for your money, much as I like the stuff, work it right up your jacksie, buster.' Then, considering the whole crazy situation, I started to laugh. In the heat of the Equatorial afternoon, the bedroom was ripe with the smell of cunt. The three of us were naked as jaybirds, with Margaret fucked as never before, and a Greek crook and an English bush pilot were squaring up to each other. I do like ordinary days that turn out to be interesting. The stuff of life. Beats the hell out of being in the office or factory.

'Please, Miklos, I really don't know who you are,' Margaret said, sitting up and worried by our antagonism, 'but I don't mind about what has happened – between you and I and Tyler. The sex thing. I'm not usually that kind of woman, although you must think I am. Can't we be friends, all of us?'

'Certainly for me, Margaret,' the slimy Greek said ingratiatingly. 'I do not think you are anything but the nicest kind of woman.'

'You've been calling her a horny-arsed bitch who loves being fucked with a big prick, among other things,' I had to jeer.

'I lost control, I admit,' Margaret protested to me. 'You both must feel entitled to speak to me that way. Both of you must take some responsibility for arousing me. I couldn't help acting like I did, so wantonly. Like a whore. But you don't need to remind me of it, Tyler.'

'That's because he is no gentleman,' Miklos said, getting one up on me, I felt, my attempt to provoke him turning against me. I even felt that Margaret was warming to him.

'You're both wicked men,' she said lightly, as if to defuse the situation. 'Doing what you did between you to a poor defenceless woman. Even if I got to like it more than I should have. Let us be friends. I'm sure Miklos will keep this afternoon's events a secret and won't cause any trouble here in Uganda for Tyler.'

'I meant you no disrespect, Margaret,' I said, 'and no one was more delighted than I when you called on me today, but don't beg or apologise to that scumbag. I'm low and I know it but he's lower. He sucks up to murdering thugs in the military to give him the muscle he used to get his way here today. Among decent locals he's as popular as a turd in a swimming pool.'

'So, I'm despicable,' Miklos grinned, reverting to his old self. 'Better not push it, Wight. You wouldn't like it, and the lady certainly wouldn't. I strongly advise both of you to remember—'

'Of course, whatever you say,' Margaret said hastily to placate him, looking extremely vulnerable with her big breasts and cunt exposed. 'We don't want trouble and I'm sure you really don't intend us any harm, now that we know each other. I said let's be friends.' She was undoubtedly wary of Miklos again, nervous in her attempt to appease him, to keep him in a good humour.

Miklos recognised this, revelling in the fact that he had her where he wanted. 'We should celebrate our friendship in a fit manner,' he suggested amiably. 'I'd be delighted to entertain you at my Kampala restaurant. You really are a most beautiful woman.'

'Thank you, kind sir,' Margaret said like a flattered schoolgirl, annoying me further. 'I'd like to accept your invitation. I was hoping to see more of Uganda while I'm here. Dining in Kampala would be nice.' She looked pointedly at me. 'Nobody else has offered.'

I gave up. 'Take your husband with you as well,' I said meanly. 'I'm sure he'd love to meet a horny Greek who's fucked you.'

In the Flesh

'You fucked me first, started me off, and I know I'll never be the same woman,' she said reasonably. 'Is Miklos so different?' A shy sly smile was allowed to flit across her full mouth. 'You're two of a kind, both bad influences. I should have nothing to do with you – should I?'

'A definite yes, you must,' Miklos said encouragingly. 'What a pleasure it is to know you, a real lady.'

'I bet you don't meet many of those in your line,' I told him. 'A lady and an enthusiastic amateur all in one. Must have made your day.'

'Don't be sarcastic, Tyler,' Margaret chided me. I was beginning to feel the stranger in my own house. The odd one out. 'It doesn't become you.'

'You'll find having anything to do with *him* won't become you, either,' I warned her. 'So I fucked you, but I'm basically harmless. He's poison.'

'If you can't stand the heat, get out of the kitchen,' Miklos said, surprising me as always with his English phrases. 'Leave us and we'll continue without you, won't we, Margaret?' He held up his flaccid prick before her face, his free hand resting on the top of her head. 'Bring it up,' he invited. 'Give it a little suck.'

Surely not, I thought, watching her face. Maybe when on heat as she had been, she would, but not from scratch. No doubt it had featured in her lurid fantasising, being made to do it, and Miklos's command to *suck* settled the issue. With a nervous giggle, she leaned over, replacing his hand on his prick with her own and taking the whole of the bulbous purple knob into her mouth.

She quickly learned to like it, it was obvious. I watched her get the hang of it, suctioning ever more earnestly at the stiffening rod in her gullet. She sucked with mounting pleasure, kneeling up on the bed while Miklos stood, hands on hips, gloating down at her bobbing head. The sight made my own unattended dong rear longingly, wishing she were chewing so avidly on mine. 'Don't be all bloody day,' I grumbled, envious of Miklos on the receiving end. 'I've got to get you home to your husband. Remember him? Don't make a meal of it.'

That was exactly what she was doing, her cheeks hollowing and expanding with each strenuous suck, taking the entire length of the engorged stalk back to her throat. I had to admire her *modus operandi*. Not bad for a beginner, I judged, noting her fingers were between her legs diddling herself. At times she let the entire length slip from her lips, licking up from the balls, wetting the knob copiously with her saliva before hungrily pulling it back into her mouth. Her entire being seemed concentrated on her cock-gorged gullet. Miklos growled and grabbed her hair, knees buckling and arse thrusting as he was taken to his limit. 'Fuck, fuck!' he howled in his extremis, her jaw and his buttocks working furiously as he saturated her throat.

Swallowing all, her tongue licking her lips, Margaret's immediate attention was turned to me and my immense stander rearing painfully. 'Fuck me, Tyler,' she urged, bright-eyed and randified by her cocksucking triumph. 'Don't waste that lovely big thing. You fuck me. Poor Miklos is no use now. Didn't I just drain him? With my mouth too,' she giggled naughtily. 'Look at him drooping. I'm learning, aren't I?'

'You are, and all the words to go with it,' I said, wondering what I had unleashed in the lady. But who was I to complain with a bursting cock? 'Sure I'll fuck you. Get on your back.'

'No,' she said. 'I want to be on top this time. I've never had it that way. *You* get on your back.'

'Be gentle with me, won't you?' I said, stretching out on the bed. She loomed over me, big boobs dangling enticingly,

In the Flesh

shaking as she laughed at me, planting her knees either side of my waist, positioning her cunt over my upright dick, grasping it as she lowered her parted thighs.

'Don't be funny, this is serious,' she said, resolute in her intent, the itch in her cunt demanding to be relieved. Easing down, guiding my tool, she gave a low moan of sheer bliss as the hard bar of flesh went all the way up a sodden channel. Jiggling over me, her tits bouncing, her pace increased. 'Oh, I just love it. Love that big cock filling me,' she groaned. 'Hold my breasts, squeeze them tight! Oh God, why did I have to do without this for so long?'

'You're making up for it now,' I groaned with her, lifting my arse from the bed to meet her downward grinding motions. She lolled forward, her nipples berry-firm, brushing my lips. *Suck them*, I heard her order. *Suck them hard. Don't you dare come, only I can come yet—*

'Come as much as you like,' I promised, determined to have her in a frenzy, working her arse like the proverbial fiddler's elbow before I came in her. Over her shoulder I saw Miklos nosing around. Craning my neck, I saw his hands cupping the sweat-glistening mounds of her buttocks. His splayed thumbs spread the hind cheeks widely, even as she rode me. I had no doubt he had a close-up view of my cock pistoning into the lippy grip of her cunt and, slightly above that, the tight corrugated ring of her arsehole.

'*Please!*' I suddenly heard Margaret cry out. 'No!' Her body stiffened over me, her gyrations stilled. 'No-o-o,' she whined, thrusting into me as if drawing away from whatever plagued her from behind, my prick rammed home by her action. 'Not there – I forbid you!'

'Forbid nothing,' Miklos said cruelly. 'The sight of that fine bouncing rear has tempted me. Relax. It's only a finger in your butt, woman. Learn to ease up and like it.'

'It – it's not right,' Margaret wailed. 'It's too far in! It's hurting!' Her arse clenched, squeezing my prick tightly in her cunt. Seeing me looking over her shoulder, he gave a broad wink, leaning over Margaret's back. I had no doubt from the lustful glint in his eye that his prick was erect again, being directed to her rear, the tradesmen's entrance. 'Help me, Tyler. H–help m–me!' she shrieked. 'H– he's trying to put his thing up my bottom—'

I felt the combined weight on me at the foot of the pile, my prick being shuttled up and down delightfully in Margaret's agitation. '*Ooh-aagh-oh*,' Margaret whined above me. 'It's going in! I can feel it! He's up my bum—' She wriggled and jiggled, getting several loud smacks for her trouble. 'It's too big to go up my behind,' she pleaded. 'Must you, must you?'

'Damn right,' Miklos said profoundly. 'When a Greek fucks, he fucks ass! What kind of a man has she married,' he queried in an aside to me, 'to have never buggered such a good piece of ass? I'm doing him a favour, opening her up. She's tight, but I'm in to the hilt.'

He certainly was, I could feel his knob nudging mine, separated by the thin membrane between arse and cunt. Both of us thrusting and poking until, with the feeling of two cocks inside her, Margaret began to respond, caution thrown to the winds. She reared her head, craning her neck, garbling out the crudest words, at times thrusting to me and then grinding her bottom back to Miklos. Sure that his deep penetration was now gratefully accepted, the Greek lengthened his strokes up her tight-straining back passage. His hoarse shout foretold he was emptying his balls into her as she screamed out she was coming again. My time had arrived too, spurting a succession of hot volleys from the eye of my deeply lodged prick.

Margaret had had climax after climax to sate her. Now, as Miklos and I rolled aside to give her air, she lay gasping like

In the Flesh

a landed fish. Her arse turned to me, I saw it still enlarged, a pulsing open ring shaped to the girth of Miklos's tool and leaking spunk. He had been right, I conceded, the woman had taken to being fucked up the arse like a veteran. While she lay recovering, Miklos rose to dress. I escorted him to the door gladly, refusing the hand he offered.

'As you wish,' he shrugged impassively. 'I've made myself late for an appointment but it was worth it. The woman shows promise. As for the business I came to discuss with you, that can wait a day.' He clapped me on the shoulder, knowing I disliked his fake bonhomie. 'Believe me, Tyler old chap, you're getting a break.'

'My arms or my legs?' I asked.

'It's a simple flying job, coming up any day now,' he said, ignoring my jibe. 'Something certain important army brass has asked me to arrange for them.'

'Why can't they use their military aircraft?'

'No doubt they have their reasons. It's not for you or I to say. I can't refuse them if I wanted to, so neither can you. Cheer up, there's money in it. A great deal.'

'I've told you where you can stick that,' I said.

He looked about him. 'You want to live in this hovel? How about one of the new bungalows on President Obote Drive?' He sniggered. 'Not that I know how long it will still be called that. Or how about a power boat on the lake? I can get you these things. Think of the good life.'

'Just staying alive suits me,' I said. 'Thanks but no thanks.'

'You're in it whether you want to or not,' he said flatly. 'We need a flyer, no questions asked. You will hear from me.'

'Don't hurry it,' I said grimly, knowing the call would come. 'As for Mrs Warren, give her a miss. Today was just an adventure for her, a one-off. She's respectable, married, a visitor, and probably right now very much regretting what she allowed us to do.'

'Too late the English gentleman,' Miklos laughed at me. 'But the rules don't apply, I'm a Greek. Like I'll be using your services, I have plans for her too. Have a nice day.'

Chapter Seven

I had to revise my opinion on returning to the bedroom and the much-ravaged Margaret. Looking anything but regretful, she was still lolling naked on my bed, smiling blissfully and misty-eyed. Her true sensual nature emancipated in one afternoon's lustful romp, she lay luscious, warm and rounded, a woman fulfilled. Erotically imaginative, our threesome session must have been the stuff of her fantasies. She stretched her whole body languidly, her arms reaching out to me.

'Oh, how I could sleep. Sleep with you,' she yawned, drowsy with sexual fulfilment. 'Just for a while, to wake beside each other.' Her look was expectant. 'Then you can fuck me again if you want to. Or,' she added almost shyly, 'I can suck you like I did for Miklos. Men enjoy a woman doing that to them, I'm sure. I don't mind – in fact I liked it too.'

That was all very well but time was passing, darkness would fall promptly on cue at seven as it did on the Equator. Arthur would probably be pacing the floor by now, heat exhaustion or not, wondering where she'd got to. 'Remember your husband?' I said firmly, taking her arm and pulling her into a sitting position. 'You've been here hours. Use my shower and dress and I'll drive you home. I didn't mean to keep you so long. Didn't know that we'd have an unexpected visitor.'

'It was – exceptional – wasn't it?' Margaret said dreamily, smiling at the memory. 'Who would have thought I would ever experience such things? When I'm with the ladies of our coffee-morning group back in Harrowgate, it's sure to come to mind what I've done. Goodness!'

'Goodness had nothing to do with it,' I had to grin at her for her recollection. 'It was an out-and-out orgy. Every woman ought to have at least one, I suppose, to remember. All the same, Miklos is a mean Greek. Have nothing more to do with him.'

'He's very handsome though,' she said wistfully. 'So dominant. Just imagine, two big strong men having me. Fantasies will never satisfy me again, will they?'

'At least you tried 'em out,' I said, intent on getting her to her feet and into the shower. Both of us still naked, I got in the cubicle with her, enjoying the cooling water that sprayed over us. She turned to the tiled wall, still unsteady from her ordeal, leaning her brow to it, sighing as the strong jet cascaded down her back and into the deep cleave of her tilted buttocks.

'*Oh*, that's so soothing,' she crooned. 'My poor bottom seems on fire. He buggered me, didn't he?' I detected it was said with almost a purr of pride. 'I was actually being fucked in the anus, wasn't I? That huge penis thrust up into my tight little bumhole. Right up. He put his big stiff cock in my arse and fucked me there.'

'That would be a fair description of what he did, give or take a thrust or two,' I conceded, certain she had savoured saying every word, relishing the fact that she'd been a partner in the act of sodomy. Taken to it like an arse-bandit's favourite bumboy, in fact, and still intrigued enough to want to talk about it. I shut off the stream of water and gave her wet rump a smack. 'Let's have you out of here and dressed,' I ordered. 'Contemplate the merits of shagging arse later. One up on the coffee-morning ladies, do you reckon?'

'Who knows?' she giggled. 'I won't be able to look at them in future without wondering. Their husbands should be so lucky. Would you have fucked my bottom, Tyler? Miklos said you would have. Would you like to?'

I began drying her with my largest, fluffiest towel while she stood and let me. 'I intended to get around to it,' I admitted, which was what she wanted to hear. 'Right now, get all of that out of your head. You're going home to Arthur like nothing has happened. Forget me, forget Miklos especially. Just remember you were on the balcony of Entebbe Club watching the tennis tourney all afternoon, and then you had tea there. That's a must. Remember – tennis and tea!'

'And lots and lots of fucking,' she said emotionally, still highly intoxicated on sex. 'I feel a real woman for the first time.' As I tried to dry her, her hand sidled between my legs, catching me off guard as she stroked my prick. Never unwilling, it thickened and stretched, in the embryo stage of a rearing erection when she dropped to her knees and gobbled it into her mouth. Her first avid sucks and the feel of my dick throbbing between her tongue and palate, made me relent and give her her head – to coin a phrase. She was good, quickly having me holding her ears and fucking her face, saturating her tonsils as I bucked uncontrollably and shot off in her mouth.

'You're getting to be quite a ball-breaker,' I said as she smirked at having her way with me. With some relief, I helped her dress, got her into my car, and was clasped in a last passionate kiss right outside her daughter's bungalow. I'd better watch it, I thought, for my own sake as well as hers. Irate husbands of debauched wives were to be avoided. There was Chloe too, who was hardly likely to be enamoured of my screwing her mother as well as herself.

'I'll pop over in the morning,' were Margaret's parting words to me but I escaped bright and early to soar up into the freedom of the sky, accompanied by Harry Saxon on his way back north to the refugee area. My aircraft was packed with medical supplies and items such as powdered milk that he and Diana had somehow procured. The old Cessna handled sluggishly.

'You ask too much of me and this crate,' I complained, hemmed in my seat behind the controls by cardboard boxes and cartons. Harry had blankets piled high on his knees. 'You could bring us down through overloading.' I glanced below at bumpy scrub and bush populated by lion, elephant and buffalo, hardly the place for an emergency landing. 'Just a bit of cargo, you said. Where the hell do you dig all this stuff up?'

'My wife chases business people while I'm away,' he said with pride. 'Begs, borrows, steals. This lot we collected in Kenya. She charms it out of 'em. Diana's good at that.'

I had to agree. 'She's got the right equipment. She was looking particularly tasty when she waved you off this morning,' I said, making him laugh. 'Beats me how you keep her so sweet, and other men from sniffing around, when you're always giving your time to lost causes. You're a bloody do-gooder.'

'Comes with the territory,' he grinned, amused by my comment. 'I could be up here a while, at least until international organisations hear about us and get in on the act. It all happened so fast, the people pouring in from southern Sudan. Political, I suspect. Whatever, I'm the UN man on the spot and must do what I can. I hope Roberta's doing her thing back home. Without real aid there'll be famine and disease.'

In the Flesh

'What do you mean – political?' I asked, knowing Harry was a very astute official. 'You mean the refugee influx was *arranged*?'

'Could be. Uganda is unsettled and what the government doesn't need right now is a refugee problem. Kept busy, they'll be ripe for a coup, undoubtedly by the army led by Amin. The refugees are real enough, however, and need shelter, food and clean water. That's my pigeon. You could do me a favour, Ty.'

'I do you enough favours,' I said, thinking of Miklos and his promise to press-gang me into clandestine flying for 'army brass,' as he'd put it. That meant plotters out to overthrow the legal government and my gut feeling was that I was in deep shit. My simple philosophy of life was if you couldn't eat it, drink it, spend it or fuck it, then avoid it. To that I would add getting involved in life-threatening situations. My eye was drawn to the sky ahead. 'See that vapour trail? It's a SAM ground-to-air fucking missile. A Russki-supplied shoulder-held launching weapon. That means there are bandits down there with your refugees.'

'Not a very good shot,' Harry said, unperturbed. 'It missed by a mile.'

'It was meant to,' I said grimly. 'They're warning us to land or we'll get one up the arse. I've been there before, mate: the old Congo, up here in Sudan, Somalia. It's the same set-up, they want your cargo, not to shoot us down. Time to turn tail, I strongly suggest.'

'Keep going,' Harry said calmly. 'I've seen it before too. We'll work out what's what when we land. I was asking you a favour.'

'This isn't one?' I asked grimly. 'Those jokers down there could tie us to anthills at best. What the hell else could you want?'

'I was thinking of Di, my wife,' he said. 'I don't know

when I can get back again. It can get lonely for her by herself. Take her for a meal at the club, look in and see she's okay. I know I can trust you.'

That was more than I could say for myself. 'She struck me as able to take care of herself,' I said, not wishing to invite temptation. I brought the aircraft in over a mass of upturned black faces, and landed on an uneven strip of baked earth. At once we were surrounded by wild-looking tribesmen, daubed in mud and in a minimum of clothing. They carried spears and buffalo-hide shields, ancient single-shot rifles with the butts painted in colourful depictions of the hunt. Among them as they gathered around the aircraft was a white man I knew. Ed Spilsby, slung with bandoliers, armed to the teeth with a new Kalashnikov AK47 and two automatic pistols, grenades dangling around his neck, was British and an ex-officer turned mercenary.

'Your reception committee,' I said to Harry as he made to alight from the plane. 'They don't look much like starving refugees to me.' In the background stood, sat and lay a mass of humanity covering several acres, patiently awaiting their fate. 'Those poor sods will be lucky to see any of your goodies,' I reckoned. 'As for the white gentleman decked out like a one-man army, you won't get any help from him. He was Long Range Desert Group and is still fighting the fucking war. For himself, this time, for loot.'

'You do meet colourful characters in Africa,' Harry said cheerfully. 'Is that your yellow streak showing, Ty? What happened to the daring air ace who won a chestful of medals against the might of the Luftwaffe?'

'I was shit-scared then too,' I said. 'Don't get out.'

'I'll survive,' he laughed, making me admire his dedication and feel worse about my desire to fuck his wife. 'These boys will be willing to negotiate.'

'This isn't a Tarzan movie,' I reminded him. 'You'll get

In the Flesh

a twig up your arse, twirled around, and brought down with your entrails. That's just for starters. If you're so determined, get 'em to unload pronto. They intend to keep it, no doubt.'

'Some aid will get through,' Harry said, jumping to the ground, 'even if I have to buy it back from them. They won't harm me, not if they want more supplies sent in for them to steal.'

'Great system,' I said, sweating as I handed down boxes and cartons to a line of warrior types.

'It won't always be like this,' Harry called up to me. 'One day, truck loads will come in and I'll have more resources to handle it. Aid helpers to see the right people get what they need. Wells will be dug, sanitation provided. This is just a start.'

When the aircraft was unloaded there was a commotion among the crowd as I prepared for take-off. Pushing his way through to get to the plane was a terrified African I recognised as Samuel Musa. He was kicking out and screaming as the mob closed in. I had seen him frequenting the night clubs and bars of Kampala. I'd been informed he was the Minister of Agriculture and Water Resources in President Milton Obote's government. Usually immaculate in starched linen safari suits, now he looked the worse for wear, scared, sweat-streaked and dishevelled. Without saying a word, he began to scramble up into the passenger seat beside me, trembling and gasping once he felt he had reached sanctuary.

'This is a top Ugandan cabinet minister beside me shitting his pants,' I called down to Harry. 'I don't fancy your chances. When I get back, what last words do you want me to tell your wife?'

He gave a wave, any words drowned out as I revved up. Once airborne, my passenger mopped his brow, eyes still wide and white with fear. 'Thank you, thank God,' he muttered, grasping my wrist. 'I thought my life was over. I said my prayers.'

'I said one or two myself back there,' I admitted. 'Friendly bunch, weren't they? Guerrilla fighters, down here for the pickings with the refugees, no doubt.'

'Many, but not all of them,' the unhappy Samuel Musa claimed. 'I myself recognised some among them as Ugandan soldiers, troops of General Amin's own Simba Regiment. He is building a force in the north. There will be others in league with him in other regions. They will march on Kampala when ready, to overthrow us. Knowing that, my life is over. I must hide! A signal will be sent and they will be waiting for me at Entebbe when you land. Can you fly me to Tanzania where the government is friendly?'

'I couldn't do that,' I had to say despite the fear in his eyes. 'I haven't the fuel aboard. If we flew on and they're after you, we could be shot down. They have MIGs at Entebbe.'

'I would pay you,' he said, begging for mercy. 'I visited the refugees as the minister concerned for their welfare. Now I know too much. On my return I'll be arrested and disappear, like so many others have. They will say that I was killed by bandits or in a car crash, even eaten by wild animals on my trip. My poor wives. I am a dead man!'

Better you than me, mate, I could have said, recognising he'd got his immediate future dead to rights. Neither did I feel too much sympathy, knowing that as an important member of the present government, with its secret police and mass arrests, Musa had been living high on the hog. On landing at Entebbe, while coming to a halt as I taxied in to the far corner allocated to Lake Airways, he leapt out and fled in Olympic qualifying time to the thick bush on our side of the airport. I checked in at the

In the Flesh

office to see my boss Bill Dove regarding me with interest.

'We've had the army here this afternoon. That's them just taken off in their armoured car after your passenger. Who was that getting the hell out?' he asked. 'Or shouldn't I know?'

'You shouldn't,' I advised. 'Better right now to keep your nose clean.' I suddenly felt starved and drove straight to the club despite needing to clean up after the day's exertions. It was good to relax on the verandah and stretch my legs with a long cool drink, hearing those around me discussing the unstable situation. If only they knew how it concerned me, I thought, going through to the dining room and devouring steak with beer chasers, like the condemned man eating a hearty meal. I was looking forward to going home, having a shower and inviting Jovial Nkutu to be my bed partner for the night, when I was approached by a furtive-looking askari employed to guard the parked cars outside the club.

'There is a lady waiting to see you, bwana,' he began, another Muganda with fear in his eyes. 'She waits for you in the bamboo grove now. Very important, she says. You must see her.' He turned, looking back at me as he left as if I carried the mark of death.

I walked out wondering who the mysterious woman was. Margaret Warren wanting more of her fantasies enacted, I presumed. With her husband laid low, confined to bed, she'd sent the askari in to contact me rather than make it obvious to others in the crowded club she was seeking me out. I intended to reproach her on two counts. One for being so besotted with sex to risk our liaison; two for being out on foot, alone in the darkness.

But on reaching the parked cars at the rear of the club premises beside the bamboo grove, I saw it was a native woman beckoning me into the thicket. With a sinking feeling, knowing it was trouble, I recognised her as Samuel Musa's chief wife, Lule. She was not unknown to me, having admired her at parties I had attended. Short and voluptuous, with a handsome round brown face, she was the kind of Ugandan beauty who attracted and married men in positions of power. She had told me once in conversation, while I vainly tried to keep my eyes off her formidable tits, that she had attended Warwick University. Now in fearful haste she drew me by the wrist into the dark of the bamboo. I saw only the wide whites of her eyes and flashing teeth of the same dazzling whiteness.

'You brought my husband back,' she began as if I was an integral part of the concern for him. 'He is in very great danger. Now you must fly him away.'

'I don't have to do anything, Mrs Musa,' I said, reluctant to be involved and making it plain from the start. It was too dangerous a country to get implicated in internal politics. Flying, fucking, lazing in the sun, was all I asked of an uncomplicated lifestyle.

'There will be much money for you,' she said. 'You like money?'

'I like living. Everybody's offering me money for doing services that could get me the chop.' I wished now it had been a randy Margaret Warren that had come for me, not the main wife of a government minister in desperate straits. 'I don't know where your husband is. He ran away soon as we landed.'

'He is with friends, hiding,' she said. 'You, a *mzungu* with an aeroplane could fly him to safety in Tanzania.'

Mzungu was the Swahili word for peeled one, a white man, but being whiter than white would not help me if caught by Amin's thugs. How come, I thought miserably, a peaceable chap like myself always gets caught up in these situations? 'The army know I brought your husband back,'

In the Flesh

I reasoned. 'They'll be watching me. You, too. Sorry, it's too much of a risk to do it.'

'But you could,' Lule Musa said, her voice subtly changed into a softly seductive appeal. 'For me? Please, for *me* you could. I remember how you look at me before. I know.'

'I had a glass in my hand. It was a party,' I said. 'Jesus!'

This last was exclaimed as she took my hands and lifted them to her breast. She had drawn aside the loose *busuti* native costume she wore, my opened palms meeting warm bare mounds, fleshy and thick-nippled. The kind that invariably made me go weak at the knees and weak in the head. More, a surreptitious hand was at my crotch, unzipping and delving inside my shorts, grasping at my penis. 'You will, *bwana*, won't you?' she ingratiated herself, the use of the servile term deliberate. 'Oh, it feels so big in my hand, you make me want to do it. Then you will fly my husband, won't you?'

'I – I – couldn't,' I replied, being expertly manipulated and fatally responding. This despite a warning voice advising a stiffening of resolve instead of a stiffening of my prick. 'What would your husband think of this?' I appealed feebly as a last resort.

'He is too frightened to think,' she said, going down on her knees – and not to beg for mercy. Hot African lips surrounded my excited tool. She licked and sucked at the knob slowly and deliberately, as if giving a sample of more delights to follow. 'It is so big and strong, like a black one,' she moaned softly as if genuinely desiring it up her. Taking my stalk out of her mouth, she nursed it between her big firm teats 'Give this to me, put it in me. You have a car near?'

'This way,' I heard myself saying hoarsely, turning a deaf

ear to the warning signals bleeping in my brain. My prick, rearing and soaked with Mrs Musa's saliva, still clasped in her hand, had ordained otherwise. I pulled open the rear door on reaching the old Morris Traveller and Lule Musa got in, drawing the *busuti* gown over her head and lying back along the seat. Dim light filtering from the club verandah showed her stretched out buck naked, arms beckoning me and parted knees raised.

'Come,' she ordered, sounding impatient. With her big pointy-ended tits thrusting up like rocket nose-cones, sleek brown body glistening as if oiled and the plump lipless slit of her hairless quim pouting at me, what was a guy to do? I faltered as the danger signals flashed, recognising it could prove a costly jump. My neck. While weighing up this prospect, Sam Musa's wife reached forward, grabbing my wrists and hauling me between her sturdy thighs.

The unexpectedness of her sudden heave had my face buried in the deep cleave of her ample breasts, with which she immediately attempted to smother me. Nose and mouth held in between mounds of pliant flesh, I felt her hand at my belt and my shorts being tugged over my arse. 'You will, you will, I make you,' I heard her mutter forcefully. I was atop the comfortable platform of her belly, sweat-soaked and hot, her legs encircling my back, a hand directing my prick to an uptilted pouting groove. 'Fuck me, *mzungu*,' she said as if desiring it for her own sake. 'Fuck me! Give me a come.'

Forced in none too gently, I was lodged up her, hauled by the arse and her upward thrusts until penetrated to the hilt with our pubic mounds grinding. She began making little muted sounds, the twin cheeks of her expansive buttocks surging up to me to get every last inch embedded up her cock-filled cunt. Giving up all resistance, I began to fuck her in earnest. A whole-hearted partner, a vocal one, she

In the Flesh

loudly screeched out her joy at being poked so vigorously, using a mix of her Luganda language and some English for my benefit.

'Oh, Samuel, Mr Musa, this one is having your wife! He is fucking her! Mama, mama, a *mzungu* is making a baby in me—' Despite these protestations, what she did was drag me closer with arms and crossed ankles, working her bottom tirelessly. No novice, she nipped me with the strong muscles of the walls of her cunt as if milking my prick. I found her a glorious ride, responding to my heaves, balls slapping against her bum cheeks and our damp bellies clapping at each impact. Engrossed with our pleasuring each other, I barely noticed the car that drew up alongside, its headlights illuminating us momentarily before abruptly switching off.

I heard the engine cut, the fire in my balls too urgent to do anything about caring who it might be. It could have been the whole Musa family or General Amin himself. Lule was gasping and humping me desperately in her anguish, coming in violent spasms as I let fly a torrent up her cunt. Such was the effort I collapsed on her belly while she lay prostrate, sighing as if in deep bliss. The noise of the nearby car door closing made me raise my head. Standing there I saw Harry Saxon's wife, Diana. From her viewpoint, I had no doubt, she had a clear view of my uptilted arse with Lule Musa's bare legs projecting out of the car. As if it had nothing to do with her, she turned quickly on her heel and made to walk away.

I could hardly leave it at that, though common sense dictated that I should. 'It's not what you think, Mrs Saxon,' I called out after her, feeling an utter clot. 'I mean, I can explain.'

She halted, coming forward, amused I was sure as I tried to drag up my shorts. Lule sat up, watching with interest, unperturbed and not attempting to cover herself. 'Very formal, Mr Wight, aren't we?' Diana Saxon said, apparently not at all shocked and finding it an effort to keep the merriment out of her voice. 'It was Diana last time we met. You don't have to explain anything to me, although I'm sure it would make interesting listening. I came to the club hoping to see you. Not quite as much of you as I have,' she could not resist adding teasingly, 'but I wanted to know that my husband arrived safely and all's well up there.'

'He arrived safe,' I told her, my pants hoisted but not daring to zip up while she watched. 'He's an old hand at looking after himself. I've no doubt I'll be flying there soon. I could take a letter for you.'

'That would be kind of you,' she smiled. 'In the meantime I'll gather up some Red Cross aid for you to take. Say goodnight to your friend for me,' she added mischievously, turning to leave. 'Sorry to disturb you.'

'Sorry you caught me with my pants down,' I returned, seeing that she obviously regarded the episode as amusing, par for the course for me, perhaps. 'First Roberta, now this. You'll never be able to take me seriously, will you?'

'You're an attractive rogue, but I rather like rogues. Obviously very virile too. I'm a married woman, often left alone for weeks on end,' she said levelly. 'Better I don't take you very seriously, I think. Goodnight, Tyler. Let me know when you'll be flying north again.'

Chapter Eight

After that, I could hardly tell Diana her husband had asked me to see she was not lonely in his absence. I felt I'd blown it, her parting words showing she was vulnerable to loneliness and open-minded enough to admit it. A sharp dig in the ribs from Mrs Musa brought me back to the present with enough problems to be getting on with.

'You give fuck to me. Now you must help Mr Musa escape,' she said in a very different tone to her utterances while being screwed. 'Arrangements will be made when you can fly him away to Tanzania.'

'Not so easy,' I said in alarm, regretting being weak enough to fall into her trap. 'The airport will be watched. Can't he make his way out overland? By car, or across the lake by boat.'

'You are afraid,' she said contemptuously.

'Too right,' I admitted as she pulled on her gown. 'We'd all end up feeding the crocs in the Nile. It's not possible. This could get us all in serious trouble.'

'You are already in trouble, *mzungu*,' she said more maliciously than I liked. 'My husband is a jealous man. You have laid with his number one wife. He would kill you for that. He is a chief of his tribe, any of his men would do it for him.' She stepped out of the car to disappear into the bamboo grove, giving a final warning. 'You will hear when it is ready to fly him. You must die for the shame you have brought taking his wife if you do not help.' As if to add substance to her threat, the car-park askari stood beside me, fingering the broad blade of his machete.

Sod my horrible luck, I cursed, starting my engine and heading for home. I found the verandah lit in welcome and the comely Jovial Nkutu waiting to greet me in her spotless kitchen as I entered by the back door. 'I can make you supper, sir,' she offered. I hugged her and kissed her for her kindness, wondering for how much longer the good life would continue.

'Never mind food, Jove,' I said. 'Join me in bed with all the beer in the house.' Lying there with a naked Jovial beside me and bottles of the ice-cold local Tusker brew on hand seemed a good way to forget my situation. 'We'll make a night of it. Who knows what tomorrow may bring?'

'I cannot go to bed with you, sir,' Jovial said, grinning her wide smile. 'Tonight has brought a lady to visit you. The one who is called Warren. Two hours she has waited in your lounge. She would not leave.' She smiled rather more wickedly, no doubt giving notice that she should be the one to occupy my bed. 'I told her that you had flown to Kenya and would not be back.'

'It obviously didn't work,' I said, going through to the other room. 'Really, Margaret,' I began as I advanced. 'Wasn't yesterday enough? We've got to be careful. This won't do.'

'What won't do, Tyler?' said an amused voice, and I saw it was not the mother but her daughter, Chloe, who was waiting. She rose from her chair, eyes mischievously alight, looking very young and desirable in her starched cap and figure-hugging white nurse's uniform. 'Whatever have you been up to with my poor mum, you dog?'

'Nothing, nothing,' I lied desperately, feeling I'd let

In the Flesh

myself be stupidly caught out. 'I told you, she's your mother.'

'And a woman,' Chloe laughed. 'A frustrated one, I know. Have you been fucking her? She seems different, looks different. I wouldn't put it past you.'

'You wrong me greatly,' I said sadly. 'I thought if it were her, it's no time to be out visiting, that's all. More to the point, what are you doing here, a newly betrothed young lady?'

'What do you think?' she answered brashly. 'What is it we always do, given the opportunity?'

'Jesus, Chlo,' I pleaded. 'I've had a hard day. You're too much. Where's your fiancé, your ma and pa?'

'Dad had to be removed to Mulago,' she laughed at my concern, referring to the general hospital in Kampala. 'It's just heat exhaustion, he'll recover. Mum is staying overnight in an hotel to be near him. It was me who made her. And Heiny is there at the hospital as duty doctor on call.' She crossed to me, her left hand at the top button of her uniform dress, the other going to my crotch and cupping my balls. She did not stop when Jovial entered the room and enquired if we required drinks, an excuse for her to take in what was going on.

'So you thought I was on duty call as well,' I said, ignoring Jovial who remained with us as an interested spectator. 'Can't you get enough, Chlo?'

'That's rich, coming from you who made me so fond of it,' the girl pouted. 'Heiny and I fly off to Germany tonight on the two o'clock flight for a whole boring fortnight to meet his parents. No nookie, not with his bloody silly idea of saving ourselves for our wedding night. I'll soon teach him; meantime I *want* it, to tide me over until I get back.'

'It's not convenient,' I said, words not usually in my

vocabulary. 'Not right now. I told you its been a tough day. I'm off to bed.'

'With *her*?' Chloe demanded, growing more insistent. 'Why else would she say you were in Nairobi unless she wants to go to your bed? I phoned Lake Airways and they said you were in Entebbe. I always *knew* you were fucking your housegirl. Not that I blame you, she *is* beautiful. Don't deny it. I heard you saying you were taking beer to bed with you.' She pulled off her nurse's cap, tossing it aside, continuing to unbutton the front of her uniform. 'So what? I'll join you both. I like the idea of drinking beer in bed, in between other things, the three of us.'

I shrugged, defeated, watching her wriggle her shapely hips and shake the unbuttoned uniform down to her ankles. She was revealed in a lacy bra constricting her succulent big tits and the briefest of matching lacy briefs, the transparent material bulging at her crotch and outlining the dark triangle of a thick pubic bush. 'Ask your girl, Ty,' she urged. 'I'm sure you can manage us both. Would she mind joining in?'

'She would not mind, miss,' Jovial said at once. 'If you both want. I would like it for myself very much.'

I had no doubt, looking at Jovial's pleased smile, remembering other occasions she'd been in my bed with another female. Aggressively bi-sexual, dominant in the lesbian role, the big African woman loved sex with her own sex every bit as much as with a male. All the more so if the partner was white and made to bend to her will. Chloe would be putty in her hands, I felt, seeing Jovial go up to the girl, caress her bare shoulders, and kiss her cheek lightly.

Chloe smiled back, unresisting as Jovial's hands went behind to unclip her bra. Unfettered, the white girl's breasts thrust out plump and pink, swollen with her excitement,

In the Flesh

the nipples taut and erect. 'You are so lovely. *They* are so lovely,' Jovial crooned, holding up both breasts from the underside of the rounded flesh, teasing the nipples with her lips. I heard Chloe give a languid sigh and say, 'Squeeze them, suck them hard.' Jovial obliged, pulling breast flesh into her mouth with the strength of her suction. When she lifted her face, they kissed long and passionately, mouths glued, bodies hard together.

'You like? Like me?' I heard Jovial ask with Chloe nodding eagerly. 'You will like this too,' my housegirl promised, slipping to her knees and drawing off Chloe's panties. *Ye-ee-ess*, came a long sigh as Jovial buried her face in Chloe's mound, kissing and drawing her tongue over the outer lips. 'It is better on the bed,' Jovial said, leading Chloe off.

I went into the kitchen to get ice for the stiff whisky I felt I was due, glad to observe that despite my recent ill-advised intimacy with Mrs Lule, the sight of two females doing their thing had resurrected my dick. In the bedroom I found the dressing-table mirror had been angled in a way that reflected the area of the bed. Chloe lay there, stark naked and diddling herself while Jovial undressed.

'She's done that before,' Chloe laughed. 'With you, no doubt. Now we can watch ourselves bonking. I like it. God, what breasts Jovial has,' she said in awe, seeing her stripped, struck by the magnificence of the black girl's figure. 'Oh, I want her to do things to me. Rude things. And I'll do things to her.'

'Things you've obviously done before yourself, Chlo, you randy young creature,' I said as Jovial joined her on the bed and their black and white bodies entwined. 'I never took you to be a switch-hitter, the way you love the dick.'

'Men!' Chloe exclaimed tauntingly, her breasts being nuzzled by Jovial's mouth and parting her thighs for the black girl's fingers to slip into her slit. 'You think only you men can do the business? I learned different as a probationary nurse with a predatory ward sister and I loved it.' She turned towards Jovial, clasping her in her arms. Their kiss was long and deliberate, as if showing me what's what. I sat down beside the bed with my whisky, more than content to save myself for the main bout.

The view was good, of lingering, erotic caresses, breasts rubbing nipple to nipple, penetrative fingers and tongues, mouths crushed together in heightened ardour. Jovial feeding a thick purplish nipple to Chloe's lips and the white girl sucking avidly. Chloe going down between her partner's thighs to lick and tongue at the source of her sex greedily. Positions were constantly changed: lying on their backs and at opposite ends of the bed, feet beside each other's heads, arms reaching and hands clasped, legs crossed like two pairs of opened scissors, cunt tight to cunt as they heaved against one another, rotating their public mounds and crying out in their lust.

It was Jovial who slipped the pillow under Chloe's arse for me to fuck her when I joined them. Later, after being revived with the girls sucking me in turn and at times together, I had Jovial while on her knees and her arse tilted over the edge of the bed, Chloe watching every thrust of my cock going into Jovial's rearward bulging cunt. Even after that, while I was content to be a spectator, the two females were still avid for each other: kissing, sucking, fingering and fondling until I was forced to prise them apart, reminding Chloe of the time. I delivered her back to her bungalow after midnight with little time to prepare for her flight. On the drive back I passed Heinz in his Volkswagen heading to collect his fiancée and leave for the airport.

I slept, too exhausted for my troubles to keep me awake,

In the Flesh

coming to in the morning to find Jovial up and about. A welcome cup of tea was brought to my bed; eggs and crisp bacon awaited me after I'd showered. After such a good start to the day, my worst fears returned as I drew up in my car before the shack that served as the office for Lake Airways. Parked in front of it were three jeeps full of heavily armed troops, surrounding the gleaming black Mercedes used by General Amin as his staff car. The soldiers were his personal bodyguard, members of the general's Kakwa tribe, clan markings carved into their ebony cheeks and looking fierce in the extreme. I hoped they were not there to cart me away, never to be seen or heard of again.

I braced myself on entering the office, seeing Amin wearing casual white shirt and shorts with a natty paisley cravat at his neck, as if he was off for a jolly game of croquet. He had commandeered the one seat the office boasted, legs as thick as tree trunks stretched out before him. I'd known him as a lowly but never humble sergeant, uneducated but confident and ambitious. Standing beside him was a tall, immaculately uniformed young officer looking the complete mean machine. His flat black features with narrowed eyes bore the Kakwa tribal warrior scars on each cheek. Bill Dove stood by, pale-faced and anxious, while our clerk Malik Singh cowered behind his counter.

'My good friend Tyler Wight,' Amin greeted me genially, offering an outsized hand in which to crush mine. 'Captain Suliman has questions to ask you. It is very bad not to tell the truth to him.'

You can say that again, I thought, shaking in my shoes while Suliman eyed me vindictively. 'I have nothing to hide,' I tried to say boldly, my voice coming out in a squeak. One slip and I knew the bastard would have me. 'What is it you want to know?'

'You brought Samuel Musa back to Entebbe?' he stated in precise English, making it sound a threat. 'Why did you do that?' He took the automatic Browning pistol from the holster on his belt as I looked around at the faces watching me, appealing for help. Bill Dove and Malik Singh looked struck dumb with horror; Amin's huge moon face was split in a grin, enjoying the proceedings.

'I had flown a United Nations' official north to where refugees from the Sudan are congregating,' I began carefully, swallowing to sound less intimidated. 'Mr Musa got in the aircraft as I was preparing to return. As a minister of the Ugandan government I could not refuse his order to be flown back.'

'What did he talk to you about?' Suliman demanded. 'What did he discuss about the situation there?'

'I don't discuss while flying, I concentrate on the controls,' I said. 'He said nothing to me.'

'Did he appear worried, frightened?'

'I took it he was scared of flying,' I answered, pleased with my response. 'Many people are.'

'He asked you to fly him to Tanzania,' Suliman said. 'I know.'

'Not that I heard him say,' I said, judging he was guessing and testing me. Throat dry as parchment, I tried to convince him further. 'I can't fly where I like. I'd need to get clearance from my manager, Mr Dove; refuel and get a new flight plan. Mr Musa said nothing about flying to Tanzania.'

Suliman glared in annoyance. How he'd love to have me in an interrogation room and question me in his own inimitable fashion. 'Where is he now?' he barked suddenly to throw me off balance, prodding me with his automatic pistol. 'You must say.'

Go fuck yourself, I longed to tell him. 'How would I

In the Flesh

know,' was what came out. 'He ran away into the bush as soon as we landed. I don't know why. You tell me.'

From his expression I knew I'd made myself an implacable enemy. The danger signs were recognised by the others present, including an interested Amin. 'Mr Wight is very good man, good pilot, good friend,' he put in to cool the threatening atmosphere. 'He has flown even for me many times. Captain Suliman is doing his duty too much, I think. But we are worried about Mr Musa. For a government minister to disappear is very bad thing. Perhaps even now he has been kidnapped by enemies of Uganda.'

He rose to leave with Suliman in attendance. 'Christ knows what kind of friends you've got,' Bill Dove said, wiping his brow. 'That Suliman, he makes even Amin look like an officer and a gentleman.'

'Sure, a military genius,' I replied. 'That's not just my opinion, it's his. Crafty as hell, though. Note the casual sports' outfit, as if nothing's going on. And worried about Musa disappearing with what he knows. You bet they are.'

'Don't tell me a thing,' Bill Dove pleaded. 'You're not finished with Suliman yet either. The Cessna's got its seats out and loaded with God knows what cargo for the Mbarara district. Russian-supplied automatic weapons is my guess. You'll be flying them in right now with Suliman beside you.'

'Lucky old me,' I said. 'Why the hell can't they use their own military aircraft?'

'Because they don't want it known among officers loyal to the government, what else?' Bill Dove said gloomily. 'I couldn't refuse the booking. Anyway, with the political situation as it is, tourists are thin on the ground. We need the business.'

I was airborne within ten minutes, Suliman beside me

and watching my every move. 'You are a friend of Miklos Dimitri,' he said, opening the conversation. 'He booked this flight in his name, saying you would do as he ordered always. That is good. Also he told me that you brought a woman to his room at the hotel. A *mzungu* woman. Then you provided another English one for him at your house. I want you to get one for me.'

'It wasn't like that,' I dared to say, seeing his eyes narrow menacingly and groaning inwardly. Another downturn in my fortunes, I considered. 'I don't provide women. Miklos turned up uninvited when I was with them.'

'That's not what he says,' Suliman said abruptly, not to be denied. 'In both cases Miklos laid with them and it was very good. Now you are his business partner, flying our cargoes, and have other duties. You will get a suitable woman for me. Bring one to the room at the hotel soon. I will be informed one is waiting.'

By mid-afternoon I was back in Entebbe, having dropped off my cargo on a strip in the bush, cleared for my arrival. As I circled overhead on leaving, I saw it being covered in loose bush and scrub to hide evidence of its existence. The unloading had been done by tough-looking tribesmen, many already in jungle-green camouflage uniforms, hidden away until the call came to take over the western area of the country. Neither were they caring what I saw, breaking open the boxes like Christmas morning to bring out new mortars and light machine guns. At Lake Airways, Bill Dove awaited me, more relieved to see his aircraft returned in one piece, I suspected.

'There's another trip north booked for you,' he greeted me. 'At least it's a *bona fide* UN booking this time made by Harry Saxon's wife. Take the rest of the day off, go home and have a relaxing time.'

A relaxing time, I considered grimly, driving off to

In the Flesh

shower the sweat of fear from me. How could I with Mrs Musa and her tribe after my blood if I didn't fly her hubby to safety? That apart from the psychopathic Suliman eager to do worse if he caught me anywhere near the unhappy Musa. Then there was the little item about providing *mzungu* women for his sexual gratification, plus Miklos Dimitri on my back, having to fly anything anywhere to his order or else. It was that *or else* I did not relish. Cheer up, I told myself, things could be worse. So I cheered up and things – naturally – got worse.

Arriving at my cottage, it was with dismay that I noted a strange car parked in my drive. 'It's getting like bloody Piccadilly Circus around my hovel,' I grumbled as Jovial met me on the verandah. 'A lady here to see you, *bwana*,' she said in exaggerated tones and grinning, as if every woman visitor came solely for me to fuck her.

Awaiting me in the barely furnished excuse for a lounge was a woman I knew by sight but had never spoken to. A buxom blonde type immaculately made-up but touching fifty, a mature and superior piece who sought to give that impression. I was aware she was the headmistress of Kampala's elite school for young ladies, which was where higher-ups in the military and government sent their daughters to be educated and cultured. Even in the searing heat she looked cool, wearing a figure-hugging white linen dress, the silk scarf tied around her throat the perfect accessory. She made no attempt to rise on my entrance, giving a look of disdain at my sweat-soaked shirt and dishevelled appearance.

'Wight, isn't it?' she said in a refined tone. 'Do you know of me? Are you aware who I am?'

'I've heard of you,' I said. 'Miss Desdemona Crane.'

'Otherwise known as the Crested Crane,' she allowed with a thin smile, referring to the thatch of yellow hair she wore high on her head, similar to that on the crested crane stork which was Uganda's national symbol. I'd also heard she was called Des the Despot by her pupils, and Des the Les by those who considered such an attractive but unmarried woman must be into female sex. 'You and I have business to discuss,' she said too meaningfully for my liking.

'Not that I'm aware of,' I replied curtly, having more than enough on my plate. 'Who let you in and why are you here?'

'It was your very sweet housegirl,' she said, rising and picking up her shoulder bag. 'So attractive, isn't she? Quite lovely. I can imagine why you employ her. Do you know the Kenyatta Apartments in Mulago Drive, Kampala?'

It was about the most prestigious building in the best area of the city. 'I've heard of it,' I said, watching her straighten her dress as she stood, unable not to be impressed by her large shapely bosom and a fine matching rear. 'What makes you say you can imagine why I employ my housegirl?'

'Your reputation,' she said simply. 'Come, it's well known both here and in Kenya. They still talk of the Gore-Blomley scandal in Nairobi. The mother, daughter *and* the aunt, wasn't it? I live in apartment six. Be there tonight. After dark, around eightish.'

'And why the hell should I?' I asked.

'You've a little problem with the Musa family, I understand, among other involvements,' she said matter-of-factly. 'I want to help. Until tonight then, goodbye for now.'

Bushed by all the day's proceedings, I sat down on the settee, left with the feeling Desdemona had not sent for me to fuck her. Good as that would have been with her well-developed figure, rather it was I who was going to get screwed. Right now I was in deeper shit than ever. Trouble I knew well from living my rude, lewd life, but

In the Flesh

the wrath of irate husbands and fathers paled beside my present set of crises. Get in the faithful Traveller and bolt for Tanzania an inner voice advised. But would I make it with road blocks and the border to negotiate? Giving up, I fell sideways on the settee and slept.

The shrill ring of the telephone awoke me, with Miklos on the line congratulating me on the 'delivery', as he put it. Payment awaited me at his restaurant. 'Suliman took a shine to you,' he added vindictively. 'Says you've promised him one of your women, a nice fresh white one. Better not disappoint the captain. I wouldn't be in your shoes.'

After showering, sitting down in my dressing gown to one of Jovial's excellent dinners of roast lamb, apple sponge, coffee and brandy, I felt a new man. Felt my housegirl too, when she came to clear the table. Her nearness beside my chair proved too tempting, my hand sidling under her cotton working dress. It smoothed its way up a firm leg and thigh to encounter warm and solid buttock cheeks. The obliging girl giggled, parting her feet to allow me full access into the hot damp cleave and the goodies beyond.

'Dip your back, Jove,' I coaxed her. 'Bend over the table. Stick that divine arse up for me.' If perchance my days were numbered, I would make every moment count. 'How hot and juicy you are in there,' I praised her, made coarse with lust. 'There's every chance I'll be compelled to empty my balls up you.' Jovial squealed her agreement with the suggestion, not only complying by going forward over the table but by drawing her dress over her head. Cast aside, it revealed her as naked and desirable as sleek flesh can get. Shrugging off my dressing gown, I was left as bare as she, brandishing a prick as hard as blue steel.

I heard low moans, the intake of breath as my fingers trailed from the moistened lips of her split to the puckered rim of her anus. 'It is too much,' she pleaded, trembling

Lesley Asquith

in her arousal, rolling over on her back among the dinner plates and cutlery. Her brown breasts were like heavy gourds, thrusting and jiggling as she turned, dark purple nipples thick and erect. 'Suck!' she demanded, pushing them up from underneath. 'And feel! Keep feeling.'

'You bet,' I answered, delighted to let her demand. It was well deserved, her spell of having the upper hand. She who never passed a comment if I came home late or even not at all, was always patient, cheerful and saw to my every need. I suckled on her right teat greedily, whilst two probing fingers worked their magic in a sodden cunt, her hips gyrating and writhing, rattling the dinner table. 'Now, *below*, suck below!' she ordered forcibly after I'd gorged on both elongated nipples. My mouth trailed down from her breasts until my tongue thrust deeply into her wet-walled interior, Jovial's back arching and her cries increasing. 'Now fuck!' came the command. 'Fuck! Fuck! Oh, mama, I want him to fuck me!'

I came up from between her sturdy thighs, my upright prick entering her slippery cunt without guidance, making her squeal at the pleasure as the bulbous knob pierced her lips. Every inch buried inside her, my balls fitted snugly between the cushiony globes of her buttocks. 'Fuck me!' she called again, impatient for me to shaft her. Slow to shunt and partially withdrawing at first, she slapped hard at my arse for more activity, hauling me close, tilting her crotch, knees raised and held under my armpits.

'Fuck harder!' I heard her grunt urgently, her thighs widening to get even more of me inside her. As I quickened my thrusting, both hands slid beneath her, cupping the cheeks of her behind. She gave a shriek and wriggled wildly as my middle finger forced a passage into the tight little ring of her arsehole. 'Y-yes, there too! Put it in there too—' she gasped. 'Both places. You must.'

In the Flesh

The telephone ringing out stopped us in mid-thrust, our sweat-wet bellies sliding together. 'Leave it,' I was about to say, when Jovial reached across the table and handed me the receiver while still penetrated. 'What do you want?' I asked gruffly, not appreciating the call although quite comfortably embedded up Jovial. 'I'm busy right now.'

'Tyler?' an excited female voice I recognised began. 'This is Margaret. Margaret Warren. The woman you did such wicked things to when I called on you at your home. How are you?'

Chapter Nine

With problems of my own to contend with, what Margaret Warren had been up to since our time together was anything but a priority in my thoughts. Now, I remembered it was I who had opened the door to her sexuality and wondered. She sounded animated, exuberant, obviously finding her visit to Uganda was what dreams were made of. Her fantasised dreams, no less.

'Never mind about me,' I replied, 'more importantly, how are things with you?' As I spoke, below me Jovial was grinding her cock-filled cunt sensually against me. 'I bumped into your daughter,' I said, motioning to Jovial to ease up. On the verge of making herself come as she pushed up against my dick, even her stifled moans sounded loud to me. 'She told me that your husband is in the hospital at Kampala.' At that moment Jovial gave her hips extra strong lunges, as if to remind me I was fucking her. My gasp could evidently be heard down the line.

'What's going on?' Margaret chuckled wickedly at her end. 'I believe you have a woman there with you.'

Trying to enjoy what is euphemistically called a table-ender, I could have agreed and put down the phone. 'More to the point,' is what I did say, 'where are you? With your husband? How is he?'

'Oh, Arthur was found to have malaria,' she replied almost dismissively, obviously eager to discuss a more important topic. I detected a giggle as she asked, 'Guess where I'm speaking from.'

'At Chloe's place, looking after it while she's in Germany?' I said. 'At the hospital with your husband? I don't know, you tell me. I know you're just dying to.'

Jovial, having come in a succession of shudders, was resuming the agitated motions with her cunt. Aiming for a second climax, she worked her arse to keep my prick shunting inside her, to maintain the feeling of being fucked. My position, with one hand holding a telephone, the other with a finger up a woman's bum, was not conducive to holding a long conversation. 'I'm going to hang up,' I told Margaret, still waiting for her to reply and hearing more girlish giggles from her end. 'I've got something outstanding I must attend to.'

'Wait, wait,' she said archly. 'I'm at Miklos's restaurant. Well, actually in his plush apartment above it. In his bedroom. He's got one of those waterbeds.' I suddenly heard her give out with an unexpected '*Oooh, aaagh*,' followed by the expelling of a long and languid sigh. 'Naughty!' I heard her gasp and it wasn't said to me. 'I didn't say you could do *that!* Oh, yesss.'

'That big bastard's up you right now,' I accused. 'Right up from the sound of it. Didn't I warn you about that Greek? He's trouble, Margaret. He'll own you body and soul. He'll fuck you about in more ways than you ever dreamed possible.'

'He does, he already has, he is!' she grunted, distracted by whatever was being inflicted on her. 'Can you guess what – *where* he is? Oh, oh, he's put it right in me.'

I could imagine the scene. Margaret on her hands and knees, clutching the phone with Miklos mounted up behind her. First the lifting of her dress and the drawing down of briefs over the twin moons of her buttocks. That's if she

In the Flesh

wore anything to begin with. Then the subtle fingering, touching up the outer lips, probing the moist flesh within, forcing the tightness of the puckered ring above.

I plainly heard Margaret's moans and whimpers, heightening my own lustful feelings as Jovial's legs wrapped around me tightly, lunging up desperately to gain her second climax. The phone in my hand gave out unintelligible grunts as I began to pay more attention to Jovial, increasing my thrusts to match the intensity of hers. 'I can hear what you're doing too,' Margaret shrieked excitedly down the line. 'Tyler, you're fucking someone!'

It could have been your precious daughter if you'd phoned last night, I remembered, getting into my stride and shafting vigorously as my partner bucked and squealed, coming violently but continuing to seek a further climax. In, out, my prick was deeply sheathed, withdrawn, then pistoned forward to force loud ecstatic cries, Jovial's ample bottom rising and falling to match my strokes. In the heat of the moment I threw aside the telephone, sensing Jovial was on the brink of her third climax. Timing it right, I let go my volley at the moment of her strongest convulsion. Immediately her legs went limp, lolling back breathlessly among the dinner plates, with me collapsed over her. In time she reached out to hand me the discarded telephone, giggling as I took it to my ear.

'You're there again, are you?' I heard Miklos speaking, the usual arrogant tone in his voice. 'I've just fucked your friend Margaret, front and back, of course. Who were you screwing at your end? Bring her to Kampala. You know I enjoy having your women.'

'You just got lucky,' I informed him, determined to sound casual. 'They weren't my women or you wouldn't have got a sniff. Do everybody a favour and drop dead.' Even sated, I could not help admiring the way Jovial's full breasts jiggled about as she rolled aside from me. 'You should see the one I've just had,' I taunted him. 'But you won't.'

I heard him tut-tutting with amusement. 'Is that any way to treat a good friend?' he asked. 'I owe you for introducing me to Margaret. In return I'm going to do you another big favour, make you more good money.'

'Favours from you I need like a hole in the head,' I said.

'Which is what you'll probably get if you don't continue to cooperate,' he laughed vindictively. 'In fact, I guarantee it. Remember Captain Suliman?'

'Unfortunately, yes,' I agreed, growing wary.

'You'll be making another trip with him tomorrow. All above board, booked by me with your Lake Airways and paid for in advance. I'm putting business in the way of your little flying outfit. Much needed revenue from the look of your office and hangar.'

'We get by,' I said. 'Tomorrow is out, anyway. I'm booked to fly Red Cross supplies to the UN man in the refugee area north.'

'There's been a slight change of plan,' Miklos said smoothly. 'We were able to persuade Lake Airways to get their priorities right. You fly for us tomorrow.'

'I can hardly wait,' I said drily, imagining the persuasion used. 'What do you intend to do about Mrs Warren?'

'Fuck her all she wants,' Miklos laughed. 'That lady has been kept short by her old man and she's making up for lost time. The original bitch in heat, can't get enough of it. She's beside me right now, naked and begging for more.'

'Send her away,' I appealed. 'She's out of her depth with the likes of you. You've got all the women you need. Let her go.'

'I've got plans for her,' Miklos said. 'So when did you get a conscience? People can see she's no whore, even if she

In the Flesh

acts like one. That's an extra in my business, like coming up with a virgin. She stays until I've finished with her.'

'Is she beside you while you're saying that?' I said.

'No, I sent her to get me a drink,' he answered indifferently. 'I'd have said the same if she had been. She's happy here, doing what comes naturally. Being trained for her own good.'

I doubted that. No doubt she would end up as a star attraction in his private whorehouse, passed around among influential friends to gain privileges.

I must have a conscience after all, I thought as I drove the twenty miles to Kampala, having decided to try to save Margaret from herself before my mysteriously arranged meeting with Desdemona Crane. The interior of *Chez Miklos*, the bar and restaurant, was like a touch of Parisienne elegance in a shabby African town. As I ordered a double Scotch at the bar, Miklos came up to me with Margaret in a fashionable evening gown by his side.

'That's on the house,' he said to the barman. 'Anything Mr Wight orders is to go on my account. We've just come down to dine,' he turned to me to say. 'Why not join us? I can recommend the food.'

'It would choke me,' I replied ungraciously, 'and I can pay for my own drinks.'

'As you wish,' he smiled, unperturbed as ever at my insults. He lifted the top flap of the pocket on my shirt, stuffing in a thick envelope. 'Plenty there to buy drinks. Plenty more to follow.'

'Hello, Tyler,' Margaret greeted me. 'This is a surprise.'

'I came to talk some sense into you,' I said. 'To leave *him*. Leave while the going's good.'

'But I have to remain in Kampala while my husband is in hospital,' she said. 'Miklos drives me there to see

Arthur twice a day. He's put me up in his apartment and given me this lovely evening dress to wear. Really, he's been so kind.'

I saw the Greek listening with amused interest. 'He's kind,' I said. 'The kind to avoid. Stay in an hotel if you have to. Get out before – *before* – the whoremaster sells your body to the kind of people he keeps in with. Or uses you in his live sex shows.'

'Now you're being ridiculous,' Margaret protested angrily. She linked her arm with Miklos's to show her affection and trust in him. 'You have no right to tell me what to do.'

'Leave before I have you thrown out,' Miklos chipped in. 'Mrs Warren has the use of my apartment while her husband is hospitalised.' This was being said for her benefit, to allay my warning. 'She is very welcome to stay.'

'I'll just bet she is,' I said sarcastically.

'So I'm sleeping with Miklos,' Margaret informed me defiantly. 'I look forward to sharing his bed tonight. I'm having a wonderful time for a change. It's our secret and one I expect you to keep to yourself. After all, you've had me too. What my husband and daughter will never know won't harm them.' She leaned her body into Miklos and he put an arm around her waist possessively. 'I know what I'm doing.'

'You haven't a clue,' I said, my arms pinioned by two of Miklos's biggest Ugandan waiters, who looked to him for the signal to eject me into the street. 'Personally, Mrs Warren, I don't give a flying fuck who you shack up with. Enjoy a holiday fling with anyone but this sleazy pimp by all means. He hasn't even started on you yet. You'll be sorry.'

At a nod from Miklos I was frogmarched to the restaurant entrance and bounced out into the gutter. I dusted myself off, got in my car, and five minutes later parked before the

In the Flesh

imposing Kenyatta Apartments wondering what else lay in store. Through double glass doors and up a deep-carpeted stairway, along a corridor hung with landscapes of Africa, I found number six. A press on the bell remained unanswered for some time and I was about to leave when Desdemona Crane opened the door, ushering me in as if not wishing my arrival to be witnessed.

I thought her fanciable in the extreme, despite her annoyed look. She was wearing a silk kimono that nicely accentuated her curvaceous figure. Eye-shadow and make-up had been applied liberally to her face, surprising me as she complained that I had got her out of bed. 'You're hours late, I'd given up on you,' she said, leading the way into her lounge. Following, eyeing the sway of impressive buttock cheeks before me, I could see that she wore nothing but skin under her Japanese robe. All choice mature female flesh, I reckoned, thinking how exciting it would be to mount that well-upholstered form. Or shag her dog-fashion with those same impressive buttock cheeks bumping back into my belly, meeting my thrusts. She smiled thinly, noting my expression, well aware it would seem of my lewd intentions toward her.

'You're wasting your time if you're thinking what I suspect you are, Wight,' she announced casually, using my name as if addressing an underling. 'At least you did finally turn up. Can I get you a drink?'

'Scotch, if that's all you're handing out,' I said, getting back at her. I accepted a fine crystal glass containing an excellent malt. Looking around the furniture, drapes and framed paintings, I decided Desdemona only went in for the best. 'Quite a pad,' I told her, 'but I didn't come here to admire the decor. Why do you want to see me?'

She sat on the settee opposite me, crossing long well-formed legs and allowing me a glimpse of a shapely milk-white thigh. She indicated that I sit in the armchair. 'You've been engaged to fly on missions arranged by the restauranteur Miklos Dimitri, on behalf of whomsoever uses a certain Captain Suliman as his boy.'

'Press-ganged,' I said. 'I'd hardly call them missions. They are bookings made with Lake Airways. I just work there. Don't ask me what it's about, they haven't told me. I prefer not to know, or have anything to do with them. Or with you.'

'Come, come,' she smiled. 'I'm sure you're aware that there is a faction intending to take over this country in a *coup d'etat*. They are arming secret forces in the regions and you are helping that build-up.'

'You could have fooled me,' I claimed. 'I know nothing.'

'I don't believe you,' she said. 'There's also the little matter of Sam Musa, the missing government minister. I know that his chief wife and others of his tribe wish you to fly him to safety in Tanzania. You can't deny that either.'

'They are threatening to cut off my balls if I don't,' I admitted. 'I've grown rather attached to them.'

'Yes, well your brains were down there when you fell into Mrs Musa's trap.' Desdemona gave another of her wry smiles. 'No pun intended. You are wondering why I know so much. It's my work.'

'So you're not just the headmistress of a girls' school?' I queried. 'You're an agent. Out here in a developing country and spying on 'em. Good for you, but why tell me?'

'Because I'm recruiting you. We need your services,' she said. 'You are a decorated ex-RAF officer and loyal subject of the crown – and now you are a provisional agent of the British Secret Service. Congratulations.'

'You can bust me back to civilian right now,' I told her forcibly. 'Jesus, I'm over my head as it is. I refuse!'

In the Flesh

'You can't,' she said pleasantly. 'I could make things much more awkward for you, believe me. We want you to carry on as you are, that's all. Fly Captain Suliman to his secret military camps but keep me informed, of course. Help Suliman willingly, and be available when your flight bookings are made.'

'Do you want a *coup* to succeed?' I asked. 'Have General Amin become President of Uganda?' I handed her my empty glass for a refill, feeling I needed one. 'Would you like him running the country?'

'Not particularly,' she said easily. 'But it's a pretty sure bet he will be. Britain wants Uganda to remain a friendly country and continue to trade with us, whoever's in charge. So we must do nothing to antagonise them, must we?' I was handed a generous refill of malt whisky. 'At the same time,' she added, 'poor Sam Musa must be flown to safety. We'll arrange for you to do that, with his family.'

'You've got to be kidding,' I said. 'Amin and Suliman are after his blood. Why bother?'

'Because we want him out,' Desdemona explained. 'And there'll be others; government ministers, civil servants, intellectuals, whose lives won't be worth a candle after a *coup*. Anyone considered a danger to a military government invariably gets rounded up and disappears. We envisage mass executions.'

'Mine among 'em,' I said gloomily.

'There is that chance,' she said cheerfully but then it wasn't her neck we were discussing. 'On the other hand, if you follow our instructions to the letter, you could come out of this quite well. I have to tell you that it's no accident that you're being used to fly certain supplies to the rebel forces. In our covert way we let Miklos Dimitri know you'd be the ideal person: always in debt, with no conscience and a bad reputation locally but an experienced pilot.'

'Well, thanks for the reference,' I said drily, 'so I'm to continue to fly Suliman about.'

'Yes. You're being well paid for it, I understand. If the overthrow of the present government succeeds, the newly installed President Idi Amin will probably pin the Order of the Nile on your chest for services rendered,' she smiled facetiously, leaning forward to take my empty glass, her cleavage revealing how snugly her big tits nestled together. 'Just think, the Order of the Nile.'

'More likely thrown in the bloody Nile,' I said, 'for knowing too much. And what about Musa and others you say must be got out? Flown by me at some risk – why?'

'We're hedging our bets,' Desdemona said, making it simple for me. 'Once safe elsewhere, the people we get out will no doubt form a government in exile and will be grateful to Britain for aiding their escape. Military governments come and go. Those we have helped will return to their former positions of power and become another government friendly to us. It's all tied up with our trade and exports.'

Further talk was cut short by the appearance of an African girl. She was young, nubile and obviously fresh from bed. She wore an almost transparent white shortie nightdress that added to her allure. I stared appreciatively. She was about seventeen, I reckoned, and plump and shapely in the way Baganda men liked their women – big melon-sized tits and nipples like thumbs, and between supple thighs a fat split quim. I could see plainly that it was shaved bare, the thick lipless cleave inrolling.

'Dessy, you never came back to bed,' the girl complained then, noticing me, covered her mouth to stifle a naughty giggle. 'Oh, I didn't know your visitor was still here.'

'Did I interrupt something?' I said in mock innocence,

In the Flesh

hoping to dent Desdemona's usual calm. My jibe was ignored.

'Let me introduce Miss Petal Musa,' she replied, getting back at me. 'You know her family. She's here for her safety. No doubt she's being sought for questioning about her father. Petal is a pupil of mine. Other safe houses have been arranged for those who may have to go into hiding before you fly them out. We have contingency plans.'

'How can we ever repay him for helping us to escape?' Petal said, to my mind rather suggestively. She sat beside Desdemona, cuddling into her, her extravagant tits wobbling. 'What can we do?'

'I could come up with something,' I promised, seeing Petal press a kiss to Desdemona's cheek lovingly, her forwardness surprising me. 'You two go right ahead, don't mind me,' I offered, content for the present to sit back and watch the proceedings. 'How handy for you, Dessy. Headmistress of a girls' school and able to take your pick. And you knocked *my* reputation, shame on you.' I felt I had nothing to lose, crossing to the sideboard to help myself to a fresh drink. 'Carry on, girls. Give me a shout when you need a big prick.'

'Big prick is right,' Desdemona said, unruffled as ever, unless by Petal's kisses to her neck and cheek plus a hand inside her kimono fondling her breasts. 'I never met a bigger one than you, Wight. Petal and I are lovers and have been for some time.' As if to impress me, she turned her face and the pair kissed full on the mouth, lingeringly with parted lips and tongues exploring. 'Does that shock your macho sensibilities?' she challenged, withdrawing her face. 'We don't need you or your disgusting penis. If you're not gentleman enough to leave, you may well learn something about pleasing a woman. Tenderness, consideration for the pleasure of a partner. Things outside your experience, I'm sure.'

The bitches wanted an audience, I was certain, seeing them go at it with further long kisses and hands fondling. Petal parted the kimono at Desdemona's neck to uncover a big ivory-white tit. Drawn in by a cradled arm, the African girl fastened her lips over the exposed pink nipple to draw it deeply into her mouth and suck greedily. Turned to Desdemona as she was, Petal's nightie rose over her hips, her fig-like cunt laid bare before my lustful eyes. A man can only stand so much.

'This is a game three can play,' I announced, advancing and dropping my pants en route, fully intending to spear something, anything. Desdemona sat up like a scalded cat while Petal stopped suckling to look around, eyes wide at the upright dick flourished before her.

'Indeed it is not!' Desdemona exclaimed stridently. 'Whatever gave you that idea?' She sat up and pulled together the neck of her kimono. 'How dare you?'

'It came to mind seeing what you two were doing,' I said, reasonably I thought. 'I'm not made of stone. I don't object to providing a gallery for a pair of outright exhibitionists but silly me took it as a come-on.'

'You thought wrong,' I was told firmly. 'Come, Petal, we are off to bed as the temptation seems too much for him.' Petal, I was pleased to note, was grinning at me cheekily, eyes still glued to my rearing cock. 'You can put that revolting thing away,' Desdemona ordered, linking her arm with her young lover's to whisk her out of my sight. 'I'll get further instructions to you as necessary. I shall keep in touch, rest assured,' she said before disappearing into her bedroom with Petal and closing it firmly behind her.

My watch told me it was almost two in the morning, late for the drive back especially with the army roadblocks. It meant explaining my business to cocky soldiers, high on bang or drink, who would demand something to let me

In the Flesh

pass – the money given to me by Miklos doubtless and my watch. Outside, torrents of rain rattled the windows at the height of a tropical downpour. Inside, the room was cosy. I settled for Desdemona's long settee, deciding to leave after dawn.

Before settling down, I had a pee in Dessy's ultra-feminine bathroom, leaving the toilet seat up just to annoy her. I paused outside her bedroom door to listen to moans and whimpers before going off aggrieved to my lonely couch. My impatience in crossing over to join the pair of lovers before they became wanton enough to allow a threesome, had been sadly misjudged. I had blown it.

Certainly nobody else had. Blown it, I mean. A blow job at least would have been some recompense for finding myself even more deeply involved in a dangerous game. I lay down wondering if sleep was possible. From the bedroom came the noises of two females in a hectic sexual coupling, the volume turned up for my benefit I was sure, disturbing me as was intended.

Chapter Ten

Sleep did come however. The pounding of the rain ceased, the sounds of love-making stopped in Desdemona's bedroom, and I dozed. I came to in the dim light of dawn to see an entirely naked Petal Musa slip quietly past and go toward the bathroom. How's that for a rude awakening? On her return she noticed me and bent over my prone form on the settee, grinning wickedly and flashing strong white teeth, her magnificent young girl's breasts swinging over me. She was undoubtedly as delighted to see me as I was her.

The tropic night was of such humidity that I had removed all my clothes for comfort – a smart move. Petal leant close, firm melon-sized tits almost in my face, her plump cunt nestling in the fork of rounded thighs within feeling-up distance. She held a finger to her lips for silence, letting me know she was as eager not to disturb her headmistress as I. She got on the settee beside me, her full lips seeking mine, her right hand going directly to grasp my prick and jiggling the outer skin, thickening and stretching it. She stifled a naughty giggle.

'Feel free, Petal,' I told her in a hoarse whisper, growing more rampant at the delightful rubbing she was giving my tool. 'One of those beats a tongue up your hungry little snatch, I bet.'

'I like both very much,' the young vixen whispered

joyfully. 'Too much!' She lifted one of my hands to a breast, warm and pliant in my palm, a solid sphere, the big nipple hard. 'You like to suck them?' I had little choice, the teat was pressed to my mouth before I could reply. My fingers found her pussy sodden and relaxed.

She moaned softly in increasing agitation and pushed me flat among the cushions to straddle me. She held my prick up between a finger and thumb, directing the knob to the cleft of her plump little cunt and thrust down on it. Impaled on the whole stem, she gave a tremendous shudder of pleasure, her whimpering growing louder. Lying beneath her, fondling her tits, I was forced to clamp a hand over her mouth as her squeals increased. She gyrated her hips, loving the feel of the length and thickness in her velvety channel.

'Whoa,' I had to say as her assault forced me to quell the surge in my balls. I wanted it to last and for her to experience several strong comes. 'Take it slower,' I ordered. 'It's not a race. Savour it.'

She slowed somewhat, whispering that she had come but wanted more. 'Lean right back, now come forward over me,' I directed, allowing her to discover different angles of penetration to titillate her hungry sex. 'Have you never had it with a man before?' I was interested to know.

'Just boys – my cousins,' she grunted, slipping into a nice steady rhythm. 'They only thought of themselves. But there were other ways, I found.'

'What ways?' I wanted to know, eager to hear her confessions. I was no longer surprised how a woman being fucked enjoyed disclosing her secrets. 'What ways do you find to get more pleasure yourself, Petal?' I asked.

'The girls at school,' she confessed, unable to prevent herself quickening as she ground down on my dick. 'We have no boys, so we learn to play with ourselves, then with others. It is good, we make each other come. Lick each

In the Flesh

other, play with each other. So much goes on at school. But your big thing in me is so much better. Let me go faster. I must!'

'In good time,' I promised, keen to hear more. 'What about your headmistress? When did she get into the act?' But my query went unanswered as Petal bucked furiously and went into spasms. She convulsed as if having a seizure, coming so strongly that I could no longer hold back and I shot my load deep into her. The girl collapsed forward over me, our sweat-covered bodies glued together. Across the room I saw Desdemona in her kimono, observing us grimly.

'How depraved,' she said, coming to stand beside the settee. 'You are entirely and utterly depraved, Wight. And as for this treacherous little bitch,' she added bitterly, 'she has been desperate for your obscene male appendage since first seeing it. She couldn't resist it, could she?' Desdemona added.

'Evidently not,' I agreed. Petal was still lolling across me in an evident state of bliss, content to remain there with the shrinking stiffness of my prick gripped in her cunt. Without turning her head to acknowledge Desdemona's presence, she recommenced working her pelvis against me. 'And unable to resist even yet,' I said. 'How long have you been observing us?'

'Enough to see it would have been cruel to have stopped her,' Desdemona admitted. 'I didn't like what I saw but that's how it is.'

'Did it arouse you, make you wish an obscene appendage otherwise known as a stiff prick was in you, Dessy?' I chanced.

'Yes,' Petal said surprisingly. 'It was so *good*.'

'Don't inflate his ego any more, please,' was the stern reply. 'And as for you, Wight, the name is Desdemona, or in your case, Miss Crane. I certainly wouldn't want *that* up me, thank you.' To Petal she added, 'Get *off* him, young madam, your time is up.' Getting no immediate response, she gave the girl's bobbing brown bum a series of hearty smacks, the deliveries sounding like pistol shots and making Petal yelp. She rolled off me, rubbing her bottom. 'To the room, now,' she was ordered, and she ran off with a final grin at me.

'You're human after all,' I said, reaching for my clothes. 'Who knows, you might enjoy a man. You've got a great body. I'm offering.'

'I don't do that sort of thing,' she said. 'You can't be serious.'

'As serious as you are about recruiting me as an agent,' I said. 'It's not nearly so bloody dangerous.'

'You'd better shower,' she said surprising me. 'There are soap and towels in my bathroom. I'll make you breakfast before you go.'

There was hope for her yet, I decided, bowling down the Entebbe road replete with good food and refreshed by a cold shower. I had shaved too, with a lady's razor I had found in the wall cabinet. Halfway down the road, passing Kajansi village, I came across a makeshift military roadblock.

It consisted of tables and chairs taken from the nearby huts along the strip of road enclosed by thick bush. I'd heard there were leopards in there but the soldiery that stopped my progress were far more dangerous to my mind. I drew up, surrounded by a sea of fierce black faces, all armed to the teeth, and my papers were demanded by a hulking sergeant in a sweat-stained uniform who placed the muzzle of a big Webley revolver to my brow. His ebony face with the usual tribal markings told me of his tribe, he was one of General Amin's loyals. I had no doubt they were out hoping to catch Sam Musa should he attempt to get to the airport.

In the Flesh

I handed over my work permit and driving licence to him while others looked over the car. With my papers I also handed over several packets of cigarettes kept in my glove compartment for such emergencies. The sergeant accepted them wordlessly, looked at my photograph on the driving licence, unable to read any words. 'Why are you out so early here?' he said, in what could only be taken as a threat.

'*Okazina*,' I said, using the local word for fucking, getting an instant roar of approval from the surrounding troops. 'A *Muganda muneni*.' I opened my arms wide to show the girth of the woman I claimed to have been with, knowing they went for fat females. The revolver was withdrawn from my brow. 'I'm on my way to work. Is it okay to leave now, sergeant sir?'

'Very good watch,' he said, lifting my wrist and admiring it. 'Give it to me, *mzungu*, I let you go.'

And up yours, I determined. The watch was an old friend, companion of many a scrape and hairy misadventure. I'd worn it through thick and thin: over Nazi Germany in heavy flak and shot at by enemy fighters; later, flying cargoes during the Berlin blockade; and in other dangerous situations in Africa. Though pawned repeatedly in hard-up days, I had always managed to redeem it. Despite the revolver, I determined to keep it.

'Do you know Captain Suliman?' I said in a different tone. 'He is my *rafiki*, my very good friend. As his pilot, I'm going to Entebbe to fly him on a mission ordered by General Amin.' I spoke in Swahili to impress him further but, from the scowl I got, I expected what brains I had to be splattered over the inside of my old Morris Traveller, already in a scruffy enough state.

'You come,' he ordered tersely and I followed him up a well-worn track among the trees. On the way we passed a group of women carrying heavy stalks of bananas on their heads, all of whom regarded me with horror in their eyes, sure that my number was up. The idea came to my mind as well as I was led deeper into the bush. I had decided to make a dash for it into the undergrowth when the path opened up to a clearing. There was a circle of poor huts with grass roofs and a larger mud-walled building boasting a corrugated tin roof. A notice over the doorway said Hotel in large letters, and there was a Coca-Cola sign on the door. Soldiers lounged before it with a group of young girls as I was led inside. Greatly intrigued as to why an apprehensive white man was being brought in by their mean-looking sarge, they followed us.

The so-called hotel contained more soldiers and girls, pairs of whom fucked openly across the tables or mattresses laid on the floor. I had no doubt the owner and his family had fled, and the place had been commandeered as a billet. Those not enjoying themselves with the girls helped themselves to the stock of drinks behind the counter, raising bottles to me as if welcoming me to the party. The temperature inside was intense, the stench of sweaty bodies overpowering. My sergeant captor pushed me into a corridor with his pistol in my back, knocked on a door and was told to enter.

In a bedroom with bare walls was a bed and a small bedside cabinet, the whole as poor as the rest of the building. Beside the bed, on which two entirely naked young girls lay giggling at our arrival, Captain Suliman stood dressing, buckling on the webbing belt which held his holstered automatic. The sergeant saluted, addressing him in a northern tribal dialect I did not understand. Whatever it was that Suliman answered, my captor put his pistol away and left me to his officer and the pair of naked girls.

'You have not brought me one of your women yet,' Suliman reproached me right away. 'I have waited but you

In the Flesh

have done nothing. That is very bad. It is not good to do bad things with me.'

You can bet your boots on that, I reckoned, as his narrowed eyes trained on me while I sought for a suitable answer. As it was, I didn't need to find one, Suliman continuing in a more reasonable tone – at least reasonable for him.

'You will get me one when I return from the northern district. I do not mind sharing my women with you,' he said, indicating the two giggling floozies on the bed. 'I say you must take them and all will be fair between us. They are Mutoro tribe girls, very good fucks.' The pair of girls understood, jumping off the bed with squeals at such fun, grabbing my arms as if they had been given a gift.

'How extremely hospitable of you,' I began, getting dragged down on the bed, 'but I couldn't. I have to get to the airport, it's you I'll be flying this morning.' This was not easy to say while my shirt was being pulled over my head and my trousers hauled down. 'Young ladies!' I protested. 'This is hardly cricket. What would your mamas say?'

'Our mamas are through in the bar,' one said, laughing delightedly, and placing her cushiony bum on my chest. 'We are massage girls from Kampala, give very good massage. You stay, *mzungu*, you like.'

'You stay,' Suliman insisted, looking down on us. 'It is fair. For myself I have important conference in Entebbe. You will see me there at nine o'clock.'

He left us, my two tittering companions eyeing me with glee. They were undoubtedly comely creatures, with ebony skins as smooth as silk, slender but with neat pear-shaped tits and tight little arses. I lay back for them to do their worst, considering it beat the bullet in the head I'd been expecting. 'What about this one?' I was asked as she held up my still-flaccid dick. 'I think he would like massage.'

Knowing *him*, he probably would, I acknowledged, the pair sitting up on their ankles either side of me, facing the object of their interest, a white dick for a change. Thus positioned, I was presented with two rounded bare bottoms, my hands going into the cleave of each and touching up their hot little cunts. This brought more squeals from one at least, the other having rubbed me up to erection and clamping her mouth over it.

'It is big now,' said the one watching her friend suck me. 'You fuck us both.' As if in accord, they fell forward on their forearms, bums tilted and on offer. 'Fuck us from back. Monkey-fuck,' the other ordered.

This was their expression for what we Brits called doggy-fashion, I presumed. I got on my knees and penetrated the girl on my left, getting an immediate response as her firm little arse bucked back against me. She was vocal in the extreme as she fucked and it brought spectators to the doorway, the soldiers lounging with bottles in hand as I shafted away. She screamed out in her language the equivalent of *I'm coming*! and hardly had she tumbled forward, her body shaking as if still in the throes, when I was pulled over by the other girl. Moments after uncunting, as they say, I was embedded up another, her arse slapping into my belly. I thrust until I fell forward with her, giving my all until I was drained and wrung out.

I wasted no time getting away and arrived in a sweaty, dishevelled state at the Lake Airways office shortly before nine with Bill Dove pacing nervously outside. 'Christ, I thought you'd bolted,' he said, relieved to see me. 'I've got that wild man Suliman inside putting the frighteners on us just through being there. Get him off my back.' Calming down somewhat, he noticed my state. 'You must give me the name of your tailor, Wight,' he said sarcastically. 'Is that any way to turn up for work? You're a disgrace.'

In the Flesh

'I'm here, aren't I?' I said. 'Is all ready for take-off?'
'Fuelled up, cargo loaded, whatever the hell it is,' he answered glumly. 'No manifest, the trip paid for in cash. At least there's a flight plan to the refugee area north but there'll be nothing for them. I've had to apologise to Mrs Saxon for her husband missing out on this flight. I said that a priority came up. An offer I couldn't refuse,' he added, knowing I was fully aware that he dare not. 'Mrs Saxon was thoughtful enough to make a packed lunch for you as well as her husband, if you see him. Go into the office and thank her, if you can bear her to see you like that.'

I entered to find Suliman sitting in the one available chair while Harry Saxon's wife stood holding two small parcels I took to be the packed lunches. 'You look like you've been dragged through a hedge backwards,' she chuckled to me, 'or was it a bed? I've made up a few chicken sandwiches for you and a piece of my home-made cake. There's some for Harry too if you see him. Tell him a convoy of aid trucks is being assembled in Nairobi. The telephone call came after he'd left. Also that the doctor promised by Roberta arrives in Entebbe today. That should please him.'

'Is that all?' I asked, thinking how absolutely lovely she looked, morning fresh despite the searing heat in a form-fitting crisp dress.

'Tell him I miss him,' she smiled. 'I fully understand about the flight being altered. It will have to be another time.'

'Later today if I get back in time,' I promised, looking at Suliman. He sat impassive, sinister in his dark glasses, his unseen eyes trained unmoving on Diana Saxon. Once in the cabin of the Cessna I noted the seating had been removed and considered the amount of cargo excessive. He sat beside me, watching my every move.

'What are you doing?' he questioned as I put on my

headset radio, pressing the button on the control wheel to transmit speech.

'Contacting the control tower as usual,' I said, resenting his presence. 'Giving my call-sign, requesting permission to take-off. It's normal procedure.'

'Not today,' he ordered. 'You fly.'

I took off, hoping no scheduled airliner was approaching. Airborne and turning north, above open country, Suliman sat back deep in thought, smiling to himself as if pleased.

'That woman back there,' he said at last. 'She was very friendly to you. That is the one I want. You will get her for me.'

'I couldn't do that, even for you,' I said horrified. 'She's the wife of a United Nations' official, a very nice lady. I wouldn't get her for you, no way. Forget it.'

He shrugged, taking off his dark glasses to look at me. 'I am sorry for you not wanting to help me,' he said, his words spoken calmly but the message plain. 'I will remember but, no matter, I can get her by myself. I shall enjoy that—'

Over my dead body, you vicious bastard, I swore, and a moment later realised it might well be.

Chapter Eleven

It was late afternoon before I was in the air on my way back, leaving Captain Suliman to continue whatever work he had been sent to oversee. It was not hard to gather something of the reason for his visit north. The long wooden boxes of our cargo were unloaded by men hardly qualifying as starving refugees. Tall, well-fed characters of the Nuba tribe, Nilotic people closely related to Amin's Kakwa, they weren't there by accident. Everything to equip a fighting force was distributed: weapons, ammo, grenades, even Ugandan Army uniforms and boots.

'Is this a recruiting drive?' I ventured to ask Suliman, who had taken complete charge with an efficiency I could not fault. A dire warning that I had seen nothing made me make myself scarce, sitting in the only shade available, under my aircraft. Earlier I'd been ordered to land on a dirt strip a mile or so away from the refugee area, so had been unable to contact Harry Saxon. I intended to warn him of Suliman's letch for his wife, advising him Diana should be kept well out of reach and leave for neighbouring Kenya at least. On my return I would seek her out, make sure she was left in no doubt about the stone-faced Captain's desire to have her.

Waiting impatiently while the unloading proceeded, I was joined in my patch of shade by Ed Spilsby, the ex-officer turned white mercenary. 'You're in on this caper too, I see,' he said genially. 'It's a fiece of cake. I've been in on the planning of it and this is one *coup* that'll succeed. When the new military government takes over, the rewards will be great. You and I will live like chiefs. Lots of wives, a couple of Mercedes, you name it.'

'Include me out,' I told him, knowing Spilsby of old to my cost. 'I'm just an aeroplane driver, doing what I'm told. I don't get involved in political situations.'

'Fuck politics,' Spilsby laughed. 'This is all about ambition and power, grabbing the good life. You know old Idi, the barefoot boy from the bundu who wants to make president; meet the Queen and the Pope, go to the White House. Not bad, eh, for my platoon sergeant in the old King's African Rifles during the Mau-Mau campaign? What do you think of these fierce-looking bastards here?'

'I wouldn't care to be around when they run amok,' I admitted.

'I'll lick 'em into shape,' Spilsby boasted, 'teach 'em discipline. They're already experienced guerillas with the Sudanese Liberation Army. The offer of a soft billet in the Uganda Army has brought 'em south and the tribes they've been protecting came with them. I see the UN and other assorted do-gooders are here to look after their welfare. It's none of our business.'

Looking after Spilsby's business was his only concern, I knew. Landing back at Entebbe, I drove straight to the Saxons' bungalow to pass on my warning. My knock at the verandah door brought the gardener out of his quarters nearby. Memsa'ab had gone to Kampala with a friend who had arrived today, I was informed. Would I like to leave a message?

I decided against it, I could hardly write Diana a note saying that a local army despot was out to debauch her. I knew she would not be hard to find if she was dining with

In the Flesh

her guest in one of the few good eating places in the city. There was *Chez Miklos* for one, I thought, remembering Margaret Warren for the first time that day. I went home to shower and change, ignoring suggestive looks from Jovial and her half-sister, Jolly, who were sitting in the kitchen exchanging gossip. The phone rang as I was about to leave, Chloe Warren's voice sounding crackly all the way from Germany.

'Tyler,' she said, 'what the hell's happened to my mother? I can't get her at the house. She wouldn't be staying with you while my dad is in hospital, would she? Don't tell me a lion's eaten her, it's more probable you have. Where is she?'

'Staying at a hotel in Kampala to be near your father, last I heard,' I said, thinking it better to lie. 'I'm going there tonight. If I see her, I'll pass on your message.'

'That's okay, as long as she's all right,' Chloe said. 'How are you doing? Who are you screwing while I'm away? Things are not going to plan here, Heiny still insists on taking a virgin bride to bed so I'm reduced to bringing myself off. At least in Hamburg they sell a great selection of vibrators. I've even considered seducing Heiny's father. The way he looks at me, I think he's game.'

'You should marry Heiny's dad, then,' I advised, hanging up. Later on, when I entered *Chez Miklos*, the tables were filled with diners and attended by a host of Ugandan waiters in long white kanzu gowns and red cummerbunds. A native band played on a small stage and, on the dance floor, I saw Fatima dressed in bangles and beads and little else performing a Turkish belly-dance routine. I saw no sign of Diana Saxon and her companion, but got a wave and a beaming smile from Chloe's mother.

Margaret sat by herself at a corner table with a glass of wine in her hand and a full bottle set before her, looking definitely tipsy. She wore yet another evening gown and too much make-up.

'Tyler,' she welcomed me exuberantly as I weaved my way through the tables. 'Where have you been hiding? Sit down and talk to me.'

'How are you doing?' I enquired, aware she was drunk and very animated. 'You don't look much like the housewife from Harrowgate, more like the prize whore of the harem. How's your husband, if you are at all interested? Your daughter Chloe phoned, saying she'd had no contact with you and was worried.'

'Well, I'm not staying at her place, am I?' she said defiantly, stifling a hiccup. 'I'm living here to be near Arthur. He's being well treated. Miklos has arranged a private room and sends in his food.'

'How convenient for you and Miklos,' I said, watching her drink her glass empty, a nearby waiter rushing forward to refill it. 'I suppose the generous Greek is fucking you rigid every chance?'

'For once in my life someone wants me,' she said, remaining defiant. 'You of all people have no right to criticise. Miklos may do as he likes. In fact, I want him to.'

I shrugged, giving up. 'What did you say to Chloe?' she went on, struggling to focus her eyes on me. 'Nothing to upset her, I hope?'

'I told her you were staying in Kampala to be near her dad,' I said. 'Nothing more. She was happy with that.'

'Dear Tyler, I knew you wouldn't let me down,' she smiled. 'It was you who changed my life.' She placed a hand on my neck, drawing me close to press soft lips to mine in a long, tongue-probing kiss. Her other hand went under the table, hidden by the cloth, to give my prick a provocative squeeze and several quick rubs.

In the Flesh

'Isn't this rather public?' I felt bound to say, my ever-eager dick nevertheless responding.

'Well, take me to my room and fuck me then,' she giggled wickedly, the hand between my thighs unzipping me, drawing out a stiff prick and doodling it. 'Miklos is at some conference or other with his political friends. I *know* you want to fuck me. *It* wants to. I've made it grow big and hard.'

The manner in which she had to lean toward me, the dipped shoulder and arm that worked away, made it patently obvious to interested onlookers at nearby tables what she was about. Trying to scrape my chair back from her, I was held in a grip that threatened to do me serious injury. I was aware of the faces turned in our direction. Then, to my mortification, I caught sight of the one face I had gone to Kampala to seek. Mrs Saxon had entered with another woman and was being shown to the table next to ours. As she took her seat I could only look at her appealingly; not my fault, my expression said. In reply she stifled an amused smile, shaking her deep chestnut curls, as if saying, 'Shame on you,' and seemingly finding my acute embarrassment fun to witness.

The woman with her took a distinctly different attitude, staring as if in disbelief as I managed to disengage myself from Margaret's grip. This, no doubt, was the doctor Roberta had said wanted to work among the refugees. She was tall, slender, thirtyish and superior-looking with large round spectacles, her pale skin marking her as a new arrival. Her dark hair was bobbed severely and her top teeth protruded slightly to part a wide mouth. She was attractive in a certain way. I noted that her breasts were small, firm and unsually pointed, the nipples embossing the jacket of her trouser suit like small round buttons.

'Was I imagining things, Diana?' I heard her say in

an icy voice. 'How *could* they in public? It was quite brazen.'

'Forget it, Cynthia,' Diana said lightly. 'They've stopped now.' The women concentrated on studying the menu, leaving me to conclude it was not the right time to approach Diana with my warning. At that moment Miklos appeared, pulling up a chair to join us.

'Glad to see you back,' he said to me affably. 'I take it your flight today went off smoothly. How did you get on with Captain Suliman? Pleasant fellow, isn't he?'

'A million laughs,' I said, adding 'What's this?' as he took a fat envelope from the inside pocket of his white tuxedo jacket, passing it to me.

'Payment for your services,' he said. 'Did you see anything of interest where you went?'

'Nothing,' I thought better to say. 'Quite a herd of giraffe had to lope off when we landed. I got my head down in the cabin and dozed off, didn't see a thing.'

'I've asked Tyler to fuck me,' Margaret piped up in a slurred tone, no doubt feeling she was being neglected. Her voice carried to the next table where Diana and Cynthia lowered their menus to glance at each other with raised eyebrows. 'You can both fuck me,' Margaret continued. 'Like we all did before. That's what I'd like.'

'You'll get all you want later,' Miklos promised quietly, taking her arm to guide her away. 'I've arranged a little party for some special friends upstairs. Too bad you're not invited, Tyler.'

Left alone, I glanced inside the envelope he had handed to me, and saw crisp new Ugandan banknotes of the 500-shilling denomination. It's an ill wind, I considered, about to get up and leave when I was joined by Fatima. She sat in Margaret's seat still dressed in the bangles and beads that barely concealed her charms. She had a lot to

In the Flesh

conceal: magnificent thrusting tits, strapping thighs and an arse one could have balanced a tray of drinks on safely. Her arrival was noted at the next table. Diana was unable to conceal her smile and her stuffy companion's eyes grew wider still.

'You worry about Mrs Warren,' Fatima said furtively, leaning to me and revealing much more of her superb breasts. 'Come.'

'Fatima, I've more than her on my mind,' I said wearily as she led me through to the rear of the restaurant. 'What can I do?' I went through beaded curtains, up a back stair and was guided into a small room stacked with spare tables and chairs. 'Why bring me here?'

'Look,' she ordered, slanting a framed picture of Murchison Falls and revealing the corner of a mirror that let me see into a large comfortably furnished lounge through the wall. 'All rooms have spying places. I don't care about this Englishwoman, only that my husband likes her too much.'

'A two-way mirror,' I said. 'Trust Miklos.' Inside the lounge I saw Margaret, drink in hand, surrounded by a group of admiring men in suits of the kind sold in cheap High Street tailors. Waiting to replenish their drinks was the restaurant's wine waiter, a tall and perfectly proportioned Nubian in red jacket and white trousers. 'I'll bet he does more than serve drinks tonight,' I said, whispering.

'He will fuck her,' Fatima agreed. 'You do not need to talk so quietly. We can hear them, they will not hear us. The men are from the Soviet Embassy. My husband keeps in with everyone, even the army people. The woman must do what he wants. She will learn.'

'I've tried telling her,' I said, hearing music from the lounge. Miklos took Margaret's glass and whispered to her. She began to sway around in what she no doubt considered a seductive manner while the four guests sat in front of her. Drawing off her dress, she cast it aside to applause, revealing herself in the tiniest, flimsiest bra, briefs, suspender-belt and sheer stockings. Shaking her shoulders, the overflowing bra's contents wobbled like jellies. There was no doubt she had been blessed with a superb figure, one inherited by her daughter, and greatly appreciated by her audience. 'She's loving it,' I had to say.

'*Bitch*!' I heard Fatima spit out. '*Amateur!*' It was spoken as if it were the biggest insult she could bestow. I thought Margaret was very good, her stripping routine having the non-professional charm of an enthusiastic exhibitionist. She unclipped her bra while facing away from her audience, turning back with her breasts covered by her hands as they begged her to show them. The next moment, she threw her arms wide and set her tits jiggling to wild cheers and stamping of feet.

'Beats the hell out of being in the Kremlin,' I reckoned, watching the Russkis drool over the performance. All eyes were on Margaret as she danced, cupping her tits and thrusting them out before slipping away as the Russians reached out for a feel. 'Miklos has been teaching her tricks.'

'Not his best ones,' Fatima said meaningfully. 'When he has done with her, given her drink and drugs, she will be just a street whore, even a five-shilling fuck in a Mombasa brothel for dhow boatmen. Her husband and family will disown her. You must get her out of here.'

Her concern, I felt, was not so much for Margaret's welfare as in wanting her gone before Fatima had to play second fiddle. Her jealousy came through loud and clear. While I agreed that Margaret was well on her way down a slippery slope and in need of rescue, watching her next bit of lewd theatre I had to admire her natural

In the Flesh

erotic talent. Turning from her audience, she lowered the remaining garment, her panties, to reveal the full cheeks of her arse. For the merest second she taunted them with the sight, waggling her rear saucily before hoisting her knickers again to cries of disapproval.

Down they came again a tantalising moment later and were kicked aside. Still facing away, her head turned to look archly over her right shoulder. Stockinged legs widely parted, she grabbed both buttock cheeks and squeezed them tightly, then gave one a resounding smack. It was a masterly come-on that had her admirers howling like wolves. To further increase their pleasure, Margaret reached forward, bending from the waist to touch fingertips to the carpet. She held this position, for a long moment, permitting a clear view into the deep cleave of her rounded cheeks and the sight of her cunt split and crinkled arsehole.

'She must go, the dirty bitch,' Fatima hissed, incensed by Margaret's brazen exhibition. 'I will not have that cow here.' It was a classic case of the pot calling the kettle black.

Margaret had now turned full frontal, shaking her breasts, jerking her pelvis in a highly suggestive fucking motion in the direction of the enraptured Soviet officials. This spectacle had my prick stirring in my pants, stretching to its full potential. It had its effect on Fatima too. Leaning into my side, looking over my shoulder at the scene through the two-way glass, a pliant breast rubbed against my arm and a hand went down to fumble for my zip. In turn, I placed my palm on the curve of her well-upholstered rump, tugging down the spangled G-string for access to a hot damp cleft.

'All the same, she's good,' I said admiringly. 'I wonder how often she's fantasised about doing this? Stripping before an audience must be the stuff of her dreams.'

'Miklos will turn it into her nightmare,' Fatima said darkly. 'The simple things she does now will not amuse him for long. Wait and see.' She had my prick in her hand, stroking it while I was in the divide of her arse cheeks up to the wrist, fingering her wet pussy. 'Look,' she pointed out savagely. 'He's got the collar for her.'

Miklos had gone behind her while she gyrated, holding a stiffened velvet dog's collar with a chain attached. It was slipped around her neck and fastened before she realised what was happening and she turned in some alarm at finding herself shackled. Whatever she said to Miklos did not reach us but he reacted by pinching one of her nipples until she flinched. Standing naked and vulnerable in the frilly suspender-belt and stockings, suddenly it was a different Margaret, apprehensive and scared as she awaited her master's next move.

'She'll obey him, just like I learned to do,' Fatima observed. 'So far that woman thinks they are true lovers. Now she is undecided. He'll make her perform for his important contacts. The big Nubian will be put to her for their amusement, then any of his guests that want her.'

Miklos tugged hard on the chain attached to the collar, pulling Margaret off her feet. He began walking around the lounge, forcing her to follow him on her hands and knees. Each time she protested, a sharp jerk on the leash made her trot forward like an obedient dog. In her reluctance and wretchedness she appealed for him to stop, to release her from the collar. His reply to this was to pick up a short riding-crop. Several sharp flicks delivered to both cheeks of her bottom had her shuffling after him with the chain slack. Thus he paraded up and down before his delighted guests, Margaret not daring to disobey.

Fatima had meanwhile moved behind me, her breasts pressed hard between my shoulder blades. She gyrated

In the Flesh

and rubbed her cunt mound against one of my arse cheeks, a hand around me stroking my prick. 'Now she is discovering the real Miklos,' she breathed in my ear with great satisfaction as she watched from over my shoulder. 'She will know him for what he really is – and she will not like it.'

Chapter Twelve

I've been guilty of inflicting indignities on female partners in the past but always with their tacit agreement. Sensing how far they'd allow me to go, I recognised that their pleas and protests were all part of the fun and added to the pleasure. But when Miklos led Margaret around like a prize exhibit at Crufts, it was without doubt sadistic and intentionally demeaning. As she paraded back and forth in front of the whooping men, she was urged on by wicked swipes of the riding crop to her exposed arse.

By now Margaret had given up asking to be released from the collar and chain, going where directed until she was brought to a halt before the central seated figure. He slid his bulk forward in the chair, legs stretched apart on either side of the kneeling victim. I heard him ask in coarse English, 'Does she know the mouth?' as he unzipped to bring out a thick limp prick.

'Sure she knows the mouth, don't you, Margaret?' Miklos sneered, using a knee to prod her closer into the fork of the official's thighs. 'Suck cock is what he means. Since you've been with me, who has learned to be an A-one cocksucker? Go ahead, show him how you've been trained, English lady. Chew on some Soviet dick.'

A jerk on the chain lifted her downcast face, lining up her mouth with the drooping sausage awaiting her attention.

'I-I-can't, I don't want to,' I heard her mumble. 'Please don't make me, not with *him*. I want to go home.'

'You are home,' Miklos said mercilessly. 'Here of your own free will and discretion. Don't disappoint us.' He gave a warning flick of the crop across her pink-striped bottom before inserting the head of it between the cheeks, probing to insert it in her cunt. Margaret took the flabby prick in her right hand, lowering her mouth slowly over the bulbous knob. I saw her brace herself, cover more of the stalk with her lips, cheeks hollowing and jaw working as she commenced suctioning.

Behind me Fatima was in a high state of agitation, about to bring herself off by grinding her tits in my back and jerking her crotch against my arse. 'The bastard,' I said grimly. 'Your husband is a bastard. Even I wouldn't sink that low.'

'Fuck his wife then,' Fatima said, moving around me and placing her back against the wall. I saw that she'd discarded her belly-dance costume, her tits swinging free as she pulled me to her, parting her thighs and directing my prick to her slit. I went in her to the hilt first thrust and continued humping her after her initial shuddering climax. With her arms fast around my neck, she raised her knees to circle my waist so that I was bearing her weight while she grunted and bobbed up and down on my stalk. My hands cupped her arse cheeks to keep her aloft as we jigged away. Through the mirror I saw Margaret sucking strenuously on a prick now stretched to its full length and girth. Her rear squirmed and jerked as Miklos worked the riding crop in her.

'Don't worry about her, the cow now likes it whether she wants to or not,' Fatima affirmed, turning her head to look. Watching Margaret sucking so avidly at one end while her arse worked feverishly at the other, made me agree. 'If she stays it will become like a drug,' Fatima warned. 'You must take her back to her husband.'

In the Flesh

As if I had nothing else to do at present, I thought, relieved that the buxom Fatima had lowered her feet to the ground to lean against the wall, recovering from her spasms. Inside the lounge the Russian was gripping the arms of his chair, shuddering as he filled Margaret's throat with his load. A tug on the leash then pulled her over onto her back, showing the hairy nest and parted cleft of her cunt. Miklos slipped off a shoe, placing the heel of his foot squarely on the exposed mound.

'Its made you want it, I know, that cock in your mouth. Made you want more than a little riding crop up your cunt,' he taunted her, caressing the vulnerable area with his stockinged foot. 'Say you want it, Mrs Warren, and you'll be in luck. Admit it and I'll give you a treat.'

I took the tortured grunt she gave as an admission, her legs stretching and widening under the incessant rubbing of Miklos's foot. Her back arched and her bottom bumped the floor. She drew her knees up to her breasts, brought to extreme arousal and urgent for relief. 'Y-You fuck me, Miklos! *Please* fuck me,' she begged. 'Or anybody . . .'

'Not just anybody,' Miklos promised and, as if on cue, I saw the magnificent ebony wine-waiter return to the room. Naked, he was a perfect physical specimen, muscled in proportion to his great size and physique. A thick bulbous-crowned circumcised prick hung curled over massive balls, an undoubted ten inches in repose.

Fatima had now recovered and wanted to continue. She was on her knees before me, taking the first tentative sucks to bring me erect for her again. She heard me expelling my breath in a low whistle of wonder at the giant Nubian's assets and raised her eyes quizzically.

'Your old man has brought in reinforcements,' I told her. 'The heavy artillery.'

A smart tug on the leash had Margaret scrambling forward on all fours, and she was brought to heel with her head level with the huge black dick of the Nubian. He stood hands on hips and trunk-like legs planted firmly apart. 'Jeez, she'll never get all *that* in her mouth,' I said. 'Not all that.'

As if to concur with my estimate, Margaret sat up on her knees, looking appealingly at Miklos, begging for his mercy. 'I-I–just couldn't,' she bleated. 'It's too big. It would choke me.'

'What's happening?' Fatima said as she licked and sucked my swelling cock. 'Keep telling me what they are doing. I want to know.'

'Miklos has called for a black Adonis to do his stuff,' I said. 'Margaret is kneeling up before him trembling at the sight and your husband is directing operations. From the red stripes on her bare arse, he's used the riding crop pretty effectively and she won't risk more of the same. He's ordered her to suck the guy. She's got the big dong in her hand but looks doubtful. I can't say I blame her. It's about a foot long before she's even started.'

'That will be Mkubwa,' Fatima agreed, massaging me to maintain the momentum prior to returning my prick to her mouth. 'She will know when he has been in her. I have taken him myself. What's happening now? Does she obey and suck him?'

'Not yet,' I observed, my stalk back between Fatima's warm wet tongue and palate, being gently suctioned to full capacity for her further use. 'She's holding his dick, looking undecided and worried, even with the threat of being punished for disobeying.'

'That's what Miklos likes,' Fatima said, deciding she had brought me up again to her satisfaction and getting to her feet to see what was going on. 'And what *she*

In the Flesh

likes too, I think,' she added shrewdly. 'Some women, huh! They have to pretend they do not want to be treated so, when all the time it is exciting for them.'

I considered she had a point. From not a few encounters with women who protested about the indignity and shame, I'd learned that these were the ingredients that made complete submission all the sweeter. 'You're not like that, are you, Fatima?' I said, grinning. Her back was to me and she ground her arse against my stiff dick. 'I take it you want this up you.'

'Why do you think I got you ready?' she asked, placing her palms on the wall below the mirror and bracing herself, buttocks tilted. Before me was a broad back streaked with sweat and my hands went around to grasp the overflowing mounds of her breasts. 'Don't rush this time,' she ordered. 'Fuck me and we will watch them. Do you like fucking Miklos's wife?'

'Who wouldn't?' I said. 'All the more so because of him.' My prick, eager to bury its nose into the hot petals of her cunt, poked its way into the cleave of her upturned rear. A push with my hips, a calculated positioning of her bottom, and I had penetrated her to the hilt, my balls nestling in the divide of her cheeks. With my chin on her shoulder, we fucked in a leisurely up-and-down motion, her arse lifting to meet my inward shunts, both of us in no hurry to complete our lewd coupling. 'You've got gorgeous big tits,' I praised her, never one to spare the compliments in mid-fuck. It was always appreciated. 'What splendid arse cheeks to thrust against. What a magnificent screw you are. Fatima, you're the fuck of the century.'

To me at that moment she was. Plump as a sucking pig, with a fat-lipped prominent quim to butt against and her inner walls gripping like a vice, I compared her to Margaret, kneeling before us, a vision of creamy white flesh.

'She has still not sucked,' Fatima said, raising her head to look. 'Mkubwa has not been made hard. She will be beaten.' Sure enough, Miklos gave her a reminder in the form of a crack across her bottom with the riding crop. Margaret yelped and drew the big black cock to her and nursed it between her breasts. Jogging her shoulders, moving it in her cleavage, she no doubt hoped to raise it as was expected of her.

This was a delaying tactic, I considered, while she was still fearful of taking the monster in her small neat mouth. Miklos allowed it to continue for no longer than a few moments, then issued another reminder with the crop, forcing her to gingerly place her lips on the bulbous knob. One more tap made her cover the plum-sized head and begin to suck. Mkubwa took her right hand and cupped it under his massive balls, and then the other to grasp the girth of his prick, for the first time taking an active part. As Margaret sucked, the slack prick thickened alarmingly. Easy forward motions of Mkubwa's powerful thighs gradually worked several inches into her mouth, her lips forming a perfect round shape and her cheeks distending.

'Watch,' Fatima said as our slow rear fuck continued. Mkubwa began to rock on his heels, his pelvis moving back and forward. In effect he was fucking her mouth. Only the first few inches of his superb rod could enter but Margaret gamely sought now to accept more, her jaw widening and her sucking rate quickening.

'It has got to her. No woman could resist the excitement it brings,' I was informed. 'Later she will think back with shame but with pride and with pleasure as well.'

I had no doubt she was right as I watched Margaret suck greedily on the big dick avidly, no doubt made wantonly lustful by the highly indecent thoughts and sensations coursing though her mind and body.

'She's all for it,' I said, thrusting harder into Fatima. As

In the Flesh

Margaret was really getting into her stride, Miklos pulled her away by the hair. Mkubwa's stimulated prick, glistening with saliva, leaped bolt upright against his flat belly. Margaret looked disappointed.

'Miklos has saved her for the chair,' Fatima grunted, our long slow screw gaining momentum with every thrust.

A tall chair had been brought to the centre of the room by Mkubwa, who sat on it as if well acquainted with the next proceeding. Brought to her feet, Miklos directed Margaret to straddle the seated man's lap with her crotch a mere inch or so above the great upstanding prick. To ensure neither cock nor cunt came into contact, Margaret had to remain poised awkwardly on the tip of her bare toes. She wavered but did not dare disobey as Miklos stood by with the crop.

'Now this is interesting,' the Greek announced wilfully, turning to his guests. 'No doubt she would like to perch on Mkubwa's prick, having tasted it and made herself aroused in the process. But she also fears this,' he laughed, holding up the riding crop. 'Which will it be? Of course, she could appeal to my better nature – promise me faithfully that in future she will be completely obedient and willing to do whatever I want. What do you say to that, Mrs Warren?'

'Please, Miklos, dear,' Margaret begged piteously. 'I really didn't mean to be with anyone but you.' To steady herself from falling, balanced precariously as she was on tiptoe, she grasped Mkubwa's rigid stander. 'Don't punish me. I'll do as you ask.'

'I'll remind you of that,' Miklos said, allowing her to totter on her toes for further long moments until she was unable to bear the ache in her calves any longer. She sat down across Mkubwa's knees, sighing with relief, her head resting on his chest. The massively erect prick projecting from his loins reared up hard against her stomach, the purple knob nestling between the divide of her breasts.

Margaret, content to recover and rest for the moment, got a flick of the crop to remind her it was still showtime.

'She'll sit on it,' Fatima declared coarsely, waggling her lush behind to urge me to fuck her harder. 'With all that hot prick against her belly and between her tits she'll want to try it. My husband won't need to beat her.'

I watched, intrigued, waiting for her to bow, or in her case lift, to the inevitable. Mkubwa made no attempt to help her, although with his strength he could easily have hoisted her over his dick. He tempted her by working his hips gently, rubbing the big cylinder of iron-hard flesh against her belly and between her breasts. With a low moan of submission, she climbed forward using his knees, lifting her parted thighs over his middle. Her nipples were thickly erect as her tits were drawn back from his chest, a sure sign of her high arousal. Grasping the big object of her desire, she directed the knob to her outer lips and lowered herself, understandingly apprehensive of its size.

Easing herself into position until cock and cunt met, the egg-sized crest nudging the entrance, Margaret gingerly eased down to allow its mass to force her lips apart. She expelled a gasp as if in pain, remaining still for a long moment as if to grow used to its girth. Then, unable to resist, she pushed down with her arse to contain a further thick-stemmed inch. That accomplished, she rested with her feet braced on the carpet, becoming accustomed to the feeling of being so widely stretched. Not a sound came from the spellbound audience. In time she began to jiggle her bottom, grunting as more prick worked its length into her, while Mkubwa sat motionless awaiting his cue. Again Margaret rested, unsure of taking more.

On the end of my prick, Fatima's arse was undulating wildly as she began another strenuous climax. Miklos, impatient for Margaret to show more spirit, gave her

In the Flesh

several whacks with the riding crop, setting her yelping and bobbing, and more stout inches forcing a passage up her in the agitation. Fatima, hearing yelps and squeals, was intrigued enough to raise her head to look even in her convulsions.

'There is no prick a cunt cannot take,' Fatima croaked as if delighted to prove her point. 'Even Mkubwa's.' Margaret was indeed getting into her stride, grinding down more confidently on the huge black stalk, almost all of its length now pistoning up her cunt. 'See, it is soon going in to his balls. She will want it all.'

Indeed, Margaret began to increase her pace, discovering in the process a method that gave her the most pleasure. She bobbed down and, fully impaled, gave a determined squirm of her arse to savour the intruder filling her cunt wall to wall and back to her stomach. It was more than Mkubwa could withstand without adding his contribution. His huge hands cupped Margaret's buttocks, lifting her as she rose and pulling her down over his prick as he thrust up on her downward lunges. Miklos stood by with a satisfied smirk. I recalled a previous boast of his that when a Greek fucked, he fucked ass. Looking down at his wife's bottom pressed to my belly, it decided me.

It was time to let go anyway and my balls were surging for release. I withdrew an already slippery dick from Fatima's cunt, drawing it out only to slide the fat knob the inch or so up to force the rear portal. Fatima groaned as I entered, my prick stretching her bottom-hole, and she squirmed on the embedded weapon. 'Yes, go on, go on,' she urged. The sight of Margaret and Mkubwa's frenzied fucking added to our lust and I was relentless in my thrusting. Fatima pushed back at me, buffeting my belly with her invaded arse. The wet sliding of my stem in the tight hole was more than enough to finish me off and I flooded her back passage as she jerked and came with grunts and agonised whines. Grasping the flesh of her hips, I humped her long after the last spurt, then rested on Fatima's broad back with both of us drawing in long breaths. Finally we both stood up.

As if enough was enough, she straightened the picture that hid the two-way mirror, shutting off Margaret jerking uncontrollably in her throes as she rode Mkubwa. 'You must leave now,' Fatima insisted, recovering her discarded bra and G-string. 'It is time for me to perform again. Get rid of that woman. Kidnap her if you have to. Make her see what is best for her.'

'I can but try,' I promised, as she led me down the back stairway. 'Her husband is in hospital and her daughter in Germany. Surely she'll come to her senses for their sake. How can I get her out of Miklos's clutches? Is she allowed to go outside?'

'Only to visit her husband and Miklos takes her,' Fatima said. 'But she always has lunch and dinner in the restaurant, usually alone. You must come in and take her, have your car waiting to drive her away.'

'That should be worth seeing,' I said grimly. 'Maybe you can help? Slip her out the back entrance one night for me. I'll be in touch, anyway. I wish I'd never met the woman.'

'You must get her away,' Fatima warned. 'There have been others, even women like her. I do not know what happened to them. They were sent to a Middle East country, I think, to be kept in some man's harem. What you saw tonight was nothing. The army here are not so well behaved as the Russians.'

'Charming,' I had to say. 'What else could happen to complicate my life?'

'You can come back and fuck me again,' Fatima suggested cheerfully. Her arms went around my neck, the pliant

In the Flesh

breasts pressed to my chest as she gave me a long kiss. 'I must shower now and prepare myself to perform my dance. If you stay and watch me, I will dance especially for you. Also the food is very good here. You must be hungry after what we did tonight. And do not worry yourself so much about the woman. She is not *your* wife.'

'True enough,' I admitted, 'but I'm not too enamoured of women being spirited off to some Arabian harem, particularly housewives from Harrowgate. How the hell does Miklos get away with it?'

'He is influential here and everyone can be bribed. It would be put down as a tourist killed by thieves and the body never found. It has happened often.' She turned to go back up the narrow stairs. 'I will talk to her if I can. But you must be the one to take her away from here.'

I walked through into the restaurant, changing my mind about going straight home as I saw people enjoying their dinner. The delicious smell reminded me I was hungry. Few tables were empty. I was deciding which was the least conspicuous, given my rather dishevelled state after screwing Fatima, when a waiter approached. He was one of the men who had recently thrown me out into the street. This time he was polite, indicating a table across the dining room.

'A memsa'ab wishes you to join her, sir,' he said, leading the way to Desdemona Crane sitting alone at a table. A chair was placed for me opposite her. As ever, she was immaculately made-up, every blonde hair in place, and wearing a silver sheath of a dress with a low neckline that accentuated the upper slopes of her big breasts and the tight ravine of her cleavage. I had to tell her she looked exceedingly attractive.

'And you always look like you've been running a marathon,' she said, handing over her menu. 'You really lower the tone of this place.'

'Dog rough, that's me,' I said. 'I can always move to another table. Should we be meeting like this, two undercover agents?'

'James Bond you're not,' she informed me without even the hint of a smile, 'but order something to make it look like we're on an evening out together. I just hope nobody I know sees me. You are simply an errand boy.'

'No secret codes or invisible ink?' I joked. 'Do I still get paid?'

She waited until we placed our order. 'What of your latest flight with Captain Suliman?' she asked. I told her what I had seen, armed men being assembled, the same as in the western province. There was no doubt the army under Amin were planning a takeover. 'I have an idea of the exact day it will be,' she said. 'It will succeed, of course. It's time to get Sam Musa and his family out. That's your next assignment. Fly them to Tanzania.'

'How do you intend to get them to the airport?' I queried, not at all pleased by the prospect. 'If I'm caught with him, I'm dead. And what's the Uganda Government doing about all this? Hasn't Musa contacted them for help? He *is* one of their ministers.'

'He didn't dare to,' Desdemona said matter-of-factly. 'He's scared some colleague seeking favour with the army would let them know he hasn't yet left the country. They all have an idea there's something in the wind but daren't upset certain parts of the military. Like ostriches they've stuck their heads in the sand, hoping it will go away and that they'll survive a coup. Or that we can get them out.'

'I don't like that *we*,' I said, noting with trepidation that Diana Saxon and her disdainful woman companion were leaving the restaurant, approaching our table en route. Desdemona had seen them as well. Obviously she was none too pleased to be found sitting with me but had

In the Flesh

to grin and bear it. 'How nice to see you again, Diana,' she said.

'I was hoping to run into you, Desdemona,' Diana replied. 'I hope you haven't forgotten my charity event tomorrow. I've put you down to run a stall.'

'I'll be there right after morning classes,' said Dessy. 'I've looked out some clothes and things to sell.'

'That's good of you,' Diana smiled, turning to me. 'And how are you, Mr Wight? I'd like the two of you to meet Dr Pellow. She's staying with me for a day or two before flying up to work with my husband among the refugees. No doubt you'll be taking her.'

'I'll look forward to that,' I said, as Cynthia Pellow stared hard at me. Desdemona was the third woman she had seen me with that evening and no doubt she was wondering what kind of a man I was. Once more there was no time to warn Diana that Captain Suliman had a letch for her and I resolved to do it the next morning. The women went on their way, my eyes following Diana Saxon's back or, more accurately, the way it curved into such fine rounded buttocks and the way they oscillated as she walked.

Desdemona too was watching, impressed. 'What are you thinking?' she asked. 'Just what is in your mind?'

'The same thing as in yours,' I said. 'How thrilling it would be to get that lovely woman into bed. Unfortunately, she seems content with her husband even though he's away so often.'

'Such a pity,' Desdemona agreed. 'She really is a remarkably beautiful creature. That gorgeous chestnut colouring, those adorable breasts—'

'Spoken like a true dyke, Dessy,' I said, grinning. 'Couldn't have put it better myself. In a way you and I are two of a kind.'

'Don't flatter yourself,' she cautioned me. 'After we've eaten, you can drive me home. I came by taxi. It's safer for a woman than travelling alone in a car. You can stay the night if you wish.'

'Don't tell me,' I laughed, 'you've had a change of inclination.'

'It would never be with you if I had,' she stated. 'It's for Petal Musa. You and that disgusting thing between your legs have ruined that young lady. She's of no more interest to me. She can't go to school because all her family are being hunted, so she has to remain in hiding at my apartment. With time on her hands, the silly girl mopes around thinking about what you did to her. I can't stand her moods. You'd better come back with me and give her what she wants.'

As I nodded agreement I wondered if she had an ulterior motive.

'In such a good cause I reckon I could throw a fuck or two in her direction,' I offered gallantly. 'It's a one-bedroom flat though. I hope you won't be too inconvenienced being put out of your bed?'

'I shall be there,' Desdemona said ominously, 'making certain you do not deprave that girl more than necessary. I shall be watching you, Wight. There are limits.'

And I bet you'll be enjoying the view, I could have said. It's a funny old world, isn't it? Our food and wine arrived at the table and I raised a glass to her. 'To whatever turns you on,' I said. 'And to remaining within limits. What are they, by the way?'

'I'm a headmistress,' she reminded me. 'See that you behave reasonably. I've had to cane naughty boys in my time.'

'Promises, promises,' I laughed, covering up a sudden

In the Flesh

feeling that her remark was entirely serious. It was not my thing, but if it was hers, what the hell? Live and let live is my philosophy.

Chapter Thirteen

Next morning, I arrived home determined to contact Diana Saxon. As ever, the faithful Jovial ignored the fact that I'd been away overnight, although I'd found my bed unmade to show she had slept there awaiting my return. I'd breakfasted too, so I changed into my best shirt and trousers, adding a tie to impress, and drove straight off to the Saxons' bungalow. It was hardly eight but the sun was fierce as I arrived in their road. Like most it was pavementless and fringed with tall hedges and trees. A pair of small boys with buckets and cloths signalled they would wash and polish my car.

This was usually my garden boy's chore, but I did not count the few shillings it would cost me as the payment from Miklos meant I was flush. I parked in the road instead of the Saxons' driveway, walking in to find Diana at breakfast on the shaded verandah with Cynthia Pellow, her companion at *Chez Miklos* the previous evening and with whom I was obviously in low esteem. The two women were sensibly attired for the heat in bikinis, sitting in cushioned wicker chairs at the breakfast table. Seen from their waists up, I contrasted Diana's shapely big breasts with the smaller pear-shaped tits of Cynthia. My interested gaze was noted, her eyes narrowing in annoyance behind her huge round spectacles. She raised a hand to cover her chest as if modesty compelled her to hide it from a lecherous man's view. As in the restaurant the night before, I found her short boyish hairstyle not unattractive and the owl-like face behind the round specs handsome.

Diana rose to greet me, forcing me to stifle a gasp of admiration at the striking beauty of her figure. Her miniscule bikini was a light primrose yellow, the strapless top inadequately accommodating a pair of perfect tits of admirable size and texture. Below the firm uptilted mounds, a smooth stomach with a neat indented navel descended to the sweep of an enticing bulge at the join of her supple thighs. The tiny briefs were held in place by strings tied in bows at the curve of her hips above her long trim legs. No one should look that good and my unruly dick stirred in full agreement.

Thankfully she indicated an empty chair for me and I sat rather gingerly. Petal had been all over me the night before and Desdemona had brought out her cane to oversee the proceedings. It seemed to me she applied it at the least excuse, Petal squealing as her arse was warmed and me accepting it as an experience I was in no hurry to repeat. I eased myself into the cushioned chair and it was noticed.

'Are you in pain?' Diana asked kindly. 'Have you hurt yourself?'

'Just a back twinge,' I lied. 'It's nothing.'

'Overdoing it, no doubt,' Cynthia Pellow said snidely.

'Anyway, what luck you arriving like this,' Diana said in her lilting Scottish accent, genuinely pleased. 'Do join us for breakfast. We were just talking about you, weren't we, Cynthia?'

'Nothing good, I presume?' I ventured, chancing a feeble joke as Cynthia eyed me with obvious distaste. 'You know, I was truly not responsible for—'

'Your appalling conduct with that woman in a crowded restaurant?' Cynthia finished for me coldly. 'It was highly offensive. There must be more private places? I imagine

In the Flesh

you found one with that Turkish dancer you went off with later.'

You tight-arsed bitch, I had to stop myself retorting. Her feeling toward me seemed to be composed of pure hate. The housegirl arrived to set a place for me and, although I had eaten breakfast at Desdemona's, I was ready for more. 'Good morning, Bwana Tyler,' she said cheerfully. 'I shall make the fried bread you like with your egg and bacon. You see, I do not forget.'

She was, of course, Jolly Ndege, my own housegirl's half-sister and a handsome Muganda I had fucked on occasion, usually when visiting Jovial and a three-in-a-bed session would ensue. I thanked her politely, hoping the ground would open and swallow me while Diana regarded me with her usual amused smile. Cynthia Pellow shook her head in disbelief. 'The girl is obviously aware of your breakfast requirements,' she said maliciously. 'But then, who isn't, I imagine.'

'I'll put you down on my waiting list,' I thought it time to answer back, pleased my riposte made Diana laugh.

'It's time you two were introduced properly and became friends,' she said, still greatly amused. 'Mr Tyler Wight, bush pilot, meet Ms Cynthia Pellow, professor of tropical medicine and an aid volunteer who's going to work with my Harry. Volunteered by Roberta Leigh-Pagett. You remember her, the Member of Parliament who came to visit.'

'He should do, from what lurid details Roberta told me about this man,' Cynthia said, distaste shining in her eyes. She rose, placing her napkin and spectacles on the table. 'If you'll excuse me, Diana, I'd like to cool off with a swim.'

I stood in a show of politeness as she descended the steps of the verandah and walked towards the sparkling pool surrounded by lawn and flower beds in the garden. Following her with my eyes, I saw a slender woman with a neat bottom and good legs. Choice meat, I had to conclude. Pity that her dislike for me bordered on the murderous.

'Penny for your thoughts,' Diana asked as if reading my mind. 'Or are they ones Cynthia would not approve of?'

'Probably not,' I contented myself saying. It was not on to admit I thought Cynthia well worthy of a fuck. 'I'm not exactly her flavour of the month, am I? What did I do?'

Again the response was a delighted laugh. 'I can't possibly think why,' Diana said with mock sincerity, 'apart from what she witnessed last evening in *Chez Miklos*. Or what her friend Roberta said to her about a recent visit to Uganda and the obliging pilot. She told all evidently, thinking it would do Cynthia a good turn. She may be brilliant in her field but I'm led to believe her experiences with men are almost non-existent.'

'So much for my reputation,' I said, giving a wry grin. The friendly housegirl returned bearing my bacon and eggs with a crisp slice of fried bread and a fresh pot of tea. When she left she gave me a beaming smile.

'At least somebody loves you,' Diana observed. 'Do eat.' She poured out tea for me. 'I've a big favour to ask of you.'

'First let me say why I've come here,' I began, getting serious.

'No,' she said, pretending to be firm with me. 'I spoke before you.' She sat back regarding me over the rim of her cup. 'I've arranged a charity event for Harry's refugees. It's at the Lake Victoria Hotel today, starting at noon. If you're not flying today, I need a volunteer.'

What a fuck this woman would make, I was thinking again, and how I'd be the first to volunteer for that. 'I'm your man,' I offered.

'There'll be stalls set around the outdoor pool,' she continued, 'and I need people to run them. Bring and buy,

In the Flesh

cakes, books, clothes, anything given that can be sold. With your charm you could sell anything. The day will end with a gala dance. I shall expect you to circulate and make sure that any lonely female gets at least one dance with you. That includes me.'

In the distance we could hear Cynthia splashing about in the pool. 'You're certainly on for a dance,' I said, 'but I don't think Cynthia would welcome one. She thinks I intend to rape her.'

'I don't think that would be her thing,' Diana laughed. 'In fact I happen to know. You're the wrong sex.'

I paused, about to raise the last forkful of bacon to my mouth, surprised at her assessment of Cynthia. 'She told you? Said she's into women? That was very honest of her.'

'It wasn't quite like that,' Diana smiled, studying my reaction. 'During the night she came into my room, complaining she couldn't get to sleep with all the strange noises. She asked if she could come in to my bed for company.'

'Lucky old Cynthia,' I felt bound to say. 'I must remember to use that line myself.'

'You would say that,' Diana teased. 'Anyway, I sleep nude in this climate. I think it proved too much for her.'

My mind pictured the scene: two hot female bodies close, the first sweet kisses to mouths, nipples; hands wandering, fondling, feeling. My prick stirred afresh. 'Of course you rebuffed her?' I asked, my interest aroused, dying to know.

'I'm not saying,' Diana smiled to perplex me. 'Would you have?'

'That's different,' I claimed. 'I'm a man.'

'Women make love,' she reminded me. 'Don't tell me I've shocked the unshockable Tyler Wight?'

'You're beautiful and you're married. I didn't think

you were the type,' I said. 'I would never have thought it.'

'Some people make the most of both worlds,' Diana laughed lightly. 'I'm not giving you the satisfaction of thinking I do, or that anything happened last night. That would be telling. You've got me on a pedestal for some reason but I wasn't born yesterday. I have a history. Some might say it's not all it should be.'

'Well, it's your future I'm here about,' I said seriously. 'Remember the young Ugandan Army officer at the Lake Airways office? He of the mean look and tribal scars on his face?'

Diana nodded. 'What about him?'

'I flew him north. On the way he told me he intended to have you. Sexually. The bastard was serious. He's powerful and dangerous.'

'I'm not likely to come in contact with him again, am I?' she remarked, unconcerned. 'He was probably expressing a desire. Men do, you know. He wouldn't mean it.'

'His kind mean it,' I warned, 'and he's more than likely to seek you out. I'll fly you to Kenya. You must go.'

'Not for him or anyone while my husband works here,' she said boldly. 'You're very sweet to be concerned and I will be on my guard. Now, I'm going to join Cynthia in the pool. You will come to run a stall at noon?'

'I said I would,' I answered, sorry I had not convinced her of the real danger she was in with Suliman. With a smile that implied I was worrying over nothing, she walked to the pool. I admired the sway of her almost bare arse cheeks. As she dived in to join Cynthia, Jolly the housegirl came up to clear the breakfast table. A broad grin on her shining black face showed me she was dying to let me in on some astounding secret.

The girl motioned me to follow, leading the way from the

In the Flesh

verandah into the bungalow. I walked behind her, making sure the swimmers did not see me. With Jolly giggling and turning to make sure I was there, she took me up a passageway and ushered me into what was Harry and Diana's bedroom. The double bed was still unmade, the pillows very crumpled and the top sheet, all that was necessary in the tropic night, seemingly kicked to the foot of the bed.

'They *sleep* together last night,' Jolly announced, her teeth flashing in a tremendous grin. She held up two fingers. 'Two *women*,' she added in case I didn't get the picture.

'The doctor *mem* was afraid by herself, she's new to Africa,' I explained. 'She came to Mrs Saxon for company.'

Jolly's grin became a wicked giggle. 'They did not have one of these,' she insisted, clasping my prick through my slacks and giving it an enthusiastic wank. 'No man for them. What do they do?'

I was certain Jolly knew, especially if she shared her sister's inclinations. 'I wouldn't know,' I had to say, not intending to share gossip with a servant, a sure means of it being spread around. I was uneasy at trespassing in Diana's room, looking through the window as the two women got out of the pool. With her fair skin glistening, Diana looked even more fanciable as she stood to rub her deep chestnut hair with a towel. The sodden bikini parts seemed moulded to the charms they barely covered: bra cups overflowing with luscious tit, the triangular patch of nylon below curved by the sublime projection of her pubic mound. Beside her, Cynthia was made to look boyish, attractively slender and athletic.

'It's time to leave,' I said, my cock now freed and responding to Jolly's manipulations. But Diana and Cynthia were placing their towels on the grass and my fear that they would return to the house abated somewhat. They lay down side by side as if intending to relax in the sun for a while. 'Get on the bed then, Jolly,' I agreed, my prick now at full stiffness and the girl telling me she wanted it inside her. 'There's time for a quickie, that's all.'

I was glad I'd parked out in the road instead of on the driveway before the verandah, where they could have seen me drive away. The giggling Jolly cast off her work overall and, stark-naked, got on the bed on hands and knees, waggling her big brown arse at me.

I got up behind her, parting the plump cheeks with my prick, directing it at the cleft of her underhanging cunt. A glance out of the window to make sure the two women were sunbathing brought me to a dead stop. Diana was lying stretched out on her back but Cynthia was sitting up looking down upon her as I know I would have, unable to resist her desires. A hand ventured to smooth Diana's hair, caress her cheek, shoulder and arm in the gentlest manner, barely touching the skin. I saw no reaction from Diana, seemingly she was content to allow Cynthia's light fondling to continue. I was brought back to the task in hand by a buffet from Jolly's solid arse, reminding me she was waiting.

'Why do you not put it in?' she complained impatiently, rolling on her back to make sure I was still erect. Beside the pool, Cynthia had paused in her stroking and caressing, lowering her face over Diana's to brush her lips to her eyes, her cheeks and, finally, with the lightest touch, to her mouth. Diana still lay unmoving, arms by her side, almost as if asleep. Cynthia, receiving no resistance and taking that as consent, or perhaps too aroused to stop, concentrated on pressing light kisses to Diana's lips. Her right hand poised, she stroked the slopes of Diana's breasts

In the Flesh

above the bikini top, lowering her lips at times to kiss the soft flesh. My eyes level with the window ledge, I saw the gentle female lovemaking proceed, glad that Jolly was on her back and unable to see. The randy girl parted the fat lips of her cunt with her fingers to encourage me to get on with it.

Outside I noted Diana's first response, returning a kiss from Cynthia that lingered, the two women's mouths crushing together with lips parted, pausing only for breath before kissing long and passionately again and again. Aroused now, I saw Diana's arms circle around the woman above her to pull her close, to continue the lewd kissing with open mouth and intruding tongue. It was Cynthia who broke it off, sitting up and looking fondly down at Diana. She reverted to the gentle gliding of her hands over her partner's breasts, pecking kisses to the heaving upper slopes, running her tongue tip up the tight line of the cleavage. It made erotic viewing, Cynthia proving adept at the art of gentle female lovemaking, a gradual process which was certainly proving effective with Harry Saxon's wife.

Careful to keep low at the window, intrigued to watch further, I got a sharp reminder from Jolly. Prone before me, bountifully naked with her whacking great teats lolling apart, thighs spread and cunt held open, she gave an impatient tug on my prick. It was if anything harder than ever. I squatted back with my arse on my ankles, hauling Jolly's hefty thighs up over mine and her comfortable bottom cheeks against my belly. Laid back on her shoulders, crotch to crotch with me, she shuffled forward, pulling down my upright dick and directing it to her crevice. Then, with a heave of her hips, I was fully sheathed, my balls nestling against the hot pillows of her arse. I cupped each cheek in my palms as she worked her bottom sensuously against the hard rod of flesh inside her, content to let her hump away as I watched the performance beyond the window.

Mouth to mouth again in sweet kisses, as Diana's shoulders lifted, Cynthia slipped a hand behind her back to unfasten the bikini top. The bra was tossed aside and Diana's glorious breasts were bared, firm and uptilted, the soft round flesh and protruding nipples an immediate target for Cynthia's mouth.

For a long moment Diana's back arched, the better to present her superb tits for Cynthia to kiss and suck. Then she sat up and protested. 'Cynthia – please – no, not now.' I heard plainly. 'The housegirl is about. The gardener's at his vegetable plot but will be returning. This isn't the time.'

'But I *must*, I want to,' Cynthia pleaded. 'Don't you like it?'

'You know very well that I do,' Diana said kindly. 'You're a wicked woman, making me like it too much. Wasn't what you did to me last night enough for you?'

'Don't make fun of me,' Cynthia begged. 'You're so beautiful I can't resist you. Last night only makes me want you more. Please, please, let me.'

Yes do, I entirely agreed, seeing the determined Cynthia lower a resisting Diana to her towel and continue her assault on mouth and nipples. As her arousal grew she sucked avidly at each teat while Diana's soft moans increased as her resistance faltered. The side strings of her bikini briefs were the next to be untied and the garment removed, leaving Diana naked and more vulnerable. It was a lesson in seduction, albeit with a willing victim. As if well aware of the next move, Diana drew up her knees and parted them widely. *I could do that just as well*, I said, speaking my thought aloud as Cynthia's head dipped low between

In the Flesh

Diana's spread thighs. *She's loving it*, I murmured, as Diana moaned and reached out to hold her partner's head, her pelvis thrusting upward.

Cradled on my thighs, Jolly was getting incensed that I was not doing my share of the work. 'What are you saying?' she demanded. 'What are you looking at?' She pulled away from me, rolling over onto elbows and knees to present her big black arse to me once more. 'I like to watch too,' she complained, eyes level with the window ledge and still on heat, worming her bottom back to me. Waste not, want not, I say and I parted the firm cheeks and went up her to the hilt while continuing my covert viewing. I began a luxurious slow stroking motion, up to the balls and back out to the crest while Jolly groaned her appreciation, eyes fixed on the outside scene.

'She likes it *too* much, I think,' she whispered in some awe, making me wonder to which woman she referred. Cynthia was obviously engrossed in lapping and licking cunt, or Diana, lying back and jerking her hips under the treatment, her hands now employed in squeezing her own breasts tightly. 'Fuck harder,' Jolly instructed me. 'Fuck faster. Make me come again. It makes me so hot to see them. Fuck, fuck, Bwana Tyler.'

I didn't dare go at it harder and faster, the bumping of the bed against the wall was already too loud. I suspected it would have been noticed but for the female lovers being so engrossed. It was easy to imagine Cynthia's long tongue probing and flicking, deep up Diana's juicy furrow, tormenting her clitty to produce the writhing and squirming we saw. A stifled cry from Diana and a shuddering of her lower torso was a clear outward sign of her initial climax. Cynthia's head continued to bob, Diana thrusting for a repeat even in the throes of a come.

'Dirty bitches,' I said, my words purely an expression of my admiration for their enthusiastic sexplay. 'Cynthia with her dykey looks, okay, but I'd never have thought it of Harry's wife. But why not? Not a word of this to anyone, Jolly,' I warned. 'You haven't seen a thing. No gossip that must reach other ears, understand?'

'I never talk,' Jolly insisted, waggling her arse to my shafting, and I believed her, knowing her sister. 'She has had others,' the girl went on to surprise me. 'Such a nice lady, others have fucked her. Men and other women. Husband away too much.'

Another glance outside made me think I'd better believe it, despite my high opinion of Diana. Flat on the towel, knees now lowered and legs straight, Cynthia was laid on top of her, breast to breast, mouth to mouth, cunt to cunt thrusting together. 'So who were the others?' I demanded, emphasising each word with a thrust up her quim to get her to oblige. I was eager to know. 'You can trust me, Jolly.'

'Many,' Jolly grunted, her second coming imminent and mine on the boil. 'Pilot, like you, only Swedish airline. German doctor and his wife. Also their son, young boy. They beat her when they find them together in bed, make it hard for her to sit.'*

'I'll bet,' I said, tickled to have learned something of Diana Saxon's history. I did not think any the less of her, more in fact. It showed she was human. To be so passionate and to bottle it up without the occasional lapse would be sinful, I considered. Now she had her legs curled around Cynthia's back, her hands pulling on her partner's pretty buttocks to haul her closer as their cunts ground furiously together.

Jolly was flat on her face, gasping, flooded with my come. I patted her bottom in thanks, deciding it was time to leave, and drew up my pants. In the garden, Diana and Cynthia now lay apart, undoubtedly sated. Looking back on my morning, I decided life can be a bitch but it does have its unforgettable moments.

---

* See *Sex and Mrs Saxon*, also published by Headline Delta.

Chapter Fourteen

At noon precisely I manned my stall at Diana's charity event which was taking place around the pool of the Lake Victoria Hotel. Diana Saxon had shown me to my site, looking wonderfully fresh and wholesome despite her hectic bout of female sex only an hour or so previously. My stall was piled with books, lampshades, clothes, odd crockery, picture frames and shoes donated by the white expatriate community. The customers were local Ugandans seeking bargains.

An enthusiastic crowd gathered and I took any money thrust in my hand as the stall's goods were depleted – only to have Diana and her helpers load the counter again. It was hard work. By three in the afternoon the sale seemed to have gone on longer than World War Two. I was inundated by eager buyers and the box at my feet was full of coins and crumpled banknotes. When Desdemona Crane arrived to assist me, I had a second-hand bra thrust in my face by a young woman demanding to know how much. We continued selling until almost four, sweat-soaked in the heat, before Diana appeared with two assistants to take over from us.

'I have orders for you,' Desdemona said as soon as we were free. It wasn't what I wanted her to say. 'Where can we talk privately?'

The very place came to mind. On the short walk to

the hotel's entrance I slipped an arm around her waist, hugging her pliant body close. 'Just keeping up our cover,' I informed her as she glared at me. For good measure I pressed a kiss to her cheek. 'Outside show.'

'People are noticing,' she hissed. 'What will they think?'

'That we've got the hots for each other,' I said, patting her bum. 'No one will suspect we're a couple of secret agents, one albeit reluctant.' Despite her trying to fend me off, I held her tight, steering her under the elephant tusk arch leading to the hotel reception. There we met Diana and Cynthia bearing trays of tea and biscuits. I returned Cynthia's icy stare with a broad wink, giving the increasingly annoyed Desdemona an extra hug.

'We're taking refreshments out to the volunteers,' Diana said, the impish smile shaping her lips. 'I presume you two intend to have your break in the hotel?'

'In the afternoon tearoom,' Desdemona said quickly. 'I have such a headache from the sun.' She almost dragged me past them. 'Did you see the look we got from that frosty bitch with Mrs Saxon? She truly suspects we're up to no good. You should be so lucky.'

'One lives in hope,' I grinned, arriving at the reception desk and slipping the African clerk a hundred-shilling note. 'The key for Mr Miklos Dimitri's private room,' I said boldly, adding a sly wink and getting the key and a wide grin in response. Taking Desdemona's elbow, I guided her up the carpeted stairway and along the passageway to the room. Throwing open the door, I stood back and invited her to enter. She did so as I locked up behind her, enjoying her amazed stare at the mirrors on the wall and ceiling and the huge silk-sheeted bed.

'My God, it's a sex maniac's boudoir,' Desdemona said coldly. 'We're here on business, nothing else.' She walked to the bathroom door, looking in on the ornate fittings, the

In the Flesh

sunken bath and glass-enclosed shower cubicle. 'The worst possible taste,' she said.

'Tempting, all the same,' I suggested. 'Cool and refreshing. You look anything but the immaculate Dessy I know and love. At this moment you're all hot and sweaty. Take a shower.' I held out my arms. 'After all, I've just about seen all there is to see of you. I'll behave, I promise.'

She reached into the shower cubicle to turn on the spray and test the water with her fingers, dabbing her cheeks to cool them. 'Running water,' she said. 'Drowns out talk if, by any chance, this harlot's parlour is bugged. You'll be flying out the Musa family tonight.' As if to allay the shock to my system she began to undress, reaching behind to unzip the back of her dress. 'Everything has been arranged. Your orders are to go to *Chez Miklos* at eleven and order a drink at the bar. You'll be contacted there.'

She lowered her dress, stepping out of it after kicking off her open-toed sandals. 'You're staring,' she said calmly, unhooking her bra and handing it to me, freeing two creamy big tits. It was not so much a stare as a look of wide-eyed horror. Down came her knickers which she handed to me along with her dress. 'Hold these for me,' she said, turning to enter the shower cubicle and allowing me a sight of her plump backside. 'You're right. A shower will be just the thing.'

The glass door was shut in my face, Desdemona becoming a shadowy figure beyond the frosted glass. 'You're not saying very much,' she called out above the running water. 'Are you scared speechless?'

'Too bloody right,' I shouted back. 'If this is going to be my lot tonight, I want to go out with a bang. Is that asking too much of you, Dessy? I'm coming in!'

It was the work of a moment to throw off my clothes and I flung open the screen door. Desdemona was soaping herself under the spray, the suds running down the slope of her breasts and dripping from her nipples.

'You said you'd behave,' she reminded me, handing me the soap. 'While you're in here, you can wash my back.' She turned from me, the sight making me forget what lay ahead of me that night. Leaning against the wall, her forehead resting against the tiles, her back swept down to her flared hips and the succulent cheeks of her naked bottom. 'Don't get any ideas,' she added, as if reading my thoughts.

I soaped her shoulders and back until the suds cascaded down her spine to find a natural channel in between the cleft of her arse. It was too much to contemplate. I nudged my cock into the slippery divide, the knob nestling snugly, surrounded by the fleshy moons.

'You're disgusting,' she told me, referring to my rapidly stiffening stalk. 'It's got big already.'

'So are these,' I said, my hands going around her and cupping the sudsy tits, my thumbs flicking the hard nipples. 'You want it,' I said, giving the slightest jiggle of my hips to remind her there was more on offer. 'Say it. Say, go ahead and fuck me.'

'There is nothing so endearing as a well-mannered gentleman,' she replied calmly. She did not, however, pull her bottom away. 'If you intend to vent your lust on me, don't expect my cooperation. You're no gentleman.'

'What's that got to do with getting fucked?' I said, determined to gain compliance. 'Have you never enjoyed a prick up your cunt, Dessy?'

'I've certainly never *enjoyed* one,' she asserted. 'I was married once and found it distinctly off-putting. It's nothing like the pleasure another woman can give. If this is a battle of wills, I can outlast you. Remember you'll be flying tonight, Wight. Does that cool your ardour?'

'Actually, it makes me more determined,' I said, my knob

In the Flesh

rubbing against the lips of her quim. Aided by the slippery suds, I pushed the plum head between the lips. I held it still to gauge her reaction. 'I'm awaiting instructions,' I said hopefully.

'Then you'll wait all night,' she answered, increasing my growing impatience, my prick urging me to penetrate properly. I thrust into her, going right up, getting no more than a grunt in response and not a move out of her. If anything, her body stiffened, making me suspect she was not entirely indifferent to being entered but would not admit it.

'You icy bitch!' I swore, angry at myself for losing my cool and her will-power proving stronger. But with my cock embedded up an admirably snug cunt and plump buttock cheeks nestling against my lower belly, I was in no mood to care about a battle of wills. 'Just you wait,' I told her forcefully. 'I'll make you admit there's no substitute for a stiff prick.'

I withdrew from her, my cock making a lewd sucking sound as it disengaged, and stepped back a pace. With room to swing my arm, my open hand cracked down with a stinging force on her bare cheeks. Two, three, four more followed and Desdemona yelped a series of cries that sounded to me more of pleasure than of pain.

'Yes, yes,' she exclaimed, her usually calm voice now hoarse with emotion. 'Oh, how I've needed a man to do that.'

I smacked her backside until my arm ached, guessing I had stumbled upon a long unfulfilled desire.

'My stupid husband wouldn't do it even when I suggested it,' she moaned, thrusting out her bottom and bracing herself for the slaps. '*Ohh*, now fuck me if you must,' she muttered.

'With pleasure,' I told her, gripping the cheeks of her

well-padded arse and thrusting forward into the sudsy cleft. I penetrated deeply without guidance. Her groan was of pure satisfaction and she climaxed immediately, shuddering and grinding her rear against me. 'Keep going,' I heard her say, tilting her bottom to get even more up her, working her hips so wildly that my prick slipped out. It rose to meet the wrinkled pucker of her arsehole in no state to care where it went. Soaped up, my merest push had the knob force an entrance and I gripped her hips while I waited for her reaction before going in full length.

'Oh, God, *that* too?' she whined. 'Haven't you got the wrong place?'

'Don't tell me what's the wrong place,' I said, enjoying the masterful role with her for once. I eased another inch inside which produced a low groan from her and an instinctive tightening of the sphincter muscle. Aided by the lubricating suds, a steady pressure made the elastic ring of her anus give way to allow my girth to enter several inches. She remained still, as if getting used to the feel of a cylindrical mass of hard flesh up her back passage. She didn't protest or complain.

'Is this something else you wanted your husband to do?' I couldn't resist asking, giving little jiggles of my hips. 'Like wanting to be spanked? Did you suggest he did this to you?'

I noted the first slight squirms in response to taking a prick up the rear. 'I *couldn't* ask him, not that,' she said hoarsely. 'The least thing shocked him. We rarely made love. He *made* me turn to my own sex.'

'Poor Dessy,' I sympathised. 'A horny young wife wasted on a wimp.' It was plain she was getting the feel of my tool in her bum, her bottom hole flexing, the motions of her arse growing more agitated as she pushed back against

In the Flesh

me. 'Would you have wanted him to do this? Was it in your mind, you naughty girl?'

To encourage her and increase my own pleasure, I pushed the last inch or two of my cock into an unresisting back passage. 'It's in,' I informed her. 'You've taken it well.' I parted her cheeks and began a slow rhythmic fucking motion, my prick gripped in a tube of velvety flesh. 'I asked if trying it up your bottom was something you fancied,' I reminded her, our movements – mine forward, hers back – gaining pace. 'Tell me.'

'Y-yes, I did,' she admitted, her breath short, her excitement mounting. 'It was the thought that it was so wicked. Never mind that now, damn you. Fuck me, fuck my bottom. Is it all in?'

'Like I said, every inch,' I assured her. 'It feels good now, doesn't it?' I had her cheeks wide apart for deeper access, on tip-toe to thrust against a now wildly gyrating arse, her grip on the shower pipes threatening to tear them from the tiled wall. Her loud scream that she was THERE! and the frenzied undulations of her flanks had me bucking from the knees and flooding her innards. She leaned against the wall with me resting on her back, my shrinking prick still gripped in the tightness of her anal ring.

'Take that out of me,' she ordered, turning once again into the old Desdemona. 'And turn on the shower again. I don't know what got into me.'

'It's known as a prick, Dessy,' I said. 'You were a great fuck.'

'Well, think yourself lucky,' she told me bitingly, 'because it won't happen again.' The shower streamed down on us and she kept apart from me. 'I still can't believe I allowed you to do that – to bugger me. To actually have it up my bottom. Only a beast would do that.'

She left the shower but stood obediently for me to towel

her dry, shaking her head at what had passed. I considered the lady did protest too much. *Fucked to a frazzle*, I thought proudly as, without dressing, she walked through to the bedroom and flopped on the bed. I joined her. I'd been short on sleep for days and nodded off before I knew it. I was wakened by Desdemona shaking me. She was up and fully dressed.

'It's gone seven,' she informed me, 'we've slept over two hours. I've got to be in Kampala to finalise the Musa exodus and you must be at the *Chez Miklos* restaurant at precisely eleven.' She paused at the door on her way out. 'Good luck tonight, Wight,' she added. 'Remember, *Chez Miklos* at eleven.'

'How could I forget?' I said, sitting up. 'It's the last place I would have thought of. Miklos is a big buddy of Amin and his cronies. It's the lion's den.'

'Don't worry, your contact is trustworthy,' she said as she left.

I returned to the foyer and handed over the room key. Outside the hotel I found that the stalls had gone and the swimming pool was covered by a dance floor with couples swaying to the resident Congolese band. The tall palms around the area were festooned with coloured lanterns that lit up a velvet night. With a flight of uncertain hazard facing me, for once I was in no mood to join in the gaiety. I sat at an empty table and ordered a double Scotch, greatly surprised to be joined by Cynthia Pellow.

'Of course, please do,' I replied to her request to sit with me. 'And here I was thinking you couldn't stand the sight of me.'

Her startlingly blue eyes regarded me icily behind the large spectacles. 'A brute of a man has been following me,' she said, sitting down in the chair I held for her. 'I've already told him I didn't want to dance.' Nearby I

In the Flesh

saw a large man I knew well. I gave him a wave and he walked off.

'Sam Bishop of Photo Safaris,' I said. 'He does look a brute with that great ginger moustache. So you considered me the lesser of two evils?' Her dark-fringed hair shone and I thought how very attractive she looked. Her slim figure with its sharply pointed tits was encased in a short black dress set off by pearls and a diamond brooch. She was showing a lot of shapely leg. 'If I may say so, Doctor Pellow,' I chanced, meaning it, 'don't be too hard on Sam. You do look very nice tonight. Extremely nice.'

'I've no doubt you tell that to every woman,' she remarked. 'You flatter them and hope to get your way. Your psychological type is well known.'

'And what's that?' I asked.

'In your case, although you are tall and good-looking, you are also an inveterate sexual deviate who has to score regularly to prove he's not inadequate.'

'An interesting theory,' I agreed, 'but could it not simply be that I like women?' I beckoned a passing waiter and ordered her a vodka orange with ice. In the silence that followed I felt bound to make conversation. 'So you're staying with Diana Saxon. I'm sure you're good company for her with Harry away.'

'She's a sweetie, isn't she?' Cynthia agreed. 'Diana of the laughing face. You like her, I know. I've noticed the way you look at her. You'd like to be intimate with her.'

'Intimate as in close friends or intimate as in sexually?' I taunted her. 'No doubt you think sexually and you're right. When you needed to avoid Sam Bishop, what made you choose my table? I know I rate very low in your esteem.'

'Diana is in the hotel counting the proceeds of the charity sale. I know no one else here. I'll move if you wish.'

'Please stay,' I said. 'It's my pleasure.' I looked at the couples swinging around to the lively Congolese rhythm. 'Perhaps you'd care to dance?'

'I think not,' Cynthia replied. 'I'm quite happy to sit. It's such a perfect night, even the air is scented.' For a change, her attitude became less hostile if not friendly. 'The sky is so huge and dark one can see the stars brilliantly. How different from London. I presume as a pilot and navigator, you know them all.'

'Well, one or two,' I confessed. 'If you look south, low in the sky, that star group is the Southern Cross. Entebbe is right on the equator. Depending on the tilt of this old Earth, at times you get to see constellations in both north and southern hemispheres. How's that for a bit of useless information?'

'As a newcomer I find it fascinating,' she said. 'It's delightful here with those coloured lanterns among the palms and not having to wrap up against the cold. It has been a lovely day in every way. I can't remember when I've enjoyed one so much.'

As well you might, I thought, recalling her naked romp on the lawn with Diana that morning. 'So you're glad you came?' I asked, meaning it in both senses.

'Yes, Africa is beautiful, isn't it?' she said pleasantly.

'Most of it,' I agreed. 'It gets to you. Not where you're going though. Refugee camps are not beautiful.'

'So Roberta informed me,' she said seriously, 'but I hope to get permission to go in a few days. Do you think you could order me another drink?' She even smiled at me, if bleakly. 'I suddenly feel the need for one.'

'I'll join you,' I said, calling a waiter. 'How well do you know Roberta Leigh-Pagett?'

'Too well,' Cynthia laughed scathingly. 'We were at school and Oxford together. She's really a dreadful woman,

In the Flesh

flaunting her affairs in front of me as if she wants to prove something. That she's more attractive to men, I suppose.'

'I'm sure you've had your admirers,' I said. 'Perhaps Roberta is all talk?'

'If she is, she has a lurid imagination,' Cynthia replied. 'She never spared me even the smallest detail of her sexual dalliances.' She took a good swallow at her second vodka as if needing it, her voice suddenly hesitant, nervy. 'Even about what she got up to with you. I could hardly believe it. Was it true?'

'Probably. I don't know exactly what she told you.'

'I mustn't blame you entirely. Roberta is a huntress, seeking out men. Whatever she wanted, of course a man would be glad to oblige.'

'Well, we men *are* so weak,' I teased her, raising my glass. 'You know me, just a sexual deviate who has to score to prove I'm not inadequate.'

'Don't be flippant,' Cynthia reproached me. 'Roberta left nothing to the imagination. Things I would not have thought possible, or even desirable. She sought to arouse me, of course. Frank sexual talk can be arousing. To think you did all those things with her.'

The conversation was getting interesting. What would this previously cool beauty want with me, except to satisfy a craving to talk with someone about sex? 'We were both consenting adults,' I said.

'She told me you gave her oral sex,' I was surprised to hear her say. 'She said it was the best she had experienced, and who would know better? Did you have oral-genital contact as she claims? I believe the proper term is cunnilingus.'

'I know the word,' I said. Our conversation was getting even more intriguing. 'Yes, I did it to her several times. She loved it and certainly didn't need to be forced.'

Lesley Asquith

'I've never experienced it,' said Cynthia, no doubt meaning with a man. She appeared calm again, her old superior self. 'My one serious relationship was sexless, with a male colleague who finally admitted he was homosexual. He refused me oral sex, although he expected me to fellate him. He said he found the female vagina quite repellant.'

'Then you missed out, doctor,' I commiserated with her, the beginning of an erection stirring. 'It's something special, bringing a woman off on your tongue. Roberta wanted me to do it to her all night.'

'She was fortunate then in having what she wanted,' Cynthia said, her speech calm again. For a spell, while broaching the subject of sexual matters, a nervous hesitancy had edged in. Now the topic was being openly discussed, the arrogant manner had returned. 'It's something I have thought about, of course, experiencing a male performing cunnilingus,' she mentioned off-handedly. 'To know what I may have missed.'

By whatever fancy names she cared to call it, Cynthia was obviously desirous of an old-fashioned licking out. I was faced with a cool customer but considered the ice-maiden had melted enough to risk getting slapped down. 'If you care to try it,' I suggested, using the same dispassionate tone as she, 'I'd be glad to oblige.'

Cynthia regarded me for a long moment as if considering the proposition. 'Where could we do it?' she enquired.

'My car,' I ventured. 'It's parked in a dark area.' I stood up from the table and she followed me to the car park. On reaching my car, I held open the rear door.

'Is this suitable?' she asked, but nevertheless sat on the rear seat. I joined her. She waited for my instructions. I told her to lean her back on the inside of the car door, to place one leg along the seat and let the other hang down, foot on floor. She did all this without comment and drew her dress

In the Flesh

up over her thighs as my head lowered. I'd forgotten one important thing but she had not.

'Surely I should take off my briefs?' she said.

'Right off,' I answered, both of us still speaking as if discussing the weather.

The light was poor but I got a glimpse of supple white thighs as she peeled her tiny knickers over her shoes. I crouched before her along the rear seat and raised her dress higher. She wore frilly suspenders and stockings. At the fork of her legs in the dimness I made out a plumply curved split mound with a tufty bush of hair. Despite her supposed indifference, I noted it was tilted forward for me.

I kissed the outer lips of her cunt several times, as if it was a mouth but got no response. Not daring to finger it first, or reach up to clasp her remarkably pointed breasts, it was almost clinical. Her cunt was bared and raised for me but she gave no sign that she was involved in proceedings. However, it was a pretty cunt and I lapped around it, sucked on it, then stiffened up my tongue and penetrated her. That at least brought a suppressed groan. Encouraged, I placed my palms over the rounded flesh of her inner thighs and opened her wider, going in to tongue-fuck her.

I licked her moist fissure, tongue flicking and probing, determined to give of my best to get her to react. I sought the hard nub of a fingertip-like clitoris and sucked it, nose and mouth hard into her. A series of stifled whimpers told me I was winning.

'Lick me, lick me out, lick me clean,' I heard her mutter through clenched teeth, her agitation mounting. Suddenly she clasped my head and forced it hard between her thighs, writhing and thrusting her pelvis to my face, gasping loudly. 'Yes, yes!' she cried, bucking wildly as the sensations palpitated through her cunt. Then her lower body went into uncontrollable spasms, undulating helplessly in a terrific orgasm.

My head was pushed away from her even in her dying convulsions. Recovered somewhat, she sat up, retrieving her panties and straightening her dress before getting out of the car. I had a monster of a hard-on and wanted to suggest she return the favour or, better still, let me fuck her. I would even have settled for a quick hand-job but she was obviously eager to depart the scene.

'I'd better go, I'm sure Diana will be looking for me,' she said, about to walk towards the coloured lanterns and the strains of dance music. I felt I'd got the short end of the stick, being treated like a handy sex toy. She added, 'Of course, this incident will remain a strictly private matter between us, Mr Wight.' As an afterthought she said, 'Thank you.'

'Think nothing of it. Be my guest. Any time,' I called after her as she strolled away. Ever had the feeling you'd been used? I had to laugh, at myself and the imperious Cynthia for wheedling a cunt-licking out of me. Laughed until I remembered what I'd be doing later that night. My hard-on and I set off on the drive to Kampala, hoping for the best – and fearing the worst.

Chapter Fifteen

When I entered *Chez Miklos* at five minutes to eleven the restaurant was crowded. Fatima was performing on the pocket-handkerchief size dance floor in front of the band. I went to the bar, noting Desdemona at a table among a group of people. She gave me the merest nod of her coiffured blonde head. As I was about to order a drink, Miklos Dimitri sidled up beside me in a white tuxedo and told the barman it was on the house. Waiting for my contact, he was the last person I wanted to see.

'How's life?' he asked. 'Having any luck?'

'Plenty. All bad,' I answered. 'Can't a customer have a quiet drink without being accosted by the biggest sleazeball in town?'

'That makes two of us then,' he laughed, his arm around my shoulder. 'Come up to my private apartment, the booze is superior to the stuff I sell here. Not waiting for someone, are you?'

'I could be,' I said cautiously.

'You've just found him,' he said cordially, grinning at the shock on my face.

I was still speechless when he ushered me into his private office upstairs. Seating himself behind a huge desk, he poured out generous malt whiskies. 'Relax,' he advised, noting my trembling hand as I accepted the drink. 'Pull up a chair. We've an hour or two before we move the Musa family out. You seem surprised?'

'You could say that,' I admitted. 'I thought you were in cahoots with Amin and Suliman, expecting great things when they take over.'

'True,' he agreed. 'A coup is bound to succeed and General Idi Amin will be the head honcho here, king of all he surveys. He won't forget his friends while it lasts. I don't expect it to. I give it a year or two before a military government runs Uganda into the ground. In that time I'll get import contracts to bring in all the machinery, modern weapons and helicopters they think they'll want. I'll be rich as another Greek called Onassis. Maybe I'll marry a socialite like Jackie Kennedy.'

'Meanwhile you're helping members of the present government to get out before they get the chop,' I said. 'Risky. But I suppose it is like taking out insurance.'

'Right,' he said, pleased with himself. 'Sam Musa and the others are professional politicians. They'll be back once the new regime collapses. No doubt they'll lie low in Tanzania plotting Amin's downfall. If and when they return, they'll remember Miklos too. The country will have to be rebuilt. World Bank loans will pour in. I intend to get my share of the gravy.' He gave me his twisted smile. 'You haven't enquired about your friend Mrs Warren?'

'I trust you haven't yet shipped her off to a Saudi harem?' I asked caustically. 'There's still a few fucks left in her, I presume?'

'Plenty, and she loves every cock put to her,' Miklos said, opening the door to the next room. I could see Margaret sprawled out face down on a bed, reflected from every angle in the multiple images of the mirror-lined walls and ceiling. Arms and legs outstretched, wrists and ankles tied by silken cords to the bed-posts, her rounded arse was raised

In the Flesh

by a cushion placed under her upper thighs, revealing her gaping cunt and arsehole.

'A little entertainment while we wait,' Miklos announced, going to her and idly dipping his fingers into the cleft of her buttocks. Making sure I was watching, he opened the drawer of a bedside cabinet and brought out a small bottle. He dripped its contents into the top of her divide, the oil running down into the fissure of her bum. Margaret gave an anguished whine, her bottom squirming until Miklos stilled her movements with a few warning smacks.

'Stay still, let it soak in,' he ordered.

'It stings and itches,' I heard Margaret protest, unable to contain the twitching of her bottom. 'Please, Miklos, you know it makes me wriggle about.'

'Then you must learn to lie still and overcome it,' Miklos said menacingly. 'Or I'll be forced to use the riding crop. Do you want to be punished, Margaret?'

'No, please, not that,' she begged him. 'I'll try not to move.'

'Good, I shall be watching,' he promised. From the drawer he next produced a thick ebony dildo, some twelve inches long and carved as an exact replica of the male organ, the shaft smooth up to the bulbous crown. He held it up for me to see, then rubbed it in the oil between her legs. Margaret's face became apprehensive.

'Don't, please, Miklos,' she asked of him. 'You know what it does to me. Why do you do this?'

'A test of your will-power,' he said, placing the knob of the big dildo against the ring of her back passage and pressing on the tight circlet until the first inch or so entered. *It's going in*, I heard Margaret grunt. 'Damn right, it's going in,' Miklos said. 'You've had bigger things in there before!'

He worked the dildo into her rear until four or five inches

remained outside, sticking lewdly from between her cheeks. 'Now, don't move,' he warned. 'Or I'll be back with the riding crop to warm your arse till it's on fire. Get the picture?'

Leaving her with the dummy prick projecting from her bottom he returned and poured more whisky. 'Sit back and watch,' he invited me. 'It gets more interesting. She'll try not to move, but she won't be able to resist.' He glanced at his gold Rolex. 'I give her no more than a few minutes before the throb in her cunt and the feel of that dildo up her arse makes her go bananas. The oil has ingredients that would make a corpse horny.'

'Miklos,' Margaret called from her spreadeagled and bound posture, 'it's so itchy, I *must* respond. It's driving me mad! Let me, let me. Do I have to beg?'

'It would do you no good,' Miklos responded. 'One movement, one twitch of that pretty arse and I'll have to thrash it. Try harder. Concentrate your mind. Think of your husband.'

'How is he, by the way?' I asked. 'Some trip to Uganda it's been for the Warrens. Him laid up in hospital with malaria and his wife with a foot of carved ebony up her jacksy. You're some kind of an evil scumbag.'

'Her old man's doing okay,' Miklos laughed, unperturbed. 'In a private room, with the best of my restaurant's food taken in to him twice a day. He doesn't even have malaria. He's suffering from heat exhaustion and stress from overwork back in England – something *you've* always dodged, Wight. The rest is doing him good, I've bribed the doctors to keep him in.'

'You think of everything,' I said. 'I hope you've got tonight's escape of the Musa family planned so well.' I sipped my whisky, deciding to go easy since I would be

In the Flesh

flying. Next door Margaret tensed her body as if in utter torment, her face reflected in the mirrors.

'Don't worry about a thing,' he assured me. 'Just enjoy the show. She's resisting longer this time, no doubt because you're here. Any time now she'll go off like a rocket. I've used this routine to entertain a few important clients before, usually with a cucumber. I forgot to bring one up from the kitchen.'

'You're slipping,' I told him, shaking my head. 'It's not like you.'

'Don't worry about her, she loves it,' Miklos sneered. 'The fucking, the humiliation, even the riding crop. She's never had it so good, it's the stuff of her wildest fantasies. Look at her.' I was, seeing her trying to control her lower torso, the occasional twitch of her pelvis showing she was losing the battle. Her bottom was jerking, making the half-buried dildo bob. 'No batteries required,' Miklos joked. 'She's been quite an asset, your Mrs Warren.'

'Let her go,' I appealed to his better nature. 'You've had good use of her. I'll come tomorrow and take her away.'

'Get that out of your head,' he warned, the dark eyes mean. 'She'll go when I say so, whenever that may be.' He drew on a long cigar, regarding me with hostility. 'Try something, Wight, and I can make you disappear too. You don't know what I can do.'

I didn't doubt it, hearing Margaret give a loud groan, her arse gyrating, cunt thrusting into the cushion, lost to all but the sensations coursing through her front and back. The spectacle caught in the ceiling mirrors, she bucked frantically in orgasm and when her spasms ceased she lay as if exhausted with the dildo still projecting from her anus.

A tentative tap on the door broke the spell and a fair-skinned Circassian girl entered bearing a tray heaped with sandwiches. She glanced into the room where Margaret lay and tried to appear unconcerned. Behind the desk Miklos crooked a finger at the girl and then pointed forcibly at his crotch. With just a moment's hesitation she knelt on the rug and unzipped him. She brought out his prick and her hair fell over her face as she began kissing it, licking up the stalk, covering the red-topped knob with her full lips. Taking more in her mouth, sucking it quickly to full thickness and length, her head bobbed as she took in every inch. She let it slip partly out and then gobbled it all in again.

'This is Anuka,' Miklos explained, nodding down at the girl now sucking him avidly. 'Her father is an old friend in Armenia and he asked me to teach her the restaurant business. She's doing well. Try the sandwiches, there's chicken or ham.' Only a tightening of his facial muscles showed he was reaching his peak, a grunt and a shudder moments later was proof that he had come in her mouth. She rose, drawing a hand across her lips and left wordlessly.

'Not eating?' he asked, rising from his chair and zipping up. 'Never mind, I've provided a selection of packed meals for your flight, with coffee and hot soup. Time to collect the Musa family and see them safe on their way. Follow me.'

I did, going with him into the bedroom where Margaret lay tethered to the bed with the dildo still projecting from her bottom. Her initial orgasm had left her inert, now as we passed her she was starting to grind her arse cheeks again, working her cunt into the cushion strategically placed below her, giving little whines that could either be of pain or pleasure. She turned her head to look at us but did not dare ask to be released. It was obvious she was on the way to reaching a second climax whether she sought it or not. Miklos ignored her, reaching into a wardrobe to hand me one of his white tuxedo jackets.

In the Flesh

'Slip it on,' he said, 'and pretend we're going partying with two bibis. Let me do the talking at any roadblocks.'

As he made to leave with me, Margaret set up a howl.

'Aren't you going to release her?' I asked. 'Are you going to leave her tied up with that thing in her?'

'She's comfortable there,' Miklos said easily. He picked up the thin bottle of oil from the bedside cabinet, adding a fresh drip to run down the join of her buttock cheeks.

'No!' Margaret protested too late, the oozy liquid trickling around the dildo and seeping on to her cunt.

'She'll have a better night there than with many a man,' Miklos observed drily. 'All the orgasms she wants and plenty extra that she may not before morning. Come on, time's wasting.'

We went down a passageway leading to the back stairs, Miklos opening the door of the storeroom piled with tables and chairs where I'd screwed Fatima. Waiting for us was Sam Musa with his chief wife Lule and daughter Petal, with both of whom my acquaintance had been intimate. The two women were dressed in Indian saris instead of their usual Ugandan busuti costume, with bangles on their wrists, large earrings. Powdered, rouged and with heavy eye make-up, I supposed it was possible in a poor light that they could have been taken for a pair of Asian ladies. Sam Musa looked as terrified as when I'd last seen him. He wore the same safari suit which was now more creased, dirty and dishevelled than ever.

In the yard behind the restaurant Miklos's large Cadillac awaited us. He opened the rear door, leaning in to lift the long seat and reveal a coffin-shaped empty space. Sam Musa climbed in and lay prone and the seat was lowered over him.

'I've used that space to my advantage a few times,' Miklos said to me as he ushered young Petal in to sit on the seat above her father. 'You name it, it's been in there. First time with an escaping politician though.'

I climbed in and sat beside Petal while Miklos took the wheel with Lule next to him. 'Hoods up, ladies,' he said as he drove off into the night and both women covered their heads with their saris.

We left the lights of Kampala and drove through pitch night, the road towards Entebbe enclosed on either side by thick bush. At Kajansi we drew up at a roadblock made out of beds, tables and chairs. We were accosted by hostile soldiers led by the intimidating sergeant I'd met before. Miklos was not the least phased as the scarred faces peered in, lowering the window and greeting them in perfect Swahili.

'Party time, boys,' he told them jovially. 'Two Asian bibis looking for a change of dick while their husbands are in Kenya on business. Look in the boot by all means. There's a little token of our appreciation for you brave soldiers guarding Uganda's interests.'

Turning my head to look through the rear window, I saw them draw out a full crate of Tusker beer to whoops of pleasure. The tough sergeant saluted me, remembering I was evidently a friend of Captain Suliman. We were waved on and drove away, Miklos chortling at his cleverness.

'Getting past the troops at the airport won't be so easy,' I reminded him. 'Everyone will be searched. We'll have our documents inspected.'

'Wait and see,' Miklos said confidently. 'Those Kakwa soldiers are Suliman's personal troops. Wouldn't he do his nut if he knew what we were up to tonight?'

'I shudder to think,' I said, wishing it were morning and I had returned safely. 'If I don't see him again it will be too soon.'

'You will,' Miklos laughed. 'He tells me you're going to

In the Flesh

fix him up with a certain lady. Mrs Saxon of the gorgeous tits. Now there's a fine woman I wouldn't mind fucking myself.'

The mention of the fucking rang a bell with Petal. Less tense after passing the checkpoint, she now leaned into me, pressing a kiss of invitation to my cheek and giving my prick a friendly squeeze. I hardly thought it was the time or place, cruising along sitting on top of her father but my unruly dick was not bothered by such incidentals. Petal dragged it out and teased it with her fist. Disregarding her ma in the front seat, she dipped her head and gave it a few delicious sucks, which only increased its urgency. She giggled even with my cock in her mouth, which added to the arousal I naturally felt. Settling back, I decided to let her drink her fill but Petal wanted more.

She rolled away from me, my prick leaping up like a springboard as it left her lips. Adjusting the sari, she lifted her left leg and slid it across my thighs, drawing the silk folds to hide her position. I felt her supple arse cheeks grinding into my lap and my prick being rudely manoeuvred until the knob rubbed against her plump cunt lips. With a determined thrust of her crotch my whole cock was buried inside her juicy folds.

She lay almost flat along the long leather seat, giving twitches of her arse muscles that served to jiggle my prick inside her. 'Petal, Petal,' her mother asked, turning her head and making me glad of the pitch darkness of the unlit road, 'are you all right back there? It won't be long now.'

'She's resting,' I answered. 'This business must be a strain for her.' Satisfied, Mrs Musa turned away, and Petal gave several jerks on my cock, acknowledging my apt reply. Her cunt channel was snug and moist, made to fuck, and as she wriggled and jiggled I lifted my hips in response, shunting up every inch to match her pushes. It was one of my more unusual fucks and made all the more erotic for having to be silent and doing it in company with her old man hidden below us. As Miklos turned into a side road onto a track, I felt her innards shudder and a series of spasms wrack her lower torso as she came. A moment later I shot my wad up her, both of us suppressing gasps and lying still until the car drew up and Miklos asked everybody to get out.

I knew where we were – the Entebbe Sailing Club, off the beaten track beside the lake. The giant wine waiter, Mkubwa, was waiting for us on Miklos's cabin-cruiser. The boat slipped its moorings and steered around the coast for the few miles to the rear of Entebbe Airport. Mkubwa grounded the boat, slipping overboard waist-deep in the lake to carry the Musa family ashore one by one, keeping them dry and bearing their weight effortlessly. Then it was my turn. Miklos stood beside me on deck, hands in pockets.

'It's all yours now,' he told me cheerfully. 'A guide will take you through the bush to come out right behind Lake Airways. Dine with me tomorrow when you get back. There'll be a bonus for you too. This is no freebie for either of us. Musa has salted money away while in office.'

When we were all ashore, Mkubwa returned to the cabin-cruiser, we watched it go astern and turn to sail away leaving us deserted on the lonely beach. Minutes later a shadowy figure joined us, a man obviously known to the Musa family who led us away into thick scrubby bush towards the outer perimeter of the airport. Thorns tugged at my sleeves as we proceeded, until what might have been called a narrow track disappeared and ahead loomed thicker bush. The man turned, silently holding up two fingers, meaning he would guide us two at a time, leading off Sam and Petal. I was left with Lule in complete darkness, the sounds of Africa at night all around,

In the Flesh

remembering it was rumoured that leopard still roamed in the area. This cloak-and-dagger stuff was not for me, I decided, and Lule Musa no doubt thought the same, cuddling up to me for company.

We sat down, hoping that we would not disturb any of the venomous snakes I knew for certain abounded there. With her arm around me tightly, I felt a big pliant breast pressing into my side. 'Do you want to fuck me like you did before?' she asked, surprising me for my mind was occupied with survival. She lay down flat on the track without waiting for an answer, drawing up the folds of the sari and placing my hand on the the join of her bared thighs. 'Feel me,' she said. 'I liked it last time with you. Fuck me quick before Okolo comes back.'

The suddenness of the invitation made the offer more arousing. Mother and daughter in one night, I thought, touching up a swollen mound with wiry hair and a moist slit. I sat up on my knees before her face, drawing an already semi-hard prick out and offering it to her face. 'A quick suck to get it stiffer,' I told her, hearing her mutter how we *mzungus* liked our cocks sucked by women. She complied, sucking hard as if impatient to get it up her cunt. When it was stiff enough, she lay back and pulled me across her.

Her hand guided my root to her cleft and she arched her back to ensure the whole length penetrated her. Feeling the urgent way she bucked against me, her ankles locked behind my back and hands hauling at my arse, I decided this was of necessity to be the quickest of quickies. It was none the less good as I thrust into her, her big breasts flattened against my chest, my pistoning cock up a throbbing cunt. She quivered, moaning and gurgling her pleasure as she climaxed, her agitation setting me off and flooding her with my tribute. It was none too soon, even while we were catching our breath we were joined by the returning guide.

A hundred yards of battling through the thick scrub and trees brought us to the wire fence of the airport perimeter. A part at a corner had been peeled back neatly, easily slotted back when not needed, and we passed through. Not far away my Cessna aircraft stood ready in front of the Lake Airways office, with a worried Bill Dove beside it. I presumed Sam Musa and his daughter were inside and I wanted to waste no time getting airborne. I was handed a flight plan and it was obvious Bill Dove wanted me to leave.

'You're supposed to fly to Mombasa,' he said. 'An emergency flight to get lobsters, fish and oysters for *Chez Miklos*. Take-off has been approved, it's a properly booked flight. What the hell you do or where you go once you are over the lake, don't tell me.'

I decided to play it by ear. Once we were well over the water and heading for Kenya, I turned south. With a map provided by Sam Musa, I landed later at a bush airstrip on the Tanzania plain. Cars were waiting and the Musa family left, shaking my hand. The assembly departed, leaving me on my own except for a large pride of lion who passed by.

I slept for several hours before returning to my Entebbe base. Come sun-up, I had never been so glad to see another day. When I reported back to Bill Dove in the office, he shook his head.

'Take the rest of the day off,' he said, mopping his brow with relief at seeing me. 'I've cancelled all flights, I'm too old to go through this too often. I've ordered a day of engine overhaul to make sure nothing else will shatter my nerves today. Captain Suliman phoned asking for you earlier. I told him you were in Mombasa. What does he want?'

'He wants to fuck Harry Saxon's wife,' I thought it best

In the Flesh

to lay on the line. 'I've warned her to leave but she won't. I'll drive by her bungalow now and try to impress on her she must. This time I'll insist she goes.'

I drove to the Saxons' villa and found Cynthia Pellow alone on the verandah. She said Diana had driven to Kampala to buy supplies to send to the refugee area.

'Sit down,' Cynthia added in a more friendly way than usual. Of course I had licked her quim the last time we met. She poured me coffee, watching me closely from behind the large round spectacles. 'I can't order you breakfast,' she said, as if cooking for me was not her bag. 'Diana took her housegirl with her. That leaves just you and I, doesn't it?' She pursed her lips as if in thought. 'I can't think what I could get you to eat.'

'Try harder,' I suggested, rising and taking her hand to lead her into the bedroom. 'I'm sure you've got something to whet my appetite.'

Chapter Sixteen

Cynthia had taken to cunt-licking – by male or female, it didn't matter. My turning up when she was alone had her senual pulses racing, although it would have been hard to tell from her set features. All the same, her urge not to waste an opportunity had been made clear and there was something about going down on such an ice-cold maiden that made it irresistible. If I could make her show some emotion it would be a triumph. In the course of time, naturally, I intended to fuck her.

In the bedroom she slipped casually out of her bikini briefs and lay across the bed without a word. She left her top on, although I would have preferred her nude. She treated it like a business arrangement, parting her legs for me and tilting her pretty cunt with its luxuriant bush of hair for my attention. As before, there was no suggestion that we should show any affection as I bent to my task.

I lapped around the inside of her upper thighs, then ran a tongue-tip over the small crinkled lips of her labia, parting them to probe inside. A stiffening of her body was her only reaction, as if she was on the point of resisting. But the free-flowing honey of her excitement on my face betrayed her apparent indifference. I stiffened up my tongue, working in and out of her like a prick, then nuzzled in to flick at her erect clitty.

A restrained gasp and a low moan told me I was making

an impression. Her hands pulled my face hard against the hairy mound now thrusting frantically as the surge of sensations in her cunt drove her over the edge. I had no intention of stopping as her pelvis undulated out of control in her first climax. I delved in to graze the stubby clitoris with my teeth, then sucked upon the distended nub to keep up the assault. Her legs went over my shoulders, heels drumming on my back as she came again with loud gasps and throaty cries, the violent spasms shaking her as she went into another strong orgasm. I continued to give her yet one more, her fourth, before her body went limp and she lolled back, drained of the energy to go for number five.

The last time she had fled almost as soon as the act was over. Now, as she recovered, her cunt still palpitating no doubt, I aimed to draw her out. I gently smoothed a hand over her thigh as I had seen her do to Diana. 'Did you like that?' I asked, my gliding hand moving on to between her legs, ever hopeful.

'You know bloody well I did,' she answered sharply, pushing my hand away from her cunt. She craned her neck, seeing me sitting there with a giant hard-on rearing out of my fly. 'And you can put that away,' she ordered. 'I don't allow men to be intimate with me. Don't ever expect it.'

'I'd call sucking you off over and over fairly intimate,' I said. 'It's all right for you, but I'm left with *this* which won't go down. You're a selfish woman, Cynthia.' I got to my feet and marched out of the room.

I quickly drove home – Jovial would welcome me, I knew. But I had hardly parked in my driveway before the Saxons' second car pulled in behind me and Cynthia got out. Jovial stood at the kitchen door with the knowing grin she always had when female visitors arrived. I'd had enough of Cynthia and stalked off into the bungalow, heading for the

In the Flesh

bathroom and a much-needed shower. I was standing in the bath under the showerhead when Cynthia was shown in by the still-grinning Jovial.

'I've come to apologise,' Cynthia said, as if it hurt her to speak. 'Of course I do appreciate what you do to me, but you must take it or leave it. I do not fuck men. That's the word you'd use, no doubt. I'm sorry,' she added, looking at my still-rampant prick, 'if it leaves you in that excited state. I realise that our particular liaison is one-sided.'

'And you came here to tell me that?' I said, my hand poised to turn on the spray. 'Well, that makes me feel a great deal better.'

'Actually I was on my way to enquire about the pass permitting me to travel upcountry to the refugee area,' she said uppishly. 'The army say it's a restricted area and I need a government official to grant permission. So far, no one I've contacted has done a thing. I merely popped in here in passing. Do I take it my apology is accepted?'

'Sure, sure,' I said acidly. 'What's a little oral-genital contact between friends? You like the tongue and I'm not complaining about being the one providing it. You've got a sweet cunt, Cynthia, even if it leaves me with a boner you could break rocks with.'

'Like all men, you're just being surly because you haven't got your own way,' she chided me. 'As a medical doctor I understand your frustration.' Stepping closer to the bath she peered at my upstanding cock through the owl-like specs. 'It does look very inflamed, I grant you. You're very well endowed too, more so than the average.'

'I got lucky when they dished them out,' I said, priding myself she was getting to like the look of it.

'Typical male chauvinism,' she answered me. 'If you wish to relieve it by hand as I advise in this case, I shall leave.'

'Better still, why don't you do it for me?' I suggested. 'That's not what you call being *really* intimate, is it? Intimate is fucking.' I took her hand and wrapped it around my rock-hard prick. 'Go ahead, it's what the doctor ordered.'

She shrugged and, perhaps won over by the hot throb in her grasp, began to rub me up in what I considered was no inexperienced manner. I groaned my pleasure, leaning against the tiled wall and buckling slightly at the knee.

'Oh, Cynthia,' I moaned, quickly brought to the boil, the jism surging from my balls as her wrist worked away energetically, the jets of spunk splashing into the bath. She turned away without a word, rinsed her hands at the washbasin and dried them before walking to the door. I felt I was making some progress as she gave me one last long look before walking out.

I ate a good breakfast, recalling with some pride the success of the night's operation in getting the Musa family to safety. Miklos rang to check that I was back and a further call came just as I was deciding how to spend my day off. It was from Margaret Warren's daughter, Chloe, in Germany, still demanding news of her mother.

'I've tried the house a dozen times,' she said. 'I presume she's still staying at a hotel in Kampala. I've tried to get through to the hospital too, but there's always a foul-up at the switchboard. What's going on? I'm stuck here in Germany worried about both my parents now. Can you tell me anything?'

'Your mother is in Kampala, near your father,' I said, which was the truth as far as it went. 'I've seen her. She visits the hospital regularly and he's improving daily, they say. He's in a private room, getting a good rest. Don't worry about a thing.'

'Are you going to Kampala today, Ty?' she asked. 'Could

you visit him and say I send him all my love and stuff like that. Tell him I'm enjoying my stay in Germany.' I heard Chloe's wicked giggle down the line. 'At last.'

'I take it that Heinz has finally come across?' I enquired, laughing with her. 'Did you have to rape the poor guy? And here I was thinking you were keeping it warm for me.'

'Couldn't wait that long,' Chloe's tinkling laugh came back. 'It wasn't Heiny either, he's still saving me for the wedding night, the idiot. Would you believe his father made a pass at me? And the first time we were in the house alone we—'

'Say no more,' I told her. 'You have that effect on men. I'll go and see your dad today and say you send your love.'

So I decided to go to Kampala. Among other reasons was the knowledge that I had to somehow rescue Margaret from the clutches of Miklos before her daughter's return. Or before her father wised up and discharged himself from hospital.

I drove straight to the large general hospital at Mulago on the outskirts of the city. Arthur Warren was sitting up in bed looking much better than I remembered him. He put down the book he was reading when I entered.

'I remember you,' he said, indicating the bedside chair for me to sit on. 'You're the pilot who knows my daughter. It's kind of you to come.'

'It's on your daughter's behalf I'm here,' I said. 'She phoned me this morning, told me to give you her love and hopes you are improving. All's well in Germany, she's having a nice time.'

'Why didn't she phone her mother to say that?' Arthur asked and I wondered if I'd put my foot in it. Arthur, it seemed, was not so dull as to be completely unaware something was amiss. 'Doesn't she know where her mother is staying? My wife says she's in an hotel nearby. Do you know if that's a fact?'

'I think so,' I lied. 'I met her once in Kampala and she said she'd visited you. I really wouldn't doubt her word.'

'I think she's having an affair and living with the man,' Arthur said bluntly. 'She visits me regularly but she looks different, like something's going on. Made-up and looking years younger. And who is paying for this room and the medical treatment and all the food? Have you ever heard of a Greek called Miklos who owns a restaurant here? I believe he's her lover.'

For a man confined to a private room in hospital, I reckoned the betrayed husband had done his sleuthing well. As if reading my thoughts, he watched me intently for a sign I knew more than I made out.

'I wouldn't know anything about that,' 'Surely, Mrs Warren is not that type of lady? You know her better than that.' As if to qualify my statement I added, 'How could you suspect she is having an affair when you're stuck in here?'

'I paid a porter to keep his eyes open for me,' he said. 'He told me my wife arrives and leaves in a large American car driven by this Miklos fellow and that the food comes from his restaurant. Besides,' he concluded darkly, 'it's not the first time. My wife has a highly sexed nature, although you may find that difficult to believe. I know it all too well from our relationship over the years.'

How many men would complain about that? I wondered. As Arthur seemed inclined to talk about his hard luck in being stuck with a horny wife, I tut-tutted to gain his confidence. 'One can never tell,' I said in sympathy. 'I mean, to look at her.'

'Yes,' Arthur agreed bitterly. She looks like the epitome of the average housewife and mother. Perhaps I've been

In the Flesh

too busy in business and local affairs to be the kind of husband she needs. I was never much interested in that side. You know, *sex*.' He uttered the word as if it was the lowest form of human activity. 'She even *masturbates* at her age,' he added. 'I've actually caught her at it.' He looked me in the eye to gauge my reaction, accepting the sad shake of my head with a nod of agreement. 'Walked in and caught her abusing herself on the living room sofa in mid-afternoon.'

'Not mid-afternoon?' I gasped. 'Good God!'

'Mid-afternoon,' he confirmed. 'What do you think of that?'

What I thought was, no wonder Margaret went off the rails when she had the chance. Looking at her tubby hubby I began to suspect this outrage at his wife's failings gave him a curious pleasure. They were still a couple after all. 'You said it wasn't the first time?' I reminded him, 'there were others?'

'One I know for certain,' Arthur said gravely. 'When I charged her with having lovers, she swore she'd only had one.' I thought the sad tone of his voice could have been disappointment. 'But, God knows, one was more than enough,' he vowed, almost brightening. 'A mere boy, the age of our daughter, in fact an ex-boyfriend of hers. Chloe knows nothing of this, of course. I hope I can trust you never to reveal it?'

'You have my word,' I promised, stifling my amusement, while thinking Margaret had been holding out on me in saying her only relief had been through fantasies and playing with herself. At that moment one of the doctors came in and, as I left, I wondered about Arthur's wife's affair with a boy young enough to be her son.

I drove into the centre of the city, with its open-fronted Asian shops and African market sellers. I stepped out of my car in the searing heat of the afternoon and heard someone call my name. Looking cool and beautiful in a lemon cotton dress that clung to her curvaceous frame, Diana Saxon came up to greet me.

'No one should look that good,' I told her, making her laugh.

'So you wouldn't object to seeing more of me?' she asked, the amusement glinting in her dark hazel eyes.

'Try me,' I said. 'Offhand I can think of less inspiring sights. Like the pyramids, the sphinx, the Taj Mahal and stuff like them. Are you having me on, like you usually do?'

'It's been unbearably hot and I feel like a swim. My car's parked in the UN compound because I'm catching the four o'clock train to Nairobi. I need a lift to a club that Harry and I belong to. You look hot and bothered too. Drive me and I'll sign you in as my guest for a dip in the pool.'

I swiftly agreed and we drove off through the dusty crowded streets. 'A swim would be great,' I said, negotiating handcarts loaded with produce and battered taxis, 'but better still is hearing you say you're leaving for Nairobi. I take it you've heeded my warning about Captain Suliman?'

'Nothing of the kind,' Diana laughed. 'There's a truck-load of Red Cross blankets and medicines going begging in Nairobi. I'm leaving by train this afternoon to drive it back.' She saw me look at her in amazement. 'I can drive a truck, you know. In my time I've been a driver-mechanic in the Wrens, that's the Women's Royal Naval Service.'

'I've heard of the Wrens,' I said. 'Take me seriously over this one thing, please. Do you want me to spell it out? Suliman intends to fuck you. At present he's involved in plotting a military takeover but he'll come for you the first chance he gets.'

In the Flesh

'I appreciate your concern but I'm not running away,' she said. We were leaving Kampala on a road fringed with high trees. 'Turn here,' I was instructed. Along a track was an iron gate in a fenced enclosure. It was opened for us by a Ugandan guard who unlocked it from the inside to let us through. Ahead I caught sight of well-kept flower beds, neat wooden chalets and a swimming pool with the bright sunlight sparkling on blue water.

'I didn't even know this place existed,' I said. 'The only thing is, I haven't brought my swimming shorts.'

'You won't need any,' Diana said jokingly. 'Look around you now. I presume you're not shy?'

She presumed correctly – which was just as well. In the pool and out of it, walking or reclining on loungers on the lawn, everybody was as naked as nature intended. The females, if anything, outnumbered the men but it was a working day and the ladies had house servants to do their chores. The whites were predominant but there were a sprinkling of Asian and African women. I got out of the car, noting with interest the different shapes – tits that thrust, nestled together, drooped and wobbled. Bottoms, too, came in a variety of sizes and contours: cheeky, chunky, pert and rounded, with prominent pubic mounds both bushy and shaved.

'I think I've died and gone to heaven,' I said. 'It beats the hell out of slaving in a factory, doesn't it? How come I've missed this joint?'

'The members have just been fortunate, I suppose,' Diana laughed. 'You're not supposed to stare, by the way.' She led me to a one-roomed chalet and began to undress, folding her clothes neatly on a chair. I stood rooted to the floor, holding my breath as each garment came off. Her smooth violin-shaped back was turned to me, her sizeable breasts swinging out under her arms as she bent to slip off her flimsy panties, allowing me to view her gorgeously curved rear. My instinct was to shuffle forward on my knees and pay tribute with hot kisses pressed to her bum.

She faced me, in turning making her breasts jiggle delightfully. The triangular patch of hair on her mound was a darker shade of the deep reddish chestnut of her hair. 'You haven't undressed,' she chided me, smiling. 'What's keeping you?'

'You really know how to hurt a guy, don't you?' I said. 'I'm not made of stone. Well, part of me feels like it is. Undressing now would be, you know, slightly embarrassing.'

'Never mind that,' Diana said, smiling as ever. 'It's quite normal here, the men get erections all the time. We females pretend to ignore it. Come on, get undressed, I'm dying for a swim.'

So I stripped, standing at last in front of her with a cockstand that refused to go down. She shook her curls at me, her eyes alight with merriment. 'It's what's known in medical terms as a dirty great hard-on,' I said, deciding to make light of it. 'It refuses to behave. You standing there looking so bloody gorgeous might have something to do with it.'

'A cold shower might help,' she suggested, leading me out reluctantly. 'It's communal, we use the showers before swimming.' In the sunlight I felt even more exposed, feeling interested eyes on my nudity. We walked to a long hut with a row of a dozen shower heads along a tiled wall. To my chagrin, the place was full of naked women and I was the only male present. Some women were showering, others stood chatting. My arrival made all turn in my direction while I had to wait for an unoccupied place under a spray. There were giggles and nudges. My dick seemed bigger than ever, inspired by the

In the Flesh

sight of over a dozen nude females ranging from sixteen to forty.

'Who's your friend, Diana?' one called out. 'Let me know when he's available.' There was general laughter. A young Asian woman with gold bangles on her wrists and ankles as her only apparel came closer. 'My goodness,' she said, laughing, 'he can't be white. What tribe is he?'

'You're embarrassing the poor chap,' Diana said. 'He *is* a big boy, isn't he? As for you, Surjit, keep your distance. Tyler is filling in for me while Harry is away.'

'I should be so lucky,' I announced, deciding it had gone far enough. 'You've had your fun, ladies, so behave. One of you make an empty space for me under a shower, please.'

'I'm next, share with me,' giggled the young Asian woman, pulling me into a vacated space and standing face to face with me as the water sprayed down. She was about twenty-two, I guessed, her skin a light coffee colour. Her breasts were full and rounded with remarkably thick nipples of dark purple. Below her flat tummy I saw a bulging mound thatched with the thickest, blackest hair I'd ever encountered on a quim. That she was of good caste and married, I noticed from the expensive engagement and wedding rings on the correct finger. Married very well too, I supposed, from the beauty of her classic Hindu features, she was just the sort of wife a rich Indian sought.

'Watch Surjit, she's after you,' the woman under the next shower head joked. 'You can always tell when her husband goes to India on a business trip. She comes to life, poor frustrated girl.'

'It's being in the company of you dissolute European women,' Surjit responded jocularly. She turned away from me, showing a long plaited pigtail of the same black hair and a lovely tight-cheeked arse. 'It's true.'

I was glad to dive into the pool, swimming beside Diana and admiring her arse cheeks breaking the surface, the way her breasts floated as she turned to do the backstroke. Later, lying beside her on the lawn under the shade of a large beach umbrella, the previous night's trip took its toll and I made up for lost sleep by dozing off. I awoke to find her gone and the afternoon passing. I was sorry I had missed her and guessed she had left for the Nairobi train.

I headed for the chalet to get dressed, deciding I would spend the evening dining at Chez Miklos and, hopefully, find a way to get Margaret out. Maybe Fatima would help me. It was with this thought in my mind that I entered the chalet to find the Asian girl, Surjit, sitting there naked.

'I'm sorry,' I said, surprised at her presence. 'I had no idea you used this place as well. My clothes are here.'

'There are not enough chalets or too many members,' she explained, her voice sounding undeniably pleased with herself. 'We share. But I have waited for you. Have you ever made sex with an Asian woman?'

'No,' I lied. If I was going to fuck her, being the first might please her. 'Are you suggesting we have sex?'

'Would you refuse?' she answered, giving me a sultry smile. 'It is safe to do it here, no one will come.' She stood and cupped her pointed tits in her hand, lifting them towards me. 'You indulge with wives, don't you? Mrs Saxon perhaps?'

'She was joking,' I said, my prick rising automatically at the offer Surjit made so openly. 'But I have been with other men's wives and I certainly wouldn't refuse a beauty like you.' Her right hand came out to hold my burgeoning dick, giving it tentative strokes. 'Are you in a hurry, may I ask?'

'No,' she said readily. 'My husband is in Bombay on business. I do not like to hurry. With him it is always

In the Flesh

hurry, if at all. He is old, more than sixty, but my parents considered it a good match with his wealth. I am young, I need to be satisfied.' She gave my prick a further squeeze, her little fist barely spanning its girth. 'When I saw this I made joke, but truly I want it.'

'Then it's what you'll get,' I promised, my hands gliding down the slope of her tits and turning over to cup the firm globes. I heard her sigh and congratulated myself on my luck. I explored the moist little slit between her thighs then fondled her bottom, giving it a little smack for luck. I carried her to a cane couch with ample cushions. Lying back, the girl stretched out one shapely leg and draped the other over the edge, her figlike cunt displayed to tempt me.

'I do not like hurry,' she repeated while I contemplated the naked charms spread before me.

'That makes two of us,' I said, pressing kisses to her leg from the knee up, my lips poised above the hair-covered mound, its lipless slit held open by her fingers to receive the tongue.

Chapter Seventeen

I like a challenge. Giving a frustrated young Asian wife what she craved was also a pleasure. This would have to be an Academy award job, I decided, as my mouth closed over her plump little quim and I inserted my tongue. I found her taste spicy, the inner walls of her cunt clam-tight despite the flow of excitement. Her clitty was surprisingly thick, just made for a roving tongue-tip to encircle it. Her moans and cries and the way her hips jerked against my face told me of her excitement. Too much too soon, I thought, my plan being to keep her on the brink until she begged for relief. I withdrew my titillating tongue and moved my body over her.

A long kiss stifled her squeak of protest at the abrupt withdrawal of my mouth. At once a sharply pointed tongue thrust into my mouth. I broke away to cup her soft swollen breasts, suckling hard on the purple nipples in turn. I drew curved flesh into my mouth, getting an almost savage growl of approval. The leg lying along the couch rose and wrapped itself tightly around my waist. Her cunt was placed directly on my hip, and she began thrusting it wantonly against the bone. Seeking nothing less than the orgasm she desperately needed, whichever way it could be achieved, she humped and bumped into my hip. Keen as I was myself to enter her, I contented myself with kissing her mouth and sucking her nipples, her agitation mounting as the intense rub-rubbing of her mound became frenzied.

Hot-cunted and determined, she howled in pleasure as the jerking of her loins indicated the strength of climax overtaking her body. She was still gasping and shuddering from the self-induced come as I grasped her ankles, hoisting her rounded arse against my belly. 'Stand,' she ordered hoarsely, shuffling forward on her back and directing my prick into her slit. 'Go on, stand up and fuck me. You can do it. Try it that way.'

I could only assume she'd been studying the *Kama Sutra* and was eager to attempt a certain position. Game for anything new, I found getting to my feet on loose cushions was not easy. Managing with the odd wobble, I lifted her with me, my cock still gripped in a vice-like cunt channel. With her knees clamped under my armpits, I looked down on her and saw only her head and shoulders resting on the couch, her cunt thrusting to take in the last inch of my cock, tits bouncing with the momentum. In mid-fuck she reached up and grasped my wrists, pulling herself forward like a contortionist until she was sitting on the impaling dick and leaning back from me with the whole length up her. Her legs curled around my waist as she gyrated her cunt, only her hold on my arms preventing her from falling backwards. Not only had she studied the *Kama Sutra*, but she was an expert practitioner, pulling herself upright and clasping her arms around my neck while she jogged urgently on the embedded bar of hard flesh within her.

She squealed as she came again, her wild up-and-down motions finally making me overbalance and sink to my knees while she continued to cling on and work her hips. Flat on my back among the cushions, she sat up over me, her tits flying as she employed a grinding movement to

In the Flesh

get the desired feel at her moment of orgasm. I found it impossible not to respond in kind, grasping the firm cheeks of her arse and firing long spurts of sperm into her clinging cunt.

As we lay prostrate and gasping from our exertions, Surjit gave a sudden yelp of surprise. She sat bolt upright over me and I saw a hand on her bare shoulder. There stood a grinning Miklos Dimitri and, standing beside him, Margaret Warren, both completely nude.

'Why, little Mrs Choudry,' he said. 'How nice to see you enjoying the amenities of the naturist club. I take it your husband is out of town on business? He's a good friend of mine, as you are aware.' The terrified girl scrambled off me, brushing past Miklos and Margaret to get to the sari she had left draped over a chair. 'You don't need to look so frightened and rush off, my dear,' he smiled. 'Young wives will play while older husbands are away, it's a fact of nature I fully understand. They get lonely.'

'Please, Mr Dimitri,' Surjit begged in abject fear. '*Please*, promise me you would never tell him?'

'Why should I?' Miklos said craftily. 'As I mentioned, you are lonely and we can't have that. One is liable to fall in with bad company,' he added, smirking at me. 'I shall give a private party for you tonight in my apartment above the restaurant. I'm sure you'll be there, won't you? Shall we say, eight o'clock?'

Surjit, now dressed in her blue sari, nodded miserably and left.

'Never miss a chance, do you, you bastard?' I said. 'How the hell did you know I was here?'

'I didn't,' he replied pleasantly. 'I'm a member. I brought Margaret along for an afternoon's sunning and swimming. We saw you come into this chalet and thought we'd say hello. What we saw was very interesting and enlightening.'

He turned to lead Margaret out. 'Pity you won't be present tonight.'

Left alone, I dressed and decided to drive home to Jovial and one of her excellent evening meals. I stopped at an Asian open-fronted shop to pick up a six-pack of the strong Carlsberg Special brew she liked, making use of the pay-phone there to tell her I was on my way and to start cooking. My hectic bout with Surjit had left me with an appetite. Over the telephone I ordered steak smothered with fried onions, mashed potatoes with gravy, mushrooms and peas.

'For two?' I heard Jovial snigger at the other end of the line. 'Bwana Tyler has a visitor, a lady.'

Why did she always assume any woman who visited came to be fucked? Probably because they were the only kind that did. 'Who is she?' I asked. 'Do you think she's there for the night?'

'I think very much,' I heard my housegirl giggle. 'She has brought a small case with her. She asked if there was a spare bedroom for her. It is the lady doctor who stays with Memsa'ab Saxon.'

When I got home I found Cynthia sitting in the best chair and Jovial busy at the table laying out the best of my cutlery on a tablecloth I didn't know I owned. In the centre was a bowl of mixed flowers, picked from the garden, and there were rolled-up napkins beside the dinner plates. A bottle of wine stood next to my seat and suitable wine glasses had been found. To complete the setting, Jovial had stuck a candle in the neck of a chianti bottle.

'Dinner is ready to be served,' the obliging housegirl said, accepting the six-pack I handed her and going off into the kitchen. I held Cynthia's seat out for her as she sat at the table, watching her flick the napkin over her lap as she took her place.

In the Flesh

'To what do I owe this honour, Cynthia?' I asked. 'Jovial tells me you've brought an overnight case.' I poured wine, grinning at her. 'Could it be my fatal attraction? More likely, I think it's because Diana is away for the night in Nairobi.'

'Thank goodness she is,' Cynthia said as if greatly relieved. 'This afternoon that awful Captain Suliman came to the house to find her and you can guess what he intended. We, the housegirl and I, saw him arrive and she told me to hide in the garden until he'd gone. He left saying he would be back. You were quite right saying Diana must leave Uganda. Meanwhile, I thought it safer to come here. Frankly, I was afraid of being in that house alone.'

'Then make yourself at home here,' I offered.

Later we sat on the verandah together and relaxed while Jovial served coffee and brandy. In front of us the enlarged tropic moon hung low over the placid lake, throwing a path of gold across the water. The flame trees and beds of exotic flowers scented the air. 'Peaceful, isn't it?' I found myself saying. 'This is the Africa that never lets you go. It gets under your skin like no other place.'

'Frankly it frightens me,' Cynthia admitted. 'I feel a constant air of menace present.' She drained her brandy and did not refuse to hold her glass out for more when I tipped up the bottle. 'I don't usually drink, at least not like this. Wine with a meal is my limit. Here it seems quite in order. I suppose you intend to get me drunk.'

'Why should I do that?' I asked. I saw her stifle a hiccup with the tips of her fingers. 'You're making a pretty good job of it yourself, doctor. It's been quite a day for you, has it?'

'I'm not accustomed to having to hide in a hedge from some predatory savage,' Cynthia stated in her defence. 'I know he came to ravage Diana but her housegirl warned me the brute would consider me fair game too.' She straightened herself in her chair, determined to be the old superior Cynthia, despite the effect of the alcohol. 'Just because I came to your home uninvited do not presume I'm here to sleep with you. I asked your girl to show me into the guest room.'

'Well, she showed you into my room,' I said. 'Jovial thought perhaps you were being coy. It's more comfortable in there. Don't worry, I'll be in the spare.'

'I'm sorry if I'm putting you out,' she said, not meaning a word. She lolled back in her chair, stretching her legs luxuriously, relaxed again now she had made the sleeping arrangements clear. 'I didn't want you to get the wrong idea. It must be the drink loosening my tongue but I'm not a man's woman. By that I mean I prefer my own sex.' She gave me a forced smile. 'It's nothing against you personally. Since my teen years I've recognised I have lesbian tendencies.'

'You could have fooled me,' I had to say. 'What about the times I've gone down on you? I didn't hear you complain.'

'I expected you to bring that up,' Cynthia censured me. 'I've done that with women in the past. I was curious to experience it with a man.'

'Purely in the interest of scientific research, of course,' I chided her. 'Come off it, doc, you're a borderline case. You're bi-sexual. You just won't own up to it.'

'No one ever calls me "doc",' she retorted. 'As for my sexual inclination, I think I'm a better judge of that than you.'

'I wonder,' I said, enjoying riling her. 'Have you never tried the real thing? Not just a tongue, I mean a dick.'

'I was a virgin,' Cynthia said. 'Sixteen and pure. What I experienced turned me from men and made other females

In the Flesh

far preferable as sexual partners. Do I need to elaborate?'

'I'm all ears if you want to,' I answered hopefully. 'Was that first time against your will? A forceful boyfriend, perhaps?'

'He was an adult, a family friend. His wife was present,' Cynthia recalled soberly. 'Neither was I forced. My parents went off for the weekend to a conference, leaving me in the care of their best friends who were medical researchers.'

'So they thought they'd do some research on a young girl, did they?' I said sympathetically. 'With friends like those, who needs enemies?'

'I was young, impressionable, wanting to be considered grown-up. The evening I arrived at their house they were throwing a party. The wife helped me to apply her own make-up to my face – lipstick, rouge and eyeshadow, which my parents didn't allow me to wear. I danced with the older men present and was fussed over by the women as a pretty young thing. I was given drink and considered myself very adult in such company.'

'The big build-up,' I said, commiserating. 'They were priming you. I can imagine how it would be for one so young and susceptible. You shouldn't feel guilty about that.'

'I don't,' Cynthia replied sharply. 'I was silly and merry, but I went along willingly. When the guests departed, my hosts both hugged and kissed me, saying there was no reason why the fun should end. The music was kept on, I was given a further glass of sherry, and the wife herself suggested we all took off our clothes and danced. I was unsure but I thought it would be naive of me to refuse.'

I could imagine the scene and how those pair of salacious lechers must have welcomed the teenage Cynthia falling into their clutches. 'So you did as they suggested?' I asked.

'I was still uncertain – shyness, I assumed. My parents no longer came into my room when I was dressing or when I took a bath. My breasts were quite grown, almost like they are now, and I had pubic hair. I felt very embarrassed about them seeing me nude but they proceeded to undress. It was a shock, seeing the woman's large breasts and such a mass of hair between her thighs. I hardly dared look at the man. He and his wife were frequent visitors to our house. I had known him for years. Then there he was with nothing on and that was my first sight of a penis. It was standing up and his balls seemed so huge. But I felt aroused too. They encouraged me to strip and the wife helped me, touching my skin and stroking my breasts, saying how pretty I was. They both danced with me. The woman pressed her breasts into mine and kissed me on the mouth. When her husband danced with me, I felt his hard penis rubbing against my stomach. It scared me but excited me too. Then the wife suggested we should continue upstairs and said I could spend the night with them in their room. Sleep with them in their bed.'

'Only there wouldn't be much sleeping done,' I said. 'They really threw you into the deep end, Cynthia.' I saw her regarding me shrewdly through her large horn spectacles, gauging my reaction. I put on my most sympathetic voice. 'No doubt he went at you like a bull at a gate. Hardly the initiation calculated to make a young virgin eager for a repeat performance. A damn shame he put you off men, you're such an attractive woman.'

'Perhaps,' Cynthia said, 'but that night I also learned how sex with a woman could be gentle and so sweet. Every bit as arousing and satisfying as with any man. In their bedroom I was placed between them on the bed. Both kissed and fondled me, getting me excited. Then he got on top of me and just thrust into me, unable to contain himself. I

In the Flesh

screamed, the pain was quite excrutiating, and I tried to throw him off. You are right, it was not an initiation a young virgin envisaged or ever wanted to experience again.'

'Was that your one and only time with him?'

'Or anyone else of the male gender,' Cynthia stated flatly. 'His wife ordered him out of the room and comforted me. I was crying and she held me and nursed me with her breasts. I found that pleasurable, also her tender fondling. Her kisses were nice too, and when she touched my breasts and sucked them I wanted her to do more things to me. Then she inserted her fingers into my vagina and when I responded to that, well, she completely surprised me by moving down to kiss me there. I had never imagined such a thing but found it very exciting. I suppose the way I responded encouraged her to go on. She used her tongue then and brought me to an unbelievable orgasm. So you can see why I turned to my own sex for satisfaction.'

'I can,' I agreed. 'That time with the wife wasn't the only time, was it?'

'I don't see why I should unburden myself to you,' Cynthia said, rising from her chair, 'but it wasn't, of course. We met secretly over the next two years without my parents ever knowing. I went up to Oxford later and found a lesbian lover. There have been others. Don't feel sorry for me, I haven't missed a thing.'

'You could have the best of both worlds,' I said hopefully, sure that recalling the eventful night had aroused her. It had certainly aroused me. 'Not all men go at it like your first.'

'You, for instance?' she smiled. 'No thank you. But if you want to perform cunnilingus on me before I retire, it would help me sleep.'

'I've heard it phrased less clinically,' I said, grinning. 'Better than a sleeping pill too. I'll look in on you later.'

I took a shower, deliberately using the time to keep her waiting, hoping it would increase her arousal. I determined to try for more and, donning my dressing gown, tapped on her door. She was on my bed in a silk robe, reading a book. Without a word she parted the lower half of the robe and raised her knees, displaying her pouting cunt. I shucked off the dressing gown and stood nude before her. I saw the surprise in her eyes.

'Is that really necessary?' she frowned.

'Very,' I said assertively. 'And if you take off that robe it will add greatly to the pleasure. Yours as well as mine.'

I was sure that, until then, she'd never considered my pleasure, unless she thought being allowed to lick her cunt was enough for me. She adjusted her spectacles, looking me over, my body firm and my prick even firmer. It reared like a pole. The circumcised head seemed to glow a reddish pink, a plum-sized knob on a bigger-than-average stalk. To my delight, Cynthia agreed to humour me and drew off her robe to reveal her sharply pointed tits and shapely thighs. She lay back on the bed in her usual posture to receive my tongue but I was set to seduce.

I bent over her, kissing her breasts while she watched me without comment. I cupped them, squeezed them, giving a good suck to each nipple, noting how tightly erect they became. Drawing back, I put my face between the widely parted thighs. For the first time I fingered the swollen outer lips, then touched up inside a very moist and warm channel. She stifled a gasp, her hand reaching out to stop me and withdrawing when I smacked her wrist. Then she shuddered as I went for the taut nub of her clitoris and strummed it with a fingertip.

'Lick me,' she urged. 'Lick out my cunt.' It was the first time she had ever spoken or used a crude term in our sessions.

In the Flesh

'You love your quim being licked, don't you, Cynthia?' I challenged her. 'Go on and say it, admit it. You want my tongue up you.' I inserted all of it, my nose deep in pubic hair on a cushiony mound, flicking at the sensitive clitty. She writhed her arse on the bed as I probed deeply, her voice strained and hoarse as she answered.

'You know bloody well I do. Get on with it. Give it to me – lick me clean.'

I fully intended to give it to her – and more than a tongue. When I'd brought her to a state of high arousal, I drew away, ignoring her cry of protest. I raised myself and aligned an impatient iron-hard prick on the pouting cleft of her sweet pussy. My entire length slipped in as smoothly as one could wish. With a minimum of guidance from me, it went tight to the hilt in a receptive cunt that throbbed and clasped naturally around the stout intruder.

'Oh, aaagh, NO!' Cynthia yelled but continued the pelvic jerks that my tongue had brought on. A split-second later she crossed her ankles hard about my waist, her hands gripping and hauling on my arse cheeks to draw me into her. As I thrust there was no mistaking her agitation as she made violent fucking motions beneath me. My balls slapped against her raised bottom as I pistoned away. Her cunt was a perfect receptacle to fuck. Used to tongues and vibrators, no doubt, it felt narrow and tight, but eager to respond and lubricating freely.

Her buffeting against me increased my urge to let go, determined as I was to give her a fuck to remember. I shifted my angle of penetration to touch other sensitive parts of her pussy, withdrew to the knob to have her rearing up to me and thrust in to her lustily, making her back arch. My palms cupped her pert bum cheeks, the middle finger of my right hand insinuating into her arsehole to the second knuckle, producing a squeal and even more frenzied thrusting. She climaxed with helpless heaves and contractions, crying out, 'Oh Lord, what's happening? My God, I'm coming! You – you've made me *come*!'

I too had been unable to hold out, shooting a full load up her. As we lay recovering, I cuddled into her side, her body hot. My hand cupped a smooth firm tit, the hard nipple impressed in my palm. She lay unmoving, her breathing becoming steadier.

'You *fucked* me, you dirty devil,' she said at last. 'I suppose with you it was inevitable.' I nodded, kissing her shoulder, asking if she had found it as good as with any woman? 'Don't be stupid, you were there too,' she replied coolly. 'Do you want me to say the earth moved? Of course it was good. Maybe we should have done it before.'

I gave her a kiss of appreciation and it was returned passionately, her open mouth and tongue responding to mine. We were set for the night, I considered, when my housegirl entered the room.

'There is a visitor, sir,' Jovial informed me, quite unfazed by the sight of us lying naked on the bed. I saw her looking down at Cynthia with interest, wishing no doubt to take my place. 'He is an African man, but not Ugandan. He says he must see you.'

I went to the verandah and recognised Mkubwa, the outsized Nubian employed by Miklos. He was the last person I expected to see. 'You must come with me to Kampala at once, bwana,' he said. 'I have been sent by Fatima. Tonight it will be safe to escape Mrs Warren away from there. I came here by taxi. Will you drive me back?'

'I guess I'd better,' I said grudgingly, thinking of Cynthia in my bed no doubt willing to enlarge her experience of the male sex. 'Miklos is your boss,' I questioned him. 'How come you're willing to help out?'

In the Flesh

'Mrs Warren is too much a lady to be with *him*,' Mkubwa said. 'She must go back to her husband and family.' I turned to get dressed. Cynthia and Jovial were anxious to find out what was up.

'I've been called to Kampala,' I explained, all of them following as I went into the spare room where I'd left my clothes. 'I can't get out of it, and I don't know how long I'll be.'

'Does that mean I'll be here in this house by myself?' Cynthia asked anxiously. 'I find it rather terrifying being alone in Africa.'

'Jovial will stay with you, won't you, Jove?' I asked, sure by the way she nodded that she would welcome the chance. 'If you find it frightening, let her sleep with you. For company,' I added. 'Jove's a kind girl, she won't mind.'

As I drove out of Entebbe, taking the Kampala road at speed, I wondered how Cynthia and Jovial would get on as bed partners. It was naughty of me to set it up, I supposed, but the idea intrigued me. No doubt Jovial would delight in giving me a full account later.

'Have you heard the news?' Mkubwa said, breaking into my reverie. 'President Obote leaves Uganda tomorrow for the Commonwealth Conference in Singapore. Once he is out of the country, General Amin will start a coup and make himself President. There will be fighting. Do not go near the airport. Stay in your house with your women.'

Sound advice, I decided, then remembered Diana Saxon would be driving back alone in a truck and fair game for the trigger-happy soldiers she was bound to meet on her return.

Chapter Eighteen

We arrived at the rear of Chez Miklos in total darkness and Mkubwa guided me up the narrow stairway. Fatima was waiting in the passageway outside Miklos's office. She was stark-naked, her big tits wobbling like jellies as she gripped my hand and shook it. She put a finger to her lips to show we should speak quietly.

'What gives, Fatima?' I asked in a whisper. 'Is Margaret ready? Where is she?' It was evident that I was eager to be on my way but she shook her head.

'You must wait,' she said. 'Miklos is here and we must make sure he can't stop you.'

'How do you intend to do that?' I wanted to know, recalling the two large waiters he'd called upon to throw me into the street.

'We will make sure he doesn't leave his bedroom,' Fatima assured me. She held up three fingers, grinning. 'He will have three women to amuse himself with tonight: Margaret, myself and a young Asian girl I think he must have blackmailed into being here. I know she is the wife of a Mr Choudry. They are with Miklos now. I left them there, saying I would get more champagne. When I return the three of us will be too much for him. Margaret will slip away and Mkubwa will lead you through the yard to your car. He will unlock the gate and then relock it. Mikos will just think Margaret walked out of the restaurant unnoticed.'

'If that's the best you can do, I'll go along with it,' I said. 'At least Mkubwa is on our side. I'd hate to tangle with him.'

'He has come to like Mrs Warren very much,' Fatima smiled slyly. 'And she like him. She goes to his bed at night to sleep with him.'

'Lucky old Mkubwa,' I acknowledged.

'Lucky for her too,' Fatima said meaningfully. The man in question returned to us carrying champagne in an ice-bucket which he handed to the buxom Turkish woman. She led me into her husband's office, the room where I'd sat watching Margaret tied up next door with a dildo up her arse. Fatima went into the mirrored room closing the door firmly behind her.

I was impatient to be gone. I sat and listened to the shrieks and cries from beyond the door, the sound of running feet and Miklos's cruel laugh. Imagining the high old time he was having in there, chasing three naked females about, I put my ear to the door. There were yelps, protests, pleas, made doubtless as he pursued the trio wielding his riding crop.

Still with an ear to the door, I heard the bumping of a bed in use, low moans from a female throat and the harsher grunts of Miklos expressing his lustful pleasure. Little Mrs Choudry was being fucked, I concluded, a fact confirmed a few moments later when Fatima came out of the bedroom.

In the brief moment of her opening and closing the door, I caught a glimpse of the young Asian girl prone across the wide bed with Miklos thrusting into her. Each lunge between her parted brown thighs jolted the breath from her body. Miklos fucked like a wild man, his tanned body glistening with the sweat of his exertion. As the door shut behind her, Fatima made a contemptuous gesture.

In the Flesh

'My husband is trying to prove what a man he is, fucking that young girl,' she said scornfully. 'He has had her twice already, determined to make her come. Each time Margaret and I have had to make him erect for her again, using our mouths. He is drinking too, and will soon be useless, unable to stop Margaret leaving. Wait and see for yourself.' She put her arms around my neck, pressing her nude body to me, her huge breasts soft against my chest. 'There is time for you to fuck me. I have been told to fetch more champagne.'

Her hand went between our bodies, grasping my dick and finding it stiff. 'Fuck me,' she urged. 'Make me come like you did before.' Sensing my apprehension she lolled back across the desk, pulling me over her and raising her knees. 'Miklos will not leave the bedroom,' she assured me. 'He has not made the Asian girl come and his pride will not let him stop until he has. Mrs Choudry is too stupid to bring it to an end – she could easily pretend she has had many orgasms.'

'At least it's wearing him out,' I conceded, tempted by the cunt on offer. 'It's hardly the time and the place but if you insist . . .'

As I penetrated her she gasped with relief and heaved her arse off the desk to get every inch. As ever, she was a magnificent fuck, her cunt muscles flexing and relaxing as I shagged her. We were both in the throes as Mkubwa appeared with a another ice bucket and more champagne. He placed it on the desk beside us, turning away wordlessly as I shot my load and Fatima spasmed in climax. Then she took the champagne and returned next door.

Again I was left to wait, putting my ear to the door to try and gauge the proceedings. Then came ribald cries and whoops and the sound of running feet, making me think Miklos had the women in full flight until I realised it was female voices that were raised. A moment later the door opened and Fatima signalled to me to look in. I saw Miklos being held face down on the bed with Margaret and Surjit Choudry sitting on his back and legs. It seemed obvious from his token struggling and feigned protests that he was enjoying the change, for once he was allowing the women to have their way. As Fatima trussed his wrists and ankles to the four corners of the bed, Margaret and Surjit danced around in delight.

It made quite a sight, the three naked women with their breasts bobbing, celebrating the taming of the beast. I caught Margaret's eye, making it plain by an urgent signal that I considered it time to leave. She shook her head, opening the bedside cabinet to bring out the ebony dildo and bottle of oil I'd seen Miklos use to torment her. Fatima handed the riding crop to Surjit. Intent on repaying him for recent indignities, the Asian girl cracked the crop across his bare arse time and time again with all her power. Miklos yelled loudly in anger and pain, ordering them to untie him.

His thrashed rear was not escaping so lightly, I saw. Margaret stepped up to trickle the oil between the cleft of his cheeks while he hollered in outrage. Big ebony dildo in hand, with one thrust Margaret worked it up his arsehole while his holler turned to a loud shriek of pain. Leaving it buried halfway in him, she turned and walked out of the room to join me, excited by her daring. Fatima followed with Margaret's clothes, urging her to dress quickly and go. I was in full agreement as I saw Miklos going berserk as he struggled to free himself.

Hardly waiting for Margaret to finish dressing, I led her down the back stairs where Mkubwa was waiting. 'Thank you for helping me get away from him,' she said, kissing Mkubwa ardently and so extensively that I plucked at her arm to break it up. 'I'll never forget you, dearest,' she told him warmly.

In the Flesh

'He's been so kind to me, Fatima too, risking so much to let me escape,' she said as I drove off into the night. There was no mention of the part I was playing. Thanks a bunch, Margaret, I stopped myself from saying, only too pleased we were on our way. 'I will have to face my husband now,' she added, as if considering that small matter for the first time. She gave a little giggle, which I put down to the champagne Miklos had so liberally supplied. 'Whatever am I going to tell him?'

'Whatever you think he'd like to hear,' I replied, recalling Arthur had appeared to enjoy discussing Margaret's previous infidelity. I was heading the car in the direction of Mulago Hospital, intending to rescue him while I was at it. 'We are going to get him now, so think fast. He's fit again and Miklos won't fork up for that private room with you out of his hands. The sooner the pair of you are together again and safe in Chloe's house in Entebbe the better.'

My words were cut short by a burst of rifle fire. The shots rang out over the sound of the car's engine, followed by the rapid burst of an automatic rifle. People began running in panic past the car as if fleeing from danger. I drew up, cursing my luck. 'What's going on?' Margaret asked cheerfully, still buoyed up by her adventure. 'What is it, Ty?'

'All I bloody need,' I swore unhappily. 'I'd say we're caught in the middle of a coup, the attempt by northern sections of the army to overthrow Obote's government. Right now you'd be safer with Miklos. It looks like General Amin's fling at making himself President is under way. The first thing we've got to do is get off the main road.'

I pulled away, drawing up in a deserted back alley filled with African shops now shuttered, bolted and barred. Inside them, no doubt, the inmates would be cowering, praying the firing would not come any closer. I switched off the car lights, sitting back to ponder my next move, uneasy in the extreme and annoyed to hear Margaret giggle.

'I'd have thought this latest spot of bother would have sobered you up,' I said sourly. 'Rampaging troops out here think it fair game to shoot up anything and anybody they catch outside. What do you find so bloody funny?'

'I was thinking of all that's happened to me since I came to Uganda. No one back home in Harrowgate would believe me,' she laughed blithely. 'Would they?'

'I just hope you live to tell the tale,' I said grimly. 'You have no idea of the seriousness of our situation.'

'Well, if I must die tonight,' Margaret answered, chuckling as she slipped an arm into mine and cuddled up against me, 'who's to say it wasn't all worth it? Believe me, the kind of life I led before wasn't worth living. Nothing ever happened.'

'Nothing?' I queried. 'That's not what I was given to understand when I visited Arthur in hospital. You've been holding out on me, Margaret, making out your only sexual relief was self-help and lurid fantasies, and I was the one to start you off.'

Her answer was to laugh lightly and reach for my crotch, unzipping me and delving in to grasp my prick. 'If I've got to end it all, I want to go out with a big one of these in my hand,' she announced lewdly. 'Or better still with it inside me.' She gave my responding stalk long slow strokes, her breasts pressed to my side as she leaned into me. 'What did my husband tell you? I've always had the feeling he got a thrill out of my having an affair.'

'You could be right,' I agreed, lolling back in my seat and letting her rub me up. When she took her hand away it was to pull off her knickers and lift her dress. The sounds of rapid firing seemed further off and I consoled

In the Flesh

myself that a back alley was hardly a strategic point to capture, unlike television and radio stations and government buildings, always prime targets in any coup. It made me feel inclined to let Margaret have her wicked way, the more so as she leaned over to give the tip of my upstanding dick kisses and sucks with her warm wet mouth. Her head lifted, a wanton look on her face in the dim light, her eyes questioning.

'You haven't said what my Arthur told you,' she demanded, hitching her dress higher and lifting her right leg across my lap. She took my hand and placed it on her cunt, jiggling it against my fingers. 'It could only have been about young Robbie.'

'He didn't mention a name,' I recalled, making her squirm as I felt up her hot and very moist cleft. 'Only that he'd been a steady boyfriend of your daughter Chloe. Am I right?'

'My toy-boy,' she giggled. 'It *was* wicked of me, wasn't it? But I was a very unhappy woman. Desperate, I suppose, like I am now.' She fell back across her seat next to me, her left foot on the floor and her right thigh shifting about to align her cunt over my prick. I helped by lifting the nearside cheek of her bottom until it rested on my right thigh. In that position, half on and half off me, she was able to guide my prick inside her. She gave a low groan of relief, putting her right arm around my neck to steady herself, working her arse slowly to savour the pleasure of being stuffed and in no hurry to want more for the present. 'I want to come, but not now,' she said, leaving it to soak. 'It's too nice a feeling. Did my husband go into details about Robbie and I?'

'He might well have,' I told her, my arm across her holding her left tit, 'but we were interrupted by a doctor. So I'll never know, will I?'

'If we're going to die,' she chuckled mischievously, 'I might as well admit it to you. Young Robert *was* my daughter's boyfriend, but I always thought he had a fancy for me too. I remember one summer afternoon I was in my bikini in the garden and I saw the way he looked at me. He was extremely handsome, well-built and in his school's rugger side. But he was Chloe's boyfriend and just seventeen, so of course I did nothing to encourage him.'

'Of course not,' I teased her. 'As if you would.'

'I didn't!' she professed, jerking her crotch into me. 'Well, maybe not until Chloe had left home to become a nurse. Robbie continued to come round, usually when Arthur was working late. One day he held me and kissed me, right out of the blue. For a moment or two I responded, kissing him back. Then I told him to leave. He went, but I can tell you he left me a shaken woman, terribly aroused and wishing I had let him continue.'

'It can happen,' I said to show I was on her side. I got a long kiss of appreciation for my understanding, plus a jiggle of her hips to shunt my prick inside her. 'A young boy with a crush on you, and Arthur not up to keeping you satisfied, what else could anyone expect? I suppose after that first kiss you couldn't wait to see him again?'

'I went round in a daze,' she said, laughing at the memory. 'I wanted to see him and yet was afraid to. Of course we did meet, and I felt my stomach melt. It's a wonderful feeling, isn't it? It was quite by accident, I was leaving a local hotel after a charity event when I met him with his parents. It was dark and quite late. They suggested he walk me home.'

'It was fate,' I acknowledged. 'You were thrown together.'

'Just like that,' she agreed. 'For a while we walked and nothing was said. I had butterflies churning my stomach.

In the Flesh

Perhaps I shouldn't have, but I linked my arm in his, then he put an arm around me and gave me a hug. We were passing a park, no one was around. We kissed.'

'And you didn't stop him that time,' I said.

'I couldn't. We kissed and kissed and I felt like a teenager again. All fluttery inside and mad for him,' she admitted. 'He blurted out that he loved me and I found myself telling him I loved him too and all the time there was passionate kissing going on. I remember thinking, my God, what *am* I doing, pressed up against the railings of a park at my age and out in the open? I'm old enough to be his mother! What if someone comes along? But the wild kissing continued between us, our tongues touching, with me more aroused and excited than I'd ever known.' She pressed against me, her hips moving to get the feel of the prick up her cunt. 'You'd better give it to me now,' she said. 'I'm ready. Fuck me and make me come.'

'In good time,' I promised. 'I want to hear more. Did young Robbie fuck you then? Against the park railings?'

'I think I would have let him,' Margaret laughed shortly at the memory. 'Good job he didn't try. As it was, I could feel his erection against me, hard as iron. He began to push it against me, moving it up and down directly on my mound, and I found myself thrusting back to him. I could hardly believe it, he was making me come so strongly that I climaxed like never before. We were hugging, kissing, gasping and thrusting and I knew he was coming against me too. When we had recovered I told him he must never mention what had happened to a living soul. He swore he wouldn't and I said it should never have happened. I was still trembling when I got home, going into the bathroom to tidy myself up and compose myself before making Arthur's supper. I couldn't stop thinking about it, and was still aroused when we went to bed. I made an advance, but Arthur said he was too tired, he wanted to sleep.'

'He really deserves an unfaithful wife,' I laughed. 'Maybe he'd have been more responsive if you'd told him you'd been canoodling with young Robbie. It didn't end there, did it?'

'Robbie called round the next afternoon,' she said simply. 'As soon as I let him in and shut the door, he took me in his arms. The first kiss set me off again. We went through to the lounge and hugged and kissed on the couch. If it had to be, it had to be, I decided, my feelings and his were too strong to be denied. I drew away and went upstairs to my bedroom, feeling eternally damned but with a desperate desire that he see me naked. I *wanted* so *badly* to show myself off to him that I stripped off, then I called him to join me upstairs. He came into the bedroom and looked at me with wonder, saying I was beautiful. His eyes were all over me. I could see myself in the wardrobe mirror, my breasts thrusting out and looking so big and my nipples too were stiff. I suddenly felt shy, seeing all the hair I've got below, but thrilled that he was seeing all of me.'

'Lucky lad,' I said, wondering how much longer I could hold out before starting to fuck. Her own motions were increasing and not helping my resolve. 'Tell me more.'

'All I could think of was that since I was undressed, so he should be,' Margaret said. 'When I suggested it he got out of his clothes and came to me. We lay on the bed and kissed while he played with my breasts. I asked if he liked them. He said he had always wanted to see them and had often imagined sucking on my nipples. While he was sucking them I took hold of his penis for the first time. It was so hard and clean-looking, as unblemished as if it were new. I asked if he was a virgin, wondering if he and my daughter had ever done it. Isn't it shameful – the lewd

In the Flesh

thoughts that come to mind when aroused? I actually hoped they had, because it made me excited.'

I believed her, the brain being a very potent sexual organ. 'And did he say you were his first?' I asked, our voices now strained and our hips working as if by mutual consent. It was not the most comfortable position but, together in our lust, we managed well, my prick going deep as she matched my heaves. 'Was he a virgin?'

'He didn't answer,' Margaret grunted, intent on reaching her climax. 'The naughty boy was too busy sucking my nipples. Then he was on me, between my legs, fucking me! He had done it before, the way he made me come. Oh Lord, I'm *coming* now! Shove it up, give it to me – y-e-s-s, *aaagh*!'

With her pubic bone hard against mine, the pair of us came together, kissing madly until she fell away from me. Only then did I notice a patrol of soldiers advancing cautiously towards the car. I sat up and gave Margaret a good shake. Surrounded on both sides, I wound down the window and a youngish officer looked in, his pistol pointed at my head. I raised my hands, noting that Margaret was sensibly doing the same. From the darker Nilotic features of the officer I knew we were in the hands of Amin's men. In good English I was asked to explain who we were and what were we doing there.

'We are doctors,' I said, an inspired reply, I felt. 'We were on our way to Mulago Hospital when we drew in here because of the shooting. No doubt our services will be needed tonight. Is it safe to proceed?' With relief on my part I saw the pistol lowered. 'Can you tell us what is going on, sir?' I added, as if I didn't know. 'Why is there fighting?'

'On behalf of the people of Uganda,' the youthful lieutenant said solemnly as if rehearsed, 'the army under the direction of Field Marshal Idi Amin is overthrowing the corrupt government of Milton Obote. We are seizing power even now in every district of the country.'

'Not before time,' I dared to say, offering my hand. It was taken and he shook it warmly. Chancing my luck even further, I said, 'I know the Field Marshal personally. He is to be congratulated. Perhaps now we can go on our way. There'll be work for us, I'm sure.'

'One of my jeeps will escort you to ensure your safe passage,' he said and, a few minutes later, we were on the road again, following a vehicle packed with armed men. 'Did I or did I not handle that well?' I said proudly to Margaret, both of us laughing in relief. 'All we have to do is collect your husband. What do you intend to tell him about your recent activities?' Before us the large white hospital loomed in sight. 'Would he settle for the truth?' I asked.

'An edited version, perhaps,' Margaret said jauntily. I had to conclude she cared neither one way or the other. She was now a changed woman. Arthur would have to shape up if she was to remain his wife. As if reading my thoughts, she added, 'He's lucky to have me.'

'Just about everyone else has,' I reminded her cheerfully. 'No regrets, I hope?'

'Only for the wasted years,' she said seriously. 'Now watch the way I intend to act with Arthur. I've got a feeling he's going to love it.'

Chapter Nineteen

Whatever Margaret intended, once she was reunited with her husband she played the contrite little wife, ashamed to admit her fall from grace. I had no doubt she knew exactly what she was doing. On going into Arthur's hospital room she had rushed into his arms. Now she sat beside him in the back of my car, holding his hand as if fearful of letting him leave her again. After we had passed through a roadblock on the outskirts of Kampala, the way ahead seemed quiet as I drove through the night towards Entebbe. I was all ears as the husband and wife pair began to clear the air.

'Who the devil was that Miklos fellow?' Arthur wanted to know. 'Why should he pay to keep me in hospital? What was he to you and how did you get to know him?'

'It's not all my fault, dear,' I heard Margaret say plaintively. 'Chloe was away and you were in hospital. I was all alone in a strange country. He offered to help when we met at the hospital. Like me, he was visiting a patient. He was very kind and I suppose I poured out my troubles to him.' *Devious bitch*, I thought as she continued. 'Do remember I was on my own and feeling vulnerable. How would I know the type of man he'd turn out to be?'

'You mean you found out and still stayed with him?' I heard Arthur say sorrowfully. 'I can't believe this. No one forced you.'

'It wasn't like that,' Margaret pleaded, earning my

admiration for her acting ability. 'He said you wouldn't get the best medical treatment without his help. I did it for your sake.'

'Did it? did *it*?' Arthur picked on the word bitterly. 'From that I can only think you – you – slept with him. Just like with young Robert, you couldn't resist that big Greek stud!'

'No, honestly—' Margaret sobbed.

'Yes, honestly,' Arthur insisted, excitement in his voice. 'That Greek fucked you! You were living with him!'

'Only to be near you, dear,' Margaret explained pitifully.

'But he fucked you!' her husband persisted, unable to contain his mounting arousal at the thought. 'Admit it, because it's obvious he did!'

And because you want to think he did, I thought as Margaret stifled her sobs. 'Y-yes, he did,' she confessed sorrowfully. 'He did what you said – f-fucked me. That first night he took me to his apartment.'

'Oh, God!' Arthur moaned lamentably. A glance in the rear mirror above the driving wheel showed him burying his face in his hands. Margaret huddled against him consolingly, catching my eye in the mirror and winking. 'How could you, my dearest?' he begged. 'How could you?'

'He *made* me,' Margaret offered. 'He just took me.' They huddled together in their supposed misery, making me almost want to applaud. 'I had no choice.'

'And after that?' Arthur asked fearfully. 'Are you going to tell me that was the only time?'

'No,' Margaret whispered as if the truth was too awful to say aloud. 'There were other times. Many of them. Whenever he wanted.'

'This gets worse,' Arthur wailed. 'Did – did he ever make – make you *come*? I couldn't bear that.'

In the Flesh

'Yes, he did, time and time again,' Margaret revealed as if to her great shame. 'I suppose he was a very experienced man – at that – at satisfying a woman. I tried not to, truly I did.'

'Don't upset yourself, my dear,' Arthur commiserated, hugging her. 'You couldn't help it if he forced you.'

'But not always,' Margaret whined. 'He – he – made me want him, made me hope he would take me. I should have hated every moment he was having me, dear, but I didn't. Please forgive me.'

'Of course I do,' Arthur assured her. 'Was that all that dirty beast did to you? I mean, fuck you and make you come?'

'If he didn't think I was willing, he put me over his knee and spanked me. He beat me with his hand or a riding crop until I gave in. He said he liked my bare bottom. Sometimes he'd kiss me there and then want to do more. Don't make me tell you,' implored the cunning bitch.

'You must,' Arthur insisted grimly. 'It's not what I think, I hope.'

'He was such a beast. He put his big hard penis in my back passage and did it to me there,' Margaret confessed. 'Miklos fucked my bumhole. I didn't think it possible, but he did. Often.' A glance in the rear mirror showed her cuddling him. 'There, there, my love,' I heard her mutter, 'I'm all right, truly. Why, Arthur, you have an erection! Goodness! It feels so big and hard!'

And not to be wasted, I noted, seeing Margaret lower Arthur along the back seat and hearing the ensuing grunts and moans of them fucking as I kept my eye on the dark road ahead. It was over before Margaret had time to get into her stride. The excited Arthur was obviously unable to contain himself after his wife's revelations. He would have to do better than that to keep Margaret from straying in future.

As they sat up from along the back seat I announced I was taking them home with me. 'There's safety in numbers,' I explained. 'There'll be fighting and looting until things settle down. It's better we all stick together. You can bunk up at my place.' The pun was unintentional.

Even driving on side roads, I still had to negotiate checkpoints manned by Amin's soldiers. As I at last drew into my driveway, bursts of heavy firing came from the direction of Entebbe airport. Inside the house I found my poor lounge crowded with others who believed in sticking together for safety. Besides Cynthia and Jovial, there was Desdemona Crane and Chloe Warren, newly arrived from Germany without her fiancé. She ran to greet her parents, saying she'd returned early because she'd been worried about them. When the shooting had started she'd come to my place for company. Looking around, it struck me that I'd screwed every female in the room.

Sleeping arrangements had to be made, if sleep were possible, and I volunteered to take the cane settee. When the lights were out, trying to get settled, I heard footsteps padding towards me. Chloe was kneeling beside me, her hand reaching for my crotch. 'I missed this while I was away,' she giggled softly. 'I bet you were giving it to my mother while dad was in hospital.' The familiar hand began stroking me. 'It's my turn now. I'm going to sit on it.'

The randy creature was throwing a leg across my middle, preparing to impale herself on the erection she'd created when her mother came into the room. In the deathly silence that followed I was saved by the bell, the shrill ring of the telephone startlingly loud in the night. I pushed Chloe aside to get to the phone, its ring summoning all the others in various stages of undress. They waited expectantly as I picked up the receiver. It was my boss, Bill Dove, calling from the Lake Airways office as fighting raged around him.

In the Flesh

'You want the good news or the bad news?' Bill asked. I asked for the good, imagining him crouched down behind the counter to evade any stray bullets. 'Everything's happened here,' he said. 'The day started with notification from the Bank of Uganda that the necessary down-payment in dollars has been forwarded to the Bell helicopter company in Texas. Lake Airways now own a Jet Ranger chopper and part of the package deal is that they train a pilot to fly it before delivery. The job's yours if you want it, Tyler. It means several months in the States at Fort Worth getting your licence to fly helicopters. If this country ever gets back to normal and tourists return, a chopper will be just the job for safari parties. Do you fancy a trip to America?'

'Try and stop me,' I said, welcoming the thought and thinking ahead about my chances with the females of Fort Worth. 'Before I get too excited about it,' I added, returning to the present, 'better hit me with the bad news. Can it wait?'

'No,' Bill said. 'It concerns your friend Mrs Saxon. You know she was bringing a truckload of Red Cross aid back from Kenya? I have news of her.'

'Which is?' I asked, fearing the worst.

'She's holed up on a side road north of Kajansi,' Bill said. 'The fighting was starting as she got there last evening on her way back. It got hectic evidently, a real battle, so she sensibly parked just off the main road. She's still there.'

'How do you know all this?' I said.

'A radio message on our frequency from a priest at the Kusubi mission,' he explained. 'He'd met her on the road and begged her to go with him for her safety. She wouldn't, saying if she left the truck it would be looted. As if she could stop rampaging troops helping themselves to her goodies. And I do mean *her* goodies as well as what's in the truck.'

'She's in trouble,' I agreed, shaking my head at the prospect of driving back into the night with an uprising in full swing. Nevertheless, I could hardly abandon Diana to her fate.

I took the main, direct road towards Kajansi, my fingers crossed as I drove at full speed. On both sides of the road flames leapt from burning villages and shots rang out as shadowy figures dodged in and out of the bush. At Kajansi I had to halt at the usual roadblock of chairs and tables and was at once surrounded by grinning troops. I was almost glad to see the big sergeant I had met before. He recognised me too, showing his elation at the night's events by offering his big black hand.

'Good evening, Sergeant,' was all I could find to say, taking his mitt and shaking it.

'Colonel now,' he informed me proudly. 'Tomorrow Uganda will have a new President, His Excellency Field Marshal Idi Amin Dada.'

'You've all done well,' I had to agree. 'What news of Captain Suliman? Is he now a general?'

The new colonel laughed heartily, pointing to one of the tables on which several severed heads were neatly displayed. 'He is one of those,' he said cheerfully. 'Always he was too ambitious. One day he would want to be President himself perhaps. He had to go.'

I couldn't say I was sorry as I was permitted to drive on. Many heads would roll as the new regime decided who was friend or foe. A mile or so up the road my headlights picked out the opening of a dirt track on my right. I drove in hopefully, relieved to see a large covered lorry parked there. From behind it I saw Diana Saxon emerge in a safari suit, a scarf tied about her head, holding a rifle at the ready.

'Whoa, hold it, it's me,' I shouted, getting out of my car and raising my hands to be on the safe side.

In the Flesh

'Tyler Wight, remember? Is this what I get for coming to save you?'

'What from? A fate worse than death?' Diana laughed, hugging me. 'All the same I've never been so glad to see a friendly face. It has been a little hairy being out here by myself.' She pressed a kiss to my cheek. 'How noble of you to turn up in my hour of need, and they all say you're no gentleman.'

'Save the jokes until I feel safer about this caper,' I said, shutting off my car lights. Darkness swallowed us up in night. The sounds of rifle fire thankfully shifted further away. A movement in the bush near us made me jump. 'What the hell is that?' I asked, certain we had been discovered.

'Elephant or buffalo. Take your pick,' Diana said, laughing at my jumpiness. 'They've been crashing around all night. They scared the wits out of me to begin with but I think I prefer their company to soldiers. I've got brandy in the truck – purely for medicinal purposes, of course. I think you could do with one.'

'You could probably force a brandy down my throat,' I agreed. 'It's the best suggestion I've heard all night.' Under the canvas canopy in the rear of the truck I saw a sleeping roll and blankets laid out across the tops of two level crates. We sat there and she poured a stiff measure of brandy into a tin mug, handing it to me. 'Aren't you joining me?' I asked.

'I've had several,' she laughed. 'Dutch courage. Although I kidded myself it was to keep out the night air. Did I tell you how very glad I am to have you here?'

I drank, the spirit warming my insides, cheering me. 'Think nothing of it,' I said grandly. 'I can think of worse places to be.' I remembered Bill's phone call had saved me from an embarrassing situation, with Margaret appearing just as her daughter was about to mount me. 'I'll be leaving Uganda for a spell in the United States,' I said as I raised the tin mug to her in salute. 'It's been a privilege to have known you, Mrs Saxon. Harry's a lucky man.'

'He'll be waiting for this truckload to arrive,' she remembered. 'The airport at Entebbe will be closed, no doubt, so we can forget about flying it to him. I shall deliver it myself. I've spare petrol, food and water. Would you help me drive north to the refugee area in this truck? If we set off at daylight, I'm sure we could make it. I'd feel much safer with you.'

'Don't count on that,' I said seriously. 'I mean being safe with me. I won't find it easy.'

'Huh! The way I look right now?' she laughed. 'I'm a mess. Will you risk it?'

'Of course I'll go with you,' I said, thinking that, mess or not, she looked gorgeous. 'It's only three days driving over dirt tracks, through bush and scrub, dodging wild beasts, crossing rivers with, not to mention, a civil war going on around us. It's a piece of cake.'

I received a spontaneous hug by way of thanks. With her ample breasts pressed to my chest and the yielding feel of her body in my arms, the moment proved too much. I sought her mouth with mine, kissing her with all my pent-up passion, my tongue probing. After a hesitation I felt her respond, clinging to me as she returned the open-mouthed kiss. Lowering her across the laid-out blankets, seeing her eyes watching me intently, I stopped while poised over her, shaking my head.

'I can't,' I heard myself say. 'Not like this – you're feeling grateful towards me. Much as I've always wanted to make love to you. More than with any other woman I've known. You're too good for that.'

'Is that what you think of me?' she asked. 'Good women

In the Flesh

do it too. They have feelings.' Looking down upon her, I saw her right hand go to the top button of her safari jacket, fingers undoing it unsteadily and proceeding to the one below. With the creamy swell of her breasts revealed so far I took over, pulling the jacket open to gaze upon her superb tits. I clasped them, kissed each firm globe and sucked on her nipples. Then she hugged me fiercely, her body shuddering. Despite the brave face she'd put on, the hours she'd passed alone must have been terrifying. As I returned her embrace I still wasn't sure about having her.

'Make me come,' she said breathlessly. 'I want to come. Make me.' Below me I sensed she was struggling to lower her trousers. 'Help me,' she commanded and I drew them off over her boots. Her briefs had come off with them and my eyes, now used to the darkness, were entranced by the pale white upthrust breasts and, between her thighs, the curved pubic delta with its bush of hair. I clamped my mouth to it, lapping, tonguing, going in deep while she moaned and squirmed beneath me. 'Fuck me, fuck me,' she said. 'That's good, but I want to come on your prick. Take off your clothes so that I can feel your body against me when you fuck me.'

I heard the words, my excitement increasing at her wantonness, and I threw off my shirt and trousers. Now both of us were naked apart from socks and boots. I moved back over her as she brought her legs up, catching them behind the knees with her hands to hold them high and spread. I entered her, my prick burrowing snugly in a warm moist channel that gripped the ingoing stalk and held it lovingly. Our bodies seemed to melt as we slowly worked together, thrusting and lifting, my cupped hands hefting her buttock cheeks, each of us savouring the fuck and in no hurry.

'That's good, very good,' she groaned. 'Don't you dare

come yet, Tyler Wight. If I'm to be unfaithful to Harry, make it worthwhile. God, it feels so big and hard up there, I can feel it filling me right up.' With her bottom grinding and moving in time with my thrusts and her breasts two mounds of cushiony flesh pressed to my chest, I fought to stop the liquid fire in my balls from erupting. I worked a finger up her gyrating arse, pleased to note her motions increasing and sensing her climax was approaching. I thrust my engorged dick savagely into the trough of her cunt, getting a squeal in response as she came off with long shuddering spasms.

'Don't stop, go on, go on,' she urged, slowing up and gathering her wits for seconds. 'My God, that was powerful. How wicked of us!' She gave a little giggle. 'It could be worse. It might have been that army captain you warned me about, the one who threatened to fuck me.'

'Suliman,' I said, our bodies blending, the strength of her desire returning as she tilted her pelvis to me for full-depth entry. 'I saw his head on a table tonight. He bloody well never looked so good.' The surge I felt was not to be denied much longer. 'Turn over,' I growled, pulling out of her and hearing a cry of protest as she obeyed.

'Hurry up and put it back,' she said urgently. Belly down, her bottom formed a gorgeous mound, inviting in the extreme. I drew her up on her knees. With her shoulders lowered, buttocks raised and held apart by my hands, I howled in delight at the delicious sensation of piercing her from the rear. I pushed past the outer cunt lips and gave her the entire length of my cock from knob to base. Her gasps and moans told me of the pleasure she was feeling. Again on a knife-edge, she whined that she was coming, *coming*, bumping her arse back to me as I moved faster and an intense orgasm shook me rigid. Even as I spouted my load into her, her cunt muscles clenched my

In the Flesh

prick as if she would never let me go. She fell face forward on to the blanket, sighing, 'Oh, that was wonderful. I must have needed it.'

Once again I heard the crack of rifle fire in the distance. 'What a way to die,' I said. 'No regrets, Mrs Saxon?'

'Not yet,' she admitted, rolling over and smiling. 'Perhaps next time. We've got to spend the next three days together, haven't we? Do you think we'll make it?'

'Are you referring to our chances of finishing this trip or of our making love again?' I said in reply. 'I'm sure there's every chance.' My hand went out to stroke her uptilted breasts, then slid down to fondle her wet cunt. 'How could I avoid the temptation?'

'By giving in to it,' Diana laughed wickedly, her arms reaching around my neck. 'As I'm going to do. Poor Harry, he'll never know, will he?' she said. 'Know that you're about to fuck his wife. You are, aren't you?'

'Once more into the breach,' I recited happily. How could I refuse?

A selection of Erotica from Headline

BLUE HEAVENS	Nick Bancroft	£4.99 ☐
MAID	Dagmar Brand	£4.99 ☐
EROS IN AUTUMN	Anonymous	£4.99 ☐
EROTICON THRILLS	Anonymous	£4.99 ☐
IN THE GROOVE	Lesley Asquith	£4.99 ☐
THE CALL OF THE FLESH	Faye Rossignol	£4.99 ☐
SWEET VIBRATIONS	Jeff Charles	£4.99 ☐
UNDER THE WHIP	Nick Aymes	£4.99 ☐
RETURN TO THE CASTING COUCH	Becky Bell	£4.99 ☐
MAIDS IN HEAVEN	Samantha Austen	£4.99 ☐
CLOSE UP	Felice Ash	£4.99 ☐
TOUCH ME, FEEL ME	Rosanna Challis	£4.99 ☐

All Headline books are available at your local bookshop or newsagent, or can be ordered direct from the publisher. Just tick the titles you want and fill in the form below. Prices and availability subject to change without notice.

Headline Book Publishing, Cash Sales Department, Bookpoint, 39 Milton Park, Abingdon, OXON, OX14 4TD, UK. If you have a credit card you may order by telephone – 01235 400400.

Please enclose a cheque or postal order made payable to Bookpoint Ltd to the value of the cover price and allow the following for postage and packing:

UK & BFPO: £1.00 for the first book, 50p for the second book and 30p for each additional book ordered up to a maximum charge of £3.00.

OVERSEAS & EIRE: £2.00 for the first book, £1.00 for the second book and 50p for each additional book.

Name ....

Address ....

....

....

If you would prefer to pay by credit card, please complete:
Please debit my Visa/Access/Diner's Card/American Express (delete as applicable) card no:

Signature .... Expiry Date ....